the Beekeeper's *wife*

LYNNE HINTON

ISBN: 978-1-7358600-4-6 (hard cover)
       978-1-7358600-5-3 (soft cover)

Edited by: Karli Jackson

Published by Warren Publishing
Charlotte, NC
www.warrenpublishing.net
Printed in the United States

*For Sue Joiner—kind woman,
hiking partner, beloved friend.*

"Trembling, I listened: the summer sun
Had the chill of snow;
For I knew she was telling the bees of one
Gone on the journey we all must go!"

–John Greenleaf Whittier

Praise for Lynne Hinton Books

"Like Rebecca Wells in *Divine Secrets of the Ya-Ya Sisterhood*,
Hinton has a knack in her novels for tapping into a woman's
longings for lifelong, authentic, messy friendships."

—PUBLISHERS WEEKLY

Friendship Cake
"I would welcome a friendship with Lynne Hinton.
I would welcome an invitation to sit down at her table,
but mostly I would welcome her next book."

—MAYA ANGELOU,
AUTHOR OF *I KNOW WHY THE CAGED BIRD SINGS*

"Friendship Cake will give you plenty to chew over. Delicious!"

—RITA MAE BROWN, AUTHOR OF *RUBYFRUIT JUNGLE*

Hope Springs
"Portrays the struggles and yearnings of the human heart
against a backdrop of small-town graces and female friendships.
It is a lovely novel filled with hope."

—SUE MONK KIDD, AUTHOR OF *THE SECRET LIVES OF BEES*

The Last Odd Day
"A story that beautifully and poignantly traces the defining
moments of one extraordinary woman's life."

—PAMELA DUNCAN, AUTHOR OF *PLANT LIFE*

Also by Lynne Hinton

Meditations for Walking

The Hope Springs Series
Friendship Cake
The Things I Know Best
Hope Springs
Forever Friends
Christmas Cake
Wedding Cake

The Last Odd Day
The Arms of God
The Order of Things
Pie Town
Welcome Back to Pie Town
The View From Here

The Divine Private Detective Mystery Series
Sister Eve, Private Eye
The Case of the Sin City Sister
Sister Eve and the Blue Nun

Written under the name, Jackie Lynn:
Down By The Riverside
Jacob's Ladder
Swing Low, Sweet Chariot

Written under the name, Lynne Branard:
The Art of Arranging Flowers
Traveling Light

Chapter One

It is morning, and everything is the same.

I wake to the familiar smells—coffee, the dark roast, the kind he buys at his favorite gourmet kitchen shop downtown; toast, buttered and turning brown in the oven; bacon, popping in my mother's iron skillet and which I say every day I do not want, but always eat. He has the radio playing—the college station at the university where he retired after thirty years. Classical, eighteenth-century composers, Haydn, Mozart, symphony, and stringed quartets.

He won't call me to breakfast; he won't tap at the door, sliding it open just a little with his foot, peeking his head through the crack where the light falls across his side, the bed grown cold because he's been awake and out for hours. He won't come and sit next to me, a cup of coffee in his hand to give me when I'm all the way up, my back straight and comfortable, resting against the stack of pillows.

He doesn't come to get me. He never has. He will wait until the smells from the kitchen move me from my slumber, until I get up on my own, until I'm ready and up and moving to my own waking rhythms. It's the way we've done mornings for twenty-two years.

Like I said, everything is the same.

Only it's not. I roll over, yanking the pillow around my head, pretending that what I know to be happening in the room down the hall will stop, go away, disappear—that he will stop, go away, disappear; forcing my eyes closed, I slide down beneath the sheet and blanket, trying to cover my face, my nose, trying not to smell him and the morning that he's already created. After all, he shouldn't be here. He shouldn't be in the kitchen having made breakfast. He shouldn't be sitting at the table waiting for me. He should be gone.

I made myself more than clear. I yelled. I threw things. I drank too much. I told the truth. I said the words out loud—those hurtful, stinging, bruising words. But I was clear. He had to go. I told him that this was nonsense what we were doing, that it was wrong and wasteful because we both know it can't work. People say so. I say so.

And yet, the coffee has brewed, and the toast is out of the oven and now on a plate with two kinds of jam beside it. The bacon is still in the skillet, and the soundtrack of my marriage is playing on strings stirring across the radio waves that bring it from a small studio at a private liberal arts college into our kitchen, four miles away. I know now what I have always known—he refuses to take me seriously. He refuses to believe what I've said.

I throw off the linens, toss aside the pillow, and get up and stand at the door. I open and close my eyes. I take a breath, steady myself, and walk down the hall to where I know he waits. My hair uncombed, my teeth unbrushed, the blanket wrapped around my shoulders because I couldn't find my robe, I wander coolly into this familiar scene of morning.

He lowers the paper, the local one he argues with every day but still buys on the last mile of his daily walk, dropping four quarters in the machine, waiting so patiently as they fall into place, and then pulling open the lid and taking out his prize. I asked him once why he didn't just subscribe since he read it every day—have somebody throw it on the lawn so he wouldn't have to keep quarters, wouldn't have to walk home with a paper to carry; but he claims he likes the machine, likes the way it feels to slide the coins into the narrow slot, likes the ritual of walking home with the news, as puny as it is, tucked under his arm. He also reminded me that he was home finishing the puzzle long before the young boy passed by on his bike, tossing the papers in the lawns of our neighbors.

"You're here," I say, walking over to the coffeepot, touching it to see if it's gotten cold; and it has. I grab the cup sitting out, pour the coffee, and stick it in the microwave to warm it since I like my hot beverages hot.

He doesn't reply, but I know he hears me. I don't turn to face him.

"There's bacon," he says.

"I don't want any," I reply, both of us knowing I lie.

The bell on the timer goes off, and I open the door and take out my mug of hot coffee. I open the refrigerator and find the milk, unscrew the top and smell, not sure how long we've had it, and pour some into my drink.

"Why do you say you like your coffee hot but then add milk, which inevitably cools it to room temperature?"

He asks me this at least once a month. I decide not to answer.

"I thought I told you to leave," I say, plopping down at the table across from him, across from the window where I watch a few cars passing by on the street—neighbors on their way to work or the gym, none of them even remotely aware of this conversation we are having, none of them having a clue as to what happens inside the yellow house at 137 Cottage Place.

"I thought I'd give you some more time to be sure," he answers, smiling.

I watch him slide a plate in my direction, but I'm not that easy. I slide it back.

"You don't really want me to go," he tells me, and this reminds me of how much I hate it when he tells me what it is that I want.

"You don't get to say that," I reply quickly.

He bites his lip as if he's sorry and nods. "So I don't," he says quietly.

That habit—telling me what he thinks I want—began in the very beginning of our relationship, when I was a junior just starting my major, and he was my professor, fifteen years my senior. At that time, early for us both, I liked being told what I wanted. I liked not having to think about it for myself. I liked the ease it gave me, the way it took me off the hook of making decisions, choices that may or may not be worth all the work required in figuring out what I want. He would name a desire as mine, each one of them foreign and alluring, and I would claim it as my own; I enjoyed believing that he was right. And of course, he loved filling my head with things, with thoughts he liked for me to have, with ideas he wanted to create and shape.

Unfortunately or fortunately, depending upon which one of us is asked, I grew out of that practice long before we were married. Once the new shine of our relationship faded, once the secret got out, and it wasn't forbidden for us to see each other any longer, the diploma on my wall, alumni and no longer student, I realized that not all of his ideas were good ones, and not all of his thoughts were mine. There were a few fights about our differences, tango lessons for one—I wanted them, he didn't—but he still managed to give them a try and even seemed to have a good time when we danced the few times; restaurants, for another, I liked to try some of the new spots; he had his list of favorites. But eventually he accepted that I did indeed have a mind of my own, and he stepped aside, giving me room to decide for myself what I wanted or didn't want, what I thought or didn't think, what I liked or didn't like. He even supported some of my choices, like listening to punk rock instead of classical music, staying up late and sleeping in, running a half-marathon when I turned forty, reading mysteries instead of literary novels, cutting my hair. Of course, being who he was and who I had been early in our dating life, he slips. He notices, sometimes judges, saying more than he should. But he never stands in my way, and he always repents.

I watch him as he raises the paper and reads, his back to the window, morning sun streaming in around him, and I realize he isn't going anywhere. He isn't going to leave. And when he glances up at me, folding the paper and dropping it at his elbows, and really looks at me, he knows that I know he's precisely where I want him to be. He smiles; this time he's right. He knows exactly what I want.

"What are you going to say to your mother?"

"I'm saying that I told you to leave. I'm saying that I meant it this time."

He nods. He understands how awkward this is for me. He knows how hard it is because he's heard what everyone has said about him—about us. He realizes that for me to choose to stay with him means turning aside the counsel and advice of practically everyone we know. He understands the cost.

He glances away, and I turn to where he is peering, at the clock on the stove.

"You should probably get dressed or someone from the office will be calling. You know how they like to check up on you."

"It's not *they*," I emphasize the pronoun. "It's Kathryn. She worries."

"And it's the other one too."

I smile. "You're jealous," I tell him. "You're jealous of the new guy."

He picks the paper up and unfolds it, slapping at the middle of it where it was creased. "I find jealousy a childish endeavor."

I take a sip of my coffee. "Jealousy is not an endeavor; it's an emotion we feel when we anticipate loss."

"It's childish," he answers, not looking at me. "And I have never been jealous."

"You've never had reason," I reply. "Until now."

"Nothing's changed," he says, hiding any emotion.

"Everything's changed," I respond as I get up from the table. "And quit cooking me bacon."

I take an apple from the bowl of fruit on the center of the table and head down the hall.

Chapter Two

"You're late; is everything okay?" Kathryn is a step behind me. I feel her nervous energy, her hot breath on my neck. She is a knot of tension.

"I stopped to check on the bees," I lie, moving as quickly as I can to my desk. I took off my coat at the door, wrapped my scarf around the hanger. It is always warm in the office, too warm for me, but setting the thermostat is above my pay grade. Kathryn likes it cozy. She thinks "cozy" makes us a better team, keeps us feeling at home and comfortable, thereby increasing a more positive experience for our customers. "Cozy" only makes me sleepy, or like this morning when I'm late and being followed to my station by my boss, cranky.

"I thought there was nothing to do for bees in the winter," she says, as if I don't know what month it is, as if I've somehow forgotten we're deep in the month of February, deep in the hold of winter. "I thought they stayed in their hives and hibernated until spring. I thought beekeepers took vacations from their little hobbies until April or May."

"I go by every couple of weeks to make sure their hives are still standing, that no strong wind or bored cowboy has knocked them over. It happens more than you think," I answer, deciding not to comment on bees and the fact that they don't hibernate. They're sluggish in winter and cluster around the queen; they don't sleep for four months.

I also do not respond to her condescending "little hobbies" jab. I take in a breath, turn around, and face her. Seeing how close she has gotten, she steps back.

For whatever reason, Kathryn has always been a little scared of me. Nathan says it's because I'm smarter than she is, that I intimidate other women with my intellect, but he's always thought I was smarter than I really am; besides, I don't think that's it. Kathryn is plenty smart, and she's not intimidated by intellect. If she was, she would not be as successful as she has been in the business world.

She's dealt with lots of bright women, seen a lot of them come and go in her field and in others, all trying to start businesses, all of them with great ideas and money to back them up; and yet, she owns one of the few shops in this town that's still open, still making a buck. She's a bright cookie without the need to be intimidated. She's fully aware of her own solid intellect.

It's not brains—mine or anyone else's that intimate her. It's something else. It's brawn. I think she knows I'm not beneath taking a swing at somebody if they push me far enough. I'm short but stocky, like a gymnast, boxy and headstrong; and I think she knows I won't retreat from a fight. I also think she's aware that I have a few unhealthy anger issues and don't always address them in the most mature fashion; and that can be intimidating for a lot of women, even women who made a career in law enforcement.

"And are they okay?"

I've forgotten what we were talking about. I stare at her.

"The bees," she reminds me. "Are their hives all right?"

"Oh, sure. All hives accounted for and in good standing order." I smile and wait for her to move a few more feet so I can take my seat at my station. She nods, and I remain in place.

"Are you okay, Emma? I mean, I just worry about you, with everything you're trying to do, with everything you've ..."

"I'm fine, Kathryn," I say, interrupting her, but then I take a breath, cooling. "I was just a little late today, and I'm sorry about that; but I'm fine." I give another smile to reassure her, and I pull out my chair, sit down, and turn on my computer. I feel her walk away, and I know I should have never told her that I was taking over the beekeeping. I should have never confided in her about Nathan's and my personal affairs.

I watch the screen come alive—the picture of us camping at the Canadian Rockies, the park near Lake Louise, Nathan grinning at the camera, which we handed to a German couple to take the shot, our dog Pistol between us. The trip we took just before Pistol died, before we knew he had cancer and would die trembling in my arms; the trip of black, starry nights and kayaking before breakfast on crystal blue lakes; the trip of deep restful nights and long sunny days.

I type in my password and wait, the home screen dissolving into folders and icons, a decades' worth of digital files.

"Hey." Jon peeks over the top of the divider between us. I didn't even know he was there.

"Hey," I reply. "How's it going?" I ask, knowing he's still learning, still trying to fit in.

"You do something different to your hair?"

I smooth down the sides and shake my head. "Just the wind," I answer him, thinking I should probably spend a little more time on my appearance. I didn't even put on mascara this morning. There's a coffee stain on my blouse.

He stares at me for a minute as if he's trying to decide if I've made a change and then decides to let it go. "I sold my first package—commercial, not home."

"That's great, Jon," I tell him, thinking it took him only six weeks longer than the last kid we hired.

"It's the dental clinic out on the interstate."

Well, that's a surprise. I thought we had already contacted all the medical and dental practices in the area, several times a year in fact. They're low-hanging fruit because most of them are well aware of the need for a security system.

"My uncle works there," he confesses, and now it makes sense.

When I started with Kathryn in customer service, I bugged every family member and friend I knew to purchase a security system. Relying on connections can keep you afloat for a few months, but then you have to start hustling strangers, doing real sales work. Your brother-in-law's barbershop and your cousin's family who owns a bar somewhere out in the county can only take you so far.

"Deluxe or standard?"

"Standard," he answers, sounding disappointed. "He actually already has a system with Alarm Guard, but he said he could use something in the parking lot."

I smile and nod. "That's still good," I say, trying to sound supportive.

"Yeah, now I'm trying to call my friend's dad; he owns the trophy shop downtown." He holds up his hand like he's saying goodbye and disappears behind the thin wall dividing us.

Jon has been working for Kathryn for three months now. He's fresh out of college, worked here as an intern last summer. He majored in business, and he doesn't really want to sell security systems. He wants to open a brewery, sell craft beer, already has names for the brands, like J.J.'s Ode to Joy. But he doesn't have any start-up money, and his father is a Baptist preacher with no intent to help his son do the work of the devil. When the reverend found out what his son planned to do with a college education, he quit paying the bills, and now Jon has a stack of loans to pay back. Jon's Joy will have to wait.

He's a good kid, though; I like him. He works hard, even though his heart isn't in it, and I have a certain amount of fondness for how he treats me like his big sister. He's a tad slow following my humor, but he's sweet and he does his job, stays out of my way and doesn't pry. That's as much as I can hope for in a colleague separated from me by only a panelboard eight hours a day while we both try to peddle alarm systems.

I've been with Kathryn since she started K-Locks Security. I interned with her while I finished my English degree, working on copy for ads and brochures. It was this or staying at the college, but with Nathan heading up the English Department at that time, no matter where I landed, it just felt like people would suspect he had a hand in what I got. So I took this job because it was convenient, a block from school, and I thought that having experience creating press release materials and writing technical pieces would help me land a job doing what I really wanted, which was writing features for a paper or short stories for a small press. I thought it might help prepare me for the novel that, at the time, I knew I had in me.

Twenty years later, having come and gone from this office more than a few times, taking a job in marketing for a local restaurant chain and then later managing a local food bank, I'm here again, for good this time, I think. And the only words I put to page are the new updates for customized security and interesting facts about our home automation solutions. I sell systems and still write the ads and brochures, the copy on our website. There never were features or editorials, only one short story that I kept tinkering with until I finally gave up; and there has certainly never been a novel, at least not one that was finished.

Nathan has always been the one who tried to get me to quit the job, always pushed me to "dream bigger," "get away and write," "just do it." In spite of our differences, he has always been supportive of my writing. He thought the papers I wrote for his class had flair, thought I had some talent; but in the end, I just lost my drive. The writing felt too hard, and I didn't have the stamina to stick with it. I always thought somebody else could do it better. Despite Nathan's support, I think I finally just decided I didn't have anything interesting to say.

Truth be told, I don't mind it here in this quaint office. No crazy restaurant hours. It's close enough to the house that I can walk. I have time for reading, trying out new recipes, going to lectures and plays at the university. No hassles from management. I do good work and am compensated for it, an end of the year bonus. And I don't mind Kathryn's hovering or her monthly breakdowns that we didn't sell enough systems to make payroll or how the big companies are stealing our market share. I don't mind talking to business owners and trying to get them to upgrade or add cameras. I don't mind the cold calls I have to make to meet quota or the customers who call and complain. I don't even mind most of my coworkers—the security guards and the installation teams, the coming and the going, the dramas that unfold in every office.

I don't mind any of that. It's soothing actually. Comfortable. Uncomplicated. I like working in the business world, working with people who care about me, feeling like my job has some merit in the community. And in my life, with this marriage, with our money troubles and unpredictable theatrics, with *his* books and contracts—and now the bees—soothing and uncomplicated isn't quite the same thing as Kathryn's need for cozy, but it works just fine. It all works just fine.

Chapter Three

I forgot to pack a lunch, and that's why I'm walking down the street toward the college. Before long I join the throes of students coming and going from their classes and almost feel like I am twenty-one again. It's energizing to be around such youthfulness; moving in stride with the crowd, I feel my mood lighten and suddenly quicken my pace to match those walking near me and notice that I am smiling.

I have exactly three dollars in my wallet, so it's the campus taco food truck for the two-buck taco or around the corner to the 7-Eleven for a candy bar or bag of chips. It seems to me the taco is a more substantial and life-affirming choice, which is what my horoscope suggested for today. I saw it in the paper before I left. Nathan had folded the page so it was easy for me to find since he knows I like it. I don't read self-help, stuff but I do follow my horoscope.

I'm Pisces—Nathan, Scorpio. Straight out of the water with a resilient vibration to triumph, surviving against all opposition. Resourceful, brave, stubborn—that's my husband.

Me, I'm also water but not as resilient; more just a go with the flow kind of gal. The fish just swimming along. Astrologists say I'm good natured, faithful, but not very interested in forming a family. I'm loyal, or so the experts say, and I prefer to take things easy. Pisces are also known for their strong boundaries, their inclination to protect what's theirs and follow restrictions. We make good prison guards.

"You must like it here." The voice comes from behind me.

"It's affordable," I respond without turning around. I recognize his voice.

I know he comes here too, just like me, about the same time at the end of the month before payday. I even saw him here a few times last year when he had apparently just arrived in town and was trying to find a job at the college. We didn't speak, however, until he came to work for Kathryn. He's a security systems technician, which is a fancy way of saying he hangs cameras and wires buildings. It's the dirtiest and most physical demanding job at K-Locks, but he hasn't seemed to mind. Every time I run into him, he's whistling or has this goofy smile plastered on his face. I used to think he was high or up to something, but I see now that's just his way of working.

"Two-buck taco, I know," he adds. "Greatest idea since supersizing at Burger King." He stops, and I think maybe he's finished. I still haven't turned to face him.

I stand at the window at the truck and place my order. I'm embarrassed to do so, but I quietly ask the girl if she would fill up my coffee thermos with water. She takes it from me without comment and turns on the spigot behind her, fills it, and hands it over. She's clearly done this before. Feeding college students as she does, I'm sure she's seen all the tricks for saving money.

"Two dollars and seventeen cents," she tells me, and I count out two bills and change, place the correct amount in her hand.

"You want chips and salsa?" The question is not from the counter but from behind.

I shake my head.

"No, share some chips and salsa with me," he says, and finally I turn around. "We can sit over there." He motions with his chin at the empty table, the one in the sun.

I shrug. I have no reason to decline, and it's just lunch after all.

My taco is ready, and I move to the other window, pick up my order, and head over to the table as I hear him say, "Two tacos with an order of chips and salsa." And then I hear him speak Spanish to the girl inside the truck. She laughs.

It's winter in North Carolina, which could mean anything these days; but today it means a perfect crisp and sunny day, a little wind, enough warmth to make you loosen your scarf, slide out of your gloves—a day of surprises, of lulling us into thinking spring is closer than it is.

The town of Elon is about center in the state, which means our cold is not quite as cold as the mountains and our hot not quite as hot as the coast. There are four distinct seasons in the Piedmont, the foothills, and I like them all. It's a pretty town, oak trees lining the streets, grassy meadows; it looks like a safe place, a place where you can send your child to school and not worry. There are more than a few big-city kids who come to school here, and I'm sure the appeal of a small village is as much a draw to Elon as the reputation for supplying a solid education.

I sit down, put my food on the table in front of me, and close my eyes. If you didn't know me, you'd think I was praying, and I don't know, maybe I am. The sun, the blue sky, the sounds of college students laughing, talking, so alive, so engaged with the world, the breeze stirring old leaves along the ground, the perfectly manicured green spaces in between the college buildings, the smell of cilantro and hot sauce; it's my favorite kind of day, and I am warmed by the lift of gratitude I feel.

When I open my eyes, he has taken his seat across from me. He's tall, skinnier than Nathan, has his black hair in a ponytail. I notice his long fingers, a small tattoo on the base of his thumb as he unwraps his first taco, slides the basket of chips in my direction, opens the top of the small, plastic container of salsa. He grins like he's happy to see me.

"I pray," he says in a matter-of-fact kind of opening.

"Oh, that's not what ..." I feel like I need to explain.

"To the four directions," he continues. "Every morning, it's a ritual I do." He takes a bite of his taco as I take mine out of the bag. "It's good to speak to the forces in the universe, to welcome the day—a way of calling your spirit to attention."

"That's what you call praying?" I ask and then take a bite. I feel the sauce run down my chin. He hands me a napkin.

"I guess," he answers. "You got a better definition?"

I shake my head, take another bite, put my taco down, and wipe my mouth.

My mother grew up Catholic but was turned away from church when she married a Methodist. He wouldn't convert, so she was not allowed to be married by the priest in the church. They eloped to South Carolina, got married in a courthouse, and even though my sister and I had our first communions and took catechism classes, we were mostly a family living on the fringes of religious institutions.

I did things with the youth at the Methodist church near where we lived, had a crush on the summer youth intern; but I just never felt at home in church. What I learned about the divine came from the early trips we took with my mother's parents—camping trips, canoeing, once even hiking a section of the Appalachian Trail. The places my grandfather would take me just before dawn, making me close my eyes in the dark and then open them just as the morning sun was peeking above the top of a mountain, the cool feel of river water as I slid my hand beside the boat, the stillness at dusk. That's where I found God. There, and sometimes in a book, when a story takes my breath away. I think God's there too.

"So you've lived here since you came to college."

I take a chip from the basket and nod.

"What was that, three or four years ago?" He grins and takes a drink from his can of soda. I'm pretty sure this is what Nathan would call flirting, which is why he doesn't like Bus Stedman, the new guy at work who really isn't all that new anymore. He's been at K-Locks about six months.

I smile, choosing not to reply, take a sip from my thermos.

"What kind of job were you searching for at the college?" I ask, turning the tables on him, changing the subject, moving the topic of conversation away from me—something I've gotten very good at.

"How did you know I was trying to find a job at the college?"

I realize my blunder. He had no idea I had seen him a year ago, watched him filling out applications as I ate my lunch on the steps of the library or here at one of the tables near the taco truck.

"Just a hunch," I say, stuffing my mouth with taco so that I can't say anything else.

He watches me as if he might read some sign in the way I dip my chip in salsa or chew and swallow my lunch.

"My girlfriend came to work on her PhD," he tells me with not a bit of apprehension. "I was searching for anything to pay the bills. It was the arrangement we made. I work, she studies. I started with maintenance for a couple of weeks when we first got here, but they had to lay me off before school ever started. Later I met Dexter, heard about an opening, and got the job with Kathryn." He takes a breath. "You like selling alarm systems?"

"Living the dream," I say sarcastically and take another bite of my lunch.

"I like it here," he tells me. "It's nice. Beautiful trees, plenty of space, easy winters." He glances around. "And I like a college town. Plenty of books and folks who actually read them. People are friendlier when there are young minds all around being educated. Brings a certain energy to a place."

I nod, stuff a chip in my mouth, remembering how it just felt to walk among students, to hear their conversations, watch them come and go. Still, I understand what he's saying, but I think this is where Nathan would roll his eyes, maybe tell some anecdote about the *young minds* he worked with.

"So, your husband taught here." It's not a question so I don't answer. "What department was he in?"

"English," I answer.

"Twentieth-century British," he adds, and I shake my head. Nathan preferred the French, the twentieth-century writers. George Sand. He's taught about every class a student can take, but he always favors the stories from France.

"My girlfriend," he explains. "I was talking about her field of study."

I take another swallow of water. "Oh."

"She likes T.S. Eliot, Ezra Pound, Gerard Manley Hopkins—poets," he adds without emotion. "What about your husband? He have a favorite? He always talk more about the dead writers than the live ones?"

I think about the four books he wrote on Amantine Lucile Aurore Dupin, but I don't comment. I don't like talking about literature with people I don't know well; it feels a bit too personal somehow.

I finish up my taco, roll up the paper, take another drink of water, and wipe my mouth. "Thanks for the chips," I respond, standing. "I should be getting back." And even though I do not understand my rush, I suddenly feel as if I need to be out of this blast of sunshine and truth-telling.

"Why the hurry?" he asks.

"Payroll," I answer, which I know is a pretty good one.

"You do that too?"

I don't reply to his question because the truth is that I gave up doing payroll last year. It was part of the new arrangement I made with Kathryn about my workload. She took some of the responsibilities off my plate, and I try to get to the office on time.

"Good luck on your installation at the pharmacy," I say as I gather up my trash, referring to his afternoon appointment that I am familiar with because I am the one who booked it. I know everywhere he goes.

"Yeah, okay," I hear as I walk away.

I head to the can, drop off my trash, tighten my scarf around my neck, and move in the direction of the office. A slight breeze pushes me ahead.

Chapter Four

"Hi, this is Emma Troxler from K-Locks." I am returning the call from a home customer. She phoned during lunch and asked for assistance. Jon passed her message on to me. I'm not sure why he didn't handle it, but I figure he thinks phone calls to present customers are a waste of time. Commissions and bonuses are only applied to new deals. He clearly sees no value in service at this point and probably for his short tenure selling security systems, never will.

"Who?" It is an older woman's voice I hear. I don't remember her, even though our records say I sold her the system used in her home.

"Emma from K-Locks," I repeat myself, speaking slightly louder.

"I'm not interested," she says, practically interrupting me.

"Mrs. Lewis, I'm returning a call you made an hour ago." There's a pause. "K-Locks. I believe you use our service." No response, and I give her a few minutes to process. "We install security systems." One more clue.

"Oh right, Kathryn's agency."

"Yes, ma'am."

"I called about an hour ago," she repeats the information I already have.

"Yes, ma'am."

"Is this Kathryn?"

"No, this is Emma. I work for Kathryn."

"She's such a nice girl. Served on the police force."

"Yes, ma'am."

I wait. Surely she remembers why she called us.

"I think something's wrong with my alarm box," she finally explains.

I check the computer screen and see that she has the basic home security package. There are alarms on her windows and four doors—one front, one back, one basement, and sliding glass doors near the kitchen. She doesn't have a garage or camera system. I assume by "alarm box" she means the passcode box we install at one of the doors, usually the front one.

"What's wrong with it?" I ask, thinking it needs batteries, or perhaps she's punched in the wrong code. These are the standard concerns.

"It won't stop beeping," she says, and I know that means the battery is low.

"Mrs. Lewis, that means you need to replace the battery. Do you have a 9 volt battery at home?"

"A what?"

"A 9 volt battery. It's the little square one."

"I just don't know, honey," she replies. "I've never heard this beeping before. I don't even know where a battery goes."

"Do you have anyone who might be able to help you with that?"

She pours a long sigh across the phone. "That was Bennie's department. You know, batteries and changing screens in the windows, cars and plumbing. He did maintenance. I did cleaning."

"Yes, ma'am." And since she said "was," I understand Bennie must not be around. Bennie's department, I assume, has closed at the Lewis residence.

"The batteries are housed in the back of the alarm box," I tell her. "Can you find that?"

I hear her fumble with the phone, placing it down somewhere so that she can check, I guess.

She picks the phone up. Her breathing is slightly labored. "I can't find it," she says, and then she starts to cry.

"Mrs. Lewis," I say as calmly as I can. "Are you okay?"

"Are you married?" she asks.

I pause. I'm not sure how this information might be helpful, but I sense what she's getting at. I know she needs a bit of cheer, some encouragement. I can tell this because we put in lots of systems for single women. It's one of the first things widows tend to do, and I would never had known this if I wasn't in this line of work. It helps, this small act of reassurance now that they're living alone.

"Yes, ma'am," I reply because this is the simplest answer. Yes or no, that's all she wants to hear.

"Then you're lucky," she says. "Don't ever forget that," she adds.

"Okay."

"Bennie and I were married fifty-three years," she tells me, and I relax in my office chair and take my hands off the keyboard. I adjust the volume on my headset. She keeps pulling the mouthpiece away, making it hard to hear her, but I know this isn't just a ten-minute fixer, and I think I might just adopt Jon's stance on service calls. Still, I don't really mind.

"He's been dead five months, and I'm lost, I tell you."

I think of the single women in my life, their stories of being alone, their sorrows, their broken hearts, their fears. I think of my mom two weeks after Daddy left her.

"He made me buy this alarm before he died, knew I'd need it." I hear the catch in her voice. "He was good that way."

I nod and then reply, "Yes."

When Daddy left, Mama had all the locks changed on our doors, but it wasn't because she was afraid of strangers breaking in; she was convinced her ex-husband would return and steal things, take the children. I, on the other hand, knew there was only a slight chance of that. Daddy never really wanted two daughters. He might break in to retrieve his baseball cards or a pair of shoes; but he would never jimmy a lock to gain custody of children—not us anyway.

"So I have this thing he wanted me to have, this thing he thought would make me feel safe and unafraid. Maybe not so sad. But half the time I forget to turn it on, and the other half I forget to turn it off. Your people call me a lot."

"Well, that's what we're here for, Mrs. Lewis, and I'm sorry about the battery. It should have lasted longer than nine months."

"Six," she corrects me.

"What?"

"I've had the alarm system for six months. Bennie made me buy it a few weeks before he died. That was September. Bennie's been dead five months, not nine, which means I've had the system for six."

I shake my head, trying to clear away the cobwebs, click on the screen again since it had gone to sleep, and scroll down to the date of installation. It was in August. I'm embarrassed for the mistake and glance around to make sure no one heard me. "Right, I'm sorry. And for sure, six months is a short life for a battery. Do you want someone to come by and help you change it?" I ask. Her unit is still on warranty after all. "One of our guys can stop sometime this week if you want."

"Will it cost much?"

"No, ma'am. It's a courtesy call. No charge."

I hear her take a breath. "Might he also take a look at the disposal? I think I've got something hung up, and I'm afraid to stick my hand in there. I think it's a bone, a chicken bone. I had chicken last night. From the fire department supper. Bennie always said I threw too much in there. I just never really pay too much attention. Do you have a disposal?"

"No, ma'am, and I think he could do that too," I say, knowing our guys have sometimes done more than just service the alarm systems for our older clients. They don't always like it, and they aren't really supposed to; but Elon is a small town with an expectation of a bit more neighborliness, more so than say the two larger towns that sandwich us, Burlington and Greensboro. And well, most of our service technicians are good guys, understand the code of small towns. They fix what they can, diagnose what they can't.

"Bennie would be so embarrassed that I can't change a battery," she confesses.

"Well, our guy will show you how, and you'll be able to do it next time," I reply, trying to sound cheerful.

She clears her throat. "Thank you, dear."

"Okay, it looks like there's an opening tomorrow. Will Thursday work, in the afternoon?" I glance over Bus's schedule. He has an installment in the morning but is free after that. I start to type in the information.

"That will work," she replies. "That will work just fine. I'll be home all day tomorrow. I used to play bridge on Thursdays, but I can't seem to keep my cards straight anymore."

I think about my own trouble with numbers, my struggle with math, the family jokes about me needing a calculator to add one plus one.

I have never played bridge.

"He will call you in the morning to confirm and then let you know about what time he'll come around." I finish adding the information into the computer. Bus will get the notification and let me know if this is a job he can do. "Will you be okay until then?" I realize even one day without a fully working system can make some customers all nerves.

"Honey, the truth is that I don't care about this alarm. I never wanted it, never asked for it. I did it for Bennie. You know how we do that for our husbands, don't you?"

I think about the bees, how I'm now taking care of Nathan's bees, how he expects me to know what to do, what they need, how he doesn't even mention them anymore but somehow knows I'll take over. "Yes, ma'am," I say and let out a breath. "You'll hear from one of our guys tomorrow, okay?"

"Okay," she says, and I wait for just a second, wondering what else we might say to each other, and then when I hear she's gone, I click off the phone.

Chapter Five

Maybe it is the phone call from Mrs. Lewis, or maybe it's because it has begun to rain, a cold steady rain that I love to share—the kind of weather that brings out mugs of tea and wood for the fire, the kind of weather that makes me happy that I'm not alone, that I have such sweet companionship; maybe it's the rain that causes me to rush. I hurry out of the office and down the street. The office isn't far from the house, and sometimes I walk to work. Today is one of those days.

I stop and get the mail out of the box—bills and magazines—and I stand at the porch, put the letters on a rocking chair, and shake out my umbrella. I take in a breath, listen to the rain as it falls on the metal roof, and feel the lightness in my heart. I want to see him. I'm glad he didn't go.

I unlock the door and stand in the foyer and take off my coat, my scarf, place a hand on the wall to steady myself, and pull my feet out of my boots. I drop off the mail and keys and suddenly, I smell dinner. I had not expected him to be cooking—not tonight, not after the fight and the joyless morning.

The thought of stew or pasta cheers me even more, and before I know it, I have hurried down the hall and turned the corner to the kitchen, smiling. "I hope you saved some for me," I call out, expecting a laugh or some witty comeback about making just enough for one, some silly thing he says that I've grown used to over time but still find humorous, adorable.

"It's soup," I hear the reply and instantly understand Nathan is not here. I know the disappointment shows, and I try to clean it up, wipe it away.

"Hey," I say as I glance around, wondering where he might have gone, wondering if they had words, if he left before she saw him, sneaking out before the weather changed.

"Hey," my mother responds, following my eyes. She seems confused, or maybe she doesn't; I don't know anymore. "You expecting someone else?" She steps to the stove and stirs whatever it is she's cooking.

"No," I answer. "Of course not." But that's a lie, and she knows it. She catches me searching again but turns to her soup.

"How was work?" she asks, and I step past her and head down the hall and into the bedroom. I wonder if he's hiding in the closet, and I feel a glimmer of hope as I open the door, but there are only blouses and skirts, my wool leggings, the boots and slippers on the floor beneath them.

"It's work," I answer loudly so she can hear me and close the door softly, holding my hand on the knob. I start for the bathroom, thinking I would check in the tub or behind the door but realize it would do no good even if he were hiding. She's here now, and she requires my attention. He would know that. He would have already left even if they did run into each other. He knows we must talk.

"What are you doing here?" I ask, having returned to the dining room. I tidy up the table, slide aside the newspaper, the small plates left from the morning. I try to sound pleasantly surprised, try disguising the disappointment.

"It's Wednesday," she announces as if this will explain why she has let herself in, come into my house, and started preparing the evening meal.

"So it is," I respond, still not understanding why she is here and perturbed that my husband is not.

"Friends of the library," she adds, jolting my memory to their gathering, the meeting she has every month—the one she had reminded me of during a phone call last week.

I assumed she would call again on Monday or Tuesday to confirm that she was coming. Truthfully, I had forgotten; I always forget what she tells me.

"I told you I would let myself in and fix us supper. I asked if it was okay to spend the night."

"Right, I remember," I lie. "So, what's the soup?" I ask, not letting on that I forgot she was coming.

"Kale," she studies me. "White beans and kale."

"You want a glass of wine?" I ask, stepping in front of her to get to the refrigerator. "I have white," I add.

"Sure," she replies. "But not much. I have to give the treasurer's report tonight. Bonnie is out sick."

My mother is the assistant treasurer and vice president of several organizations. She claims that she never likes to be in charge, but she's happy to be second in command of anything. Nathan has always said it was a blatant act of passive aggressiveness on her part—a way to push ahead her agenda without taking the full burden of leadership.

My mother has always enjoyed being behind the scenes, moving things along without taking any real responsibility. He's right about her in so many aspects.

I grab the bottle and two glasses, pour her one, and hand it to her. She watches me as I pour myself more than I gave her, but I don't explain. I'm not making excuses. I don't have a treasurer's report to make. I see no reason for me not to have as much wine as I want.

"You seem like you weren't expecting me," she notes, peering closely at my face, my body language.

I take my glass and head over to the table, pull out Nathan's chair, and sit, shaking my head. "No," and I take a swallow. "I remembered."

She turns to the stove. She stirs, and her concern manifests in the way she straightens her spine.

"You didn't have other plans, did you?" She asks, her shoulders held too high, her neck rigid, her voice tight, stretched over a knot of emotions. She wears judgment like a new dress.

"Now, Mama, what other plans do you think I might have?"

She turns down the temperature and doesn't look at me.

"She threw the ball," Nathan would always say after I explained another of our fights. "But that doesn't mean you had to take the swing."

My mother hated it when I married Nathan. She claimed I threw my life away the moment I handed over more to my English professor than just my midterm paper. She fought this relationship from the very beginning, said I was only heading to heartbreak, that I was a fool and that I was ridiculous for what I was giving up. She tried as hard as she could to keep me and Violet from ever finding love or getting married. She remains convinced that marriage destroys a woman's life.

"Look at your sister; see how well she is doing," she would say time after time before the wedding; and I would argue that Violet was a totally different person than I, that she always intended to have a life in the military, climbing up that ladder, rank after rank, appointment after appointment. Although I wasn't sure of what might be on my horizon, Violet's choices were never what I had planned for myself.

She turns down the temperature, and I see her searching for an oven mitt since the handle of the pot has surely gotten hot. I start to get up to show her where they are, but she figures it out, and I take another long drink of wine.

She pulls bowls out of the cabinet, ladles soup into them, and brings them over, setting one bowl in front of me. She returns to the kitchen, finds bread I had wrapped in the bread box and cheese from the refrigerator, brings it all to the table, spreads out dinner in front of me, and then waits. She watches as I lean in to take a whiff of the soup.

When we were children, she always wanted us to pay attention to what she set on the table. She liked it when her daughters acknowledged what she cooked, always expecting a compliment before we ate.

"It smells good, Ma. Thank you."

And she blows out a breath, places her hand across her chest, contented, slides out the chair across from me, and sits, reminding me of how little things change.

Chapter Six

*T*t's late.

Mama has gone to her meeting at the county library and returned, but I am already in bed. My door is closed, only a small lamp on, a thread of light beneath my door. It is my way of announcing my unavailability. I said all I wanted to say to my mother before she left. We covered it all—reports about my job, the winterizing of the house I was having done even though it is so late in the season, my decision not to get a cat, and an assurance that I will think about an alarm system now that I am alone.

I hear her. She's close, probably standing at the bedroom door, listening, trying to decide if she will walk in, trying to decide how far to push; she is a bit more careful than she used to be, but in truth, it won't matter. I learned how to play possum when I was ten. I am still very good at pretending to be asleep, and she never seems to catch on. She has always barged in after bedtime, hunting company. It took Violet longer, but she finally got the hang of it too. It has been a wildly profitable game our father taught us well.

To say that my mother is needy is being polite. She wanted to be my best friend when I was still in day care; I just didn't understand it at the time. I thought she was kind and interested in my schooling, my lessons and play, my thoughts about the teachers and the other children; but then her questions, the hovering, her hanging on every word of my reports grew tiresome, and I quit telling her things. It wasn't that I intended to leave her out; I just didn't want to discuss everything with her. I have always needed a certain amount of solitude, time to myself. Nathan claims I have the makeup of a sturdy hermit, but since he shares my love for silence, my quiet ways have never been a problem in our marriage. Before then, however, I struggled mightily since I lived with a chatty and persistent parent.

My mother often called me secretive, even cruel at times when I wouldn't talk to her, when I wouldn't tell her everything from my day at school or what I found during my walks in the woods; but privacy has always mattered to me. It's not that I have things to hide or reason not to share; I simply see no point in small talk or what feels to me like senseless chatter. My sister Violet was better at a relationship with Mama than I was, but even she became weary at times. Our mother has great need for companionship and to feel connected and involved in her daughters' lives. It often pinches and can feel overwhelming.

Nathan was kind to her for a long time when we were first married. He coddled her, engaged her, asked what she thought about things, told her about his own ideas, fed her with attention; but that was not enough. She never really forgave him for our relationship, for pursuing me when I was so much younger than he, for making me smile the way she had never really seen me smile; and whatever he gave her—whatever he tried to give her—was still not what she sought. She still wanted all that from me. She wanted it all from me.

I hear her tiptoe away from the door. She'll go into the kitchen, probably clean out the refrigerator or sweep and mop the floor. It'll take her hours, going through the crispers, pulling out the bags of wilted lettuce, the takeout cartons from China City, checking the dates on yogurt and milk. Then when she's finished with that, she will stack the chairs on the table, pull up the rugs, roll them into piles by the door, and have to search in the washroom for the bucket and mop. She will work until ten or eleven, and I hate it when she does this, but I finally quit fighting her on that. Besides, the kitchen is dirty. It has been for months. I'll let her win this battle. I'm happy to have the help.

I hear her emptying the dishwasher, bowls and silverware clanging, and I roll over and punch up the pillow.

Nathan and I bought this house in our third year of marriage. His ex-wife got the one on Elm Street—the big white colonial with the wraparound porch, the peonies and magnolia tree out front, the porch swing, the antique dressers and beds, the oak dining table, the stereo, prints and paintings, and the new appliances. She got it all, he told me, when I asked why he didn't have any furniture; but even five years after his divorce, when we first started dating, he was still living like a grad student—like someone who either didn't have any money or simply didn't know how to furnish a place for just himself. He stayed in the basement of a colleague's home, owned only a stereo and a futon, boxes of books and albums, a few trinkets from places he had traveled, a cabinet full of files.

Nathan moved into my apartment near campus, displacing my two roommates and filling up most of the space on my shelves. His books and music were really all he brought with him into this marriage, so even though he was older and had purchased plenty more household items than I, we started pretty much with the same number of things. In fact, as I think about it now, I probably had more stuff than he did.

I didn't mind that, of course. In fact, I considered it a plus. It was the only real aspect in our relationship that was level for us. In everything else, he always outscored me, had more points, more experience, brought so much that I didn't have. But not when it came to our home.

I close my eyes and think about finding this house, how we had been talking about it for months, discussing everything we wanted, making lists, calling realtors, and how I had just happened upon this street—our new home.

I burst into his office with the flier I picked up from the clear plastic box posted beside the front steps. It was the end of the term, quiet in the English department. He was grading papers, glanced up from his desk as I flew in, flier in hand, needing to talk, wanting to explain, suddenly appearing very much like my mother, although I would never say this out loud.

"Here it is," I shouted. "Here is our place!"

And we drank champagne I had bought from the convenience store in paper cups he kept for morning coffee, even before we made an appointment to see it because I was so certain this house was meant to be ours.

"It's perfect, Emma," he said when we walked in for the first time. "Absolutely perfect." And I felt like I had just turned in the smartest term paper ever written.

Those were the best days, I think.

We pulled down paper and painted the walls together. We built shelves, hung curtains, made a little garden, added outdoor green plants, baskets of flowers. We filled the house up, room, by room with furniture we bought on Saturday mornings at consignment shops and yard sales. It took us years, but finally it is decorated with all the things that are us, just us. Not an ex-wife, not the in-laws, not mine—me more than him or his, he more than me. Us. Everything here is only us.

I remember the kitchen table, finding it behind an old restaurant downtown that was closing. The owner didn't want it but said he couldn't hold it for us until we rented a truck, so we carried it all the way home. We walked with a table, laughing and teasing each other, Nathan walking backward for three quarters of a mile, me making us stop every couple hundred yards because it was so heavy, and my shoulders were sore.

We carried that table down the street, through a park, over sidewalks, up the front steps, and put it right where it still sits. It fit perfectly in front of the window, and we set it down and walked around and around it, moving it a little this way, a little that, and then turned around and walked right down to the restaurant to get the chairs. We laughed later that we could have fit them in our car, that we didn't need to walk the rest of the furniture home, but we were so excited, so thrilled with our find, we didn't think of it until we were already home sitting at our new table. Sitting in our new dining room chairs.

I smile to think of that now.

The bed, I recall, arrived in almost the same way. A student, a mutual friend told me, was moving out of her apartment—had a bed, a queen with matching linens, and it was ours if we wanted and could pick it up that afternoon. I was excited, left work early to meet him there, and the two of us pushed and shoved and yanked and pulled the frame and slats, mattress and box spring, headboard and footboard down three flights of stairs. This time, I remember, we did have a truck, but still, the move, the find, the exact location for its place here in our room was something that just the two of us did together.

As I think about it now, every piece of furniture, every doily of lace, every pot and pan, bowl and plate and glass, everything speaks to who we were in the beginning and who we still are.

It's true that we didn't build this sweet nest at 137 Cottage Place; it went up in the 1950s with all the other quaint homes on this street. But we certainly made it what it is today. We certainly added the charm and character with every bit of remodeling and furnishing that's here. We did all that, and I love it. I love this place even in its upended state.

"It's a good house," I say to nobody. "It's a real good house." And as I hear my mother scrape the chairs across the floor, I know it is being cleaned.

Chapter Seven

I've slept late again, and I scramble from the bed. I check his side, just to see if he might have crawled in after Mama went to sleep, crawled in and slipped beneath the covers, holding tight to the edge like he did when he came to bed late.

He did not show up.

I can tell because his pillow remains on my side, down near where I tucked it between my knees before I fell off to sleep—a way to relieve a backache but also a way to generate a little comfort. I realize that he could have slept without his pillow, or he could have woken me up and retrieved his. He could have gotten up and found another one, but he didn't. His side is cold. His pillow untouched.

He hasn't shown up; I can tell.

"Well, aren't you the sleeper peeper?'

"I don't even know what that means," I tell Mama as she hands me a mug of coffee. I pull out a chair with my foot and sit. I hold onto the mug with both hands.

"Aren't you going to be late?" She is dressed for the day, her hair and makeup perfect. She's wearing a different dress than the one she was wearing last night.

I check the clock on the wall above the window. *Probably,* I think but don't answer. I take a sip of coffee. She's added milk and this softens my sour mood a little.

"How was your meeting?" I ask, trying to sound cheerful, interested.

"Hardly had a quorum," she announces. "But it was fine."

I lift my chin, declaring mild interest.

"Would you like some oatmeal?"

I glance over to the kitchen at the small saucepan on the burner. I didn't even know we had oatmeal, and this makes me wonder if she bought groceries at some point in this stay—bought groceries and has unpacked and shelved them in the pantry. Once he retired, Nathan insisted on buying the groceries.

I nod. *Why not?* I think. She's here. It's been prepared, just sitting in a pan on the stove; and I like oatmeal. It'd be nice to have breakfast. I can tell my answer makes her happy, and she hurries to the stove, pulls out a bowl from the cabinet, spoons the oats in it, adds brown sugar, honey, and a few other things I can't see from where I am sitting. She walks my breakfast to my table along with a carton of milk. I move my arms out of the way, creating a place in front of me, and she sets both the milk and the bowl down.

I make a small hole in the center of the oatmeal and pour in the milk while she watches. She stays standing across from me as I take my first bite. "Yum," I say because she's waiting.

"You want dried cranberries or pecans?"

I swallow the bite. "We have cranberries?"

"You have cranberries," she answers. "I bought some things for you last night on my way home."

I shake my head and take another spoonful.

She pulls out the chair across from me and sits, watching me closely.

"You already ate?" I ask, wondering why she isn't joining me.

She nods, still watching.

I lift my eyebrows at her. "Good," I tell her, meaning the oatmeal.

She smiles, clears her throat to get my attention.

"Em, I cleaned out a few things in your pantry."

I shrug. I heard her last night. This doesn't surprise me.

"I cleaned out some of Nathan's things," she adds.

I hold the spoonful of oatmeal over the bowl. I do not take the bite.

"What things?" I ask, trying not to sound concerned.

She leans away from me in her chair, drops her eyes. She picks up her mug and takes a drink.

I rest the spoon on the bowl. "What things?" I ask again.

"It's just some things you don't use." She fidgets slightly in her chair. "I just thought after the talk we all had ..."

"What things?" I ask again as I sit up taller.

"His coffee grinder, that weird wine opener you never use, those Middle Eastern teas." She pauses. "A few other things."

I place my hands on my lap, trying to steady myself. "Why would you do that?" I take in a breath as I feel the tightness in my chest, the hard thud of the words as they fall.

"You don't have enough room in there, and so many things are out of date. I was just trying to make some more space for you, tidy things up a bit."

I push myself away from the table, stand, and head over to the pantry, open the door. It's practically empty. It's not just the grinder. She's also cleared out the bags of coffee we got for Christmas last year and the set of small cups—demitasse, *fincan, pocillo*—a professor from Europe, somewhere in France or the southern tip of Spain, I forget, sent us when we got married, the set we cherished and saved but never actually used.

There were four of them, I remember—four small cups, pale yellow with a narrow, red lip painted on each one. They were dainty and fragile, and I always worried I would break one, so I never brought them out of the box, never used them for fear I would hold my cup too tight or set it too close to the edge of a counter or table, accidently touch it and cause it to fall.

She moved out the cans of chickpeas and spinach Nathan bought for an Indian meal he was planning at one time, several boxes of long grain rice—brown and black that I love but never cook—long, plastic bags of pinto beans that I'm sure have gone bad, a six-pack of Austrian beer neither one of us particularly liked, and the six jars of honey that I kept on the bottom shelf. There was more, I'm sure; but as soon as I realized the honey was gone, I slammed the door and headed to the table.

"Where is it?"

"What?" she asked, her voice soft, innocent.

"All of it. What did you do with it all?"

"Well, Em, love, it's in different places."

"Tell me," I say, folding my arms across my chest. "Tell me where you put everything."

"Most of it was old, Em," she explains, her voice meek and tinny. "The rice had bugs, and the beans were molding. The grinder, well, you never use that. You told me you liked ground coffee. You grind it in the stores—you told me that. The honey was rancid."

"Where?" I ask again, not bending.

She sighs and pushes away from the table. She walks in front of me, opens the cabinet under the sink, pulls out the trash can to show me.

There are bags and boxes and containers of food.

I pull it out and set the can in the corner, leaving both cabinet doors opened.

"Emma, you can't save that. It's all out of date. It's no good."

"Where else?"

"What?"

"The wine bottle opener."

She closes her eyes and shakes her head, but she walks to the back door, exits to the small landing, and returns with a large box. She sets it on the counter in front of me, and I open the top. I see everything she's taken out. There are small kitchen accessories, a few of his cookbooks, the box of cups, which I open to see if any have broken, tins of sardines, and the mason jars of honey. I return the cups to the box and take out a jar.

"Emma, that honey is too old. You need to get rid of it. You need to get rid of all of this. It's no good to have all this stuff sitting around."

"Thank you, Mother, for coming over. It's always a pleasure to have you visit." My smile is forced, tight. "I'm going to go to work now so you need to get ready to leave."

"Emma, I just cleaned out a few things that I don't think you need anymore."

"I'm going to get ready for work so you can see yourself out." I put the box on the counter, slide it next to the stove. I keep the trash can out and close the cabinet doors. I walk out of the room and hear what I think is her small breath of resignation. Then I know she is taking my bowl of oatmeal and dumping it in the sink.

Chapter Eight

*S*ince I was going to be late to work anyway, I just called in sick. I don't want to go to the office today; I don't want to see Kathryn and try to explain once again why it is I have such difficulty getting to work on time. I don't want to tell her my mother stayed the night and then be pushed to say more than I really want to say, pushed to complain about how she meddles and has been doing more of it in the last few months. I just can't do it today; so I've come to the hives. I've come to be with the bees.

Nathan started his latest project in his last year at the college. He knew he was going to retire, so he spent some extra time researching his interests, the ideas he had kept for years for what to do in his free time, and decided that beekeeping showed the most promise. My husband has always fancied himself a farmer of sorts even if it is of the urban variety. In our small garden behind the house, he has grown German Johnson, beefsteak, and Roma tomatoes. He has had trestles of beans strung above rows of sugar snaps and lettuce, spring onions and turnips. He likes herbs, has a small garden of rosemary, thyme, basil, and mint; and every summer he tries to find something new to plant, some rare long-necked squash or seedless cucumber, a melon that no one around here has ever heard of.

Until these past two springs and summers, he usually worked his gardens in the early hours of the evening, finishing with his weeding and harvesting before dusk. I would come home from work and find him hoeing the rows, as thrilled as a child in kindergarten with a new craft project. He'd hold up every pepper and potato, smiling, rotating them in the fading sunlight, turning them one way and another, later placing all the produce in bowls and baskets all around the house. Our home in the summers has always been filled with color, and I missed that when he stopped.

I remember the day that summer when I told him things in the kitchen felt gray, that I hadn't realized how much I looked forward to the yellows and deep greens, the bright reds and small bursts of white that used to line our shelves and fill the countertops. It was late June, tomatoes just turning, corn not quite ready, and I saw immediately how my words made him sad. And even though the doctor restricted his mobility after that second surgery, the one that was meant to repair the damage from the first one, he limped out to the yard and tried to yank up the weeds, trying to force a garden that was not there.

It was, however, hopeless. With the long rains and the late frost, the neglect we both showed to what was or could have been growing, the hospital visits and the therapy sessions, the depression we both battled, there was nothing coming to life in our backyard. And even though I know he wanted me to keep things growing, asked me several times to plant a few seeds, find the tomato cages and set them out, I told him I would keep the bees, but I could not manage the gardens.

I knew he was disappointed, that he struggled with what had been taken out of him, taken from him, the verve he was known for, the ability to work tirelessly outside in the sun, the simple way to bring seeds to life; and I knew he was disappointed in me, that I didn't share this love to make things grow, and I wasn't willing to do it for him.

I take in a deep breath and open the door of the truck. I walk around and pull open the tailgate to retrieve my suit and smoker and then change my mind. I decide I don't need either item. Today I know that I can do this without protection.

It's true; in the beginning I was very nervous around the bees. Nathan told me that the bees can register emotional energy and that if I can just steady my nerves, invoke within myself a spirit of patience and gentleness before I go to the hives, the bees won't even notice me. He claimed they are more irritable if the beekeeper is irritable, that they pick up and respond to the emotional state of anybody near them. He said, in fact, that he took up beekeeping for that very reason. He thought the work would steady him, which is something he expected he would need when he no longer relied upon the benefits of tenure and teaching.

When he bought his first hive, and I helped him set it up, I kept getting stung. I didn't like it, didn't want to be around them. But after his accident, when he began to realize that it was too much for him, that the beekeeping, like the gardens, required unrestricted mobility and a physical strength he no longer had, when he became sullen and withdrawn, moody and hard to please, the bees took notice. He was stung every time he came to the hives, and finally, it just got to be too hard for him. Once I got the hang of it, kept a steady breath and put aside my fears, when I ultimately got to the stage where I didn't mind the stings so much, I discovered I liked beekeeping. I found the bees good company, and I kept the hives. It became something I looked forward to. So I took over the work, and I eventually quit getting stung.

It's quite cold today—there was a brief storm in the night and a thin layer of snow covers the ground—and I imagine the bees will be so sluggish and reluctant to leave their warm, dry houses that I won't be at great risk for stings. I may not be as steady as I should be while standing in their proximity; but the weather will have a lulling effect on them.

I close the tailgate and head over to the hives.

The beeyard Nathan started is about twenty miles from town. It sits near a line of hardwood trees at the back of a large family farm that used to grow hay and alfalfa but has been idle for years.

The old farmer who owned the land died, and none of his children intend to work the fields and pastures again. It was for sale and then taken off the market because one of the sons, now nearing sixty years of age, has thoughts that he might want to return to the area, build a house, and retire to the country. Nathan met the man when he stopped to ask if he might keep his bees on the property, and he claims the sixty-year-old from Washington, DC, wouldn't last two weeks out here in such a rural and forsaken area; but I guess the farmer's son still carries the romantic illusion because he hasn't yet put the property up for sale again.

We pay him thirty dollars a month to keep the bees. Three hundred and sixty dollars a year and a case of honey that we ship to him at his apartment in Georgetown every August. It's an arrangement I plan to continue, even though this summer will be my first time actually harvesting the honey. Last spring a college student did most of the work. He was studying biology, found out about Nathan's bees from a professor, and wanted the chance to work on his senior paper about bee farming; so Nathan let him do all the box cleaning, teaching him how to use the bee blower to keep the bees away, the pulling and stacking of the supers to collect the honey later. The young man was devoted to Nathan and did everything required to keep the bees last spring and summer; but now that he's graduated and gone, this year I'll be on my own.

I, too, was given a few lessons from Nathan, like when he explained the options a keeper has for removing the bees so that the honey can be extracted. He made sure I understood how to use the blower and a bee brush, a chemical repellant if necessary, and even the fume boards. Still, as hopeful as we both might have been at the time he taught me, I have no idea if I'll even be able to manage the hives past April and May and into the summer.

I walk the path down to the hives and notice that the morning sun is warming the ground and expect the bees will be tempted to come out. Bees are very clean creatures and will not defecate in their hives. I learned that they can hold onto their waste for days at a time, choosing sickness or even death before the elimination of their waste materials inside their homes. In winters past, Nathan called attention to the marks of droppings outside the hive entrances, evidence of their extreme dedication to keeping tidy living quarters.

The bees, Nathan explained, will also remove the bodies of dead sisters, dropping the tiny carcasses some distance from the entrance of the hives—clearly a difficult task since the worker bees are dealing with bodies nearly the same weight as their own. Nathan used this as another example of the bees' tidiness and how eliminating the dead from the hives is an important task as well as a sign of a healthy colony. I remember thinking when he told me about this that it's possible it's more than just about being clean— the action of the bees at the time of death might also speak to their rituals around loss in the colony; but I didn't say anything that day because I knew so little about the bees and even less about grief.

Today there is not much movement around the hives, and I get closer just to make sure the bees are still there. I notice the entrances and now see some activity, though I imagine because of the cold, the bees are clustering, metabolizing, and creating heat for themselves, staying warm by being conservative and holding up together.

"The bees offer us great lessons in community life," Nathan would say as he puffed the smoker a few times, watching the bees leave the hive so that he could work on the frames or check the supply of honey.

"They work and live, somehow knowing the survival of the colony is completely dependent on how well they can perform their necessary functions together. No bee can exist in isolation," he would say, and I would think about him, about the few friends he kept close, the one or two colleagues from work or old college roommates he met from time to time—still not so many as to call them his colony, his community.

I never called him on it, my isolated husband, because I basically chose the same life as he; and even though he nudged me at times to join some group, maybe hang out with a few women my age, I preferred to be with him, to enjoy our simple life, enjoy what we made and had together. I don't need sister bees, I would say; and he would nod and smile and appear to accept my assessment of my needs and desires. He rarely argued his point.

He did tell me once, though, that he felt guilty he had somehow taken me away from the true college experience the other students enjoyed, that because of him I was somehow missing out on something wonderful, something necessary to my development and my general well-being. I promised him that how I spent my free time, how I chose to be with him instead of at parties or women's groups was not something I did because he pressured me but was purely my own preference and that I never thought of myself as missing out on anything. Being with him, alone with him, was what I wanted, what I cherished most. Since I have always been a loner, I never envisioned some tantalizing community life for myself anyway; I never really needed friends. I think my willingness to become intimate with him, joining a relationship, choosing to fall and be in love—even this surprises me. I always expected to be alone. I always expected a life of solitude.

No, I love the bees and enjoy what I've learned about them, but even today I do not feel the need for friends, have never longed for my own colony; I have never had need for some great buzz of activity.

I bend down near the entrance for a better view and watch as a few workers slowly emerge from the hive, nosy a bit around me, their intruder, without harm or malice, and then sensing the cold wind, hurry again inside.

I stand up and lift my face east toward the late morning sun and then glance down to see a dead bee, dropped by a worker, I'm sure, rolling across the fine snow.

Chapter Nine

"I changed the battery for Mrs. Lewis." Bus is standing beside my desk.

Today I made it on time to work. I was even here before Kathryn, which meant I was busy when she came in, already on the phone with customers and therefore didn't have to talk about what kept me away yesterday. It's a strategy I learned when I missed all those days in the summer and fall.

I don't recall Mrs. Lewis. I shake my head, wait for more information.

"The woman on Church Street. The widow," he says, and I suddenly remember the conversation I had late on the afternoon he and I shared chips, ate our tacos together.

"Oh." I don't really have much to add.

"She doesn't know how to operate the system," he tells me.

"Well, did you help her?" I am going through my database of recently purchased business licenses. It's a matter of public record, and I read the list every month. This is where I start making my cold calls.

"She didn't really seem to be listening," he explains. "She's still pretty mired in her grief."

I look up at him, wonder how much he knows about being mired. He's wearing his service uniform for winter: a long-sleeved denim shirt with our logo embroidered on the upper left corner, khakis, black closed-toe shoes. There is a tiny smear of shaving lotion just under his ear, but I don't make mention of it or stare at that part of his neck too long.

"He's only been dead a few months," he says, his hands resting on his hips.

I nod. I remember the conversation. She bought the system one month before he died; it was still under warranty. I now recall everything I know about Mrs. Lewis, the muddled way she talked, the confused manner in which she answered my return call; she didn't seem so much mired to me as just lost. That's what I remember thinking when I got off the phone with her—she seems lost.

"I made an appointment to go again and show her how to arm and disarm. I think she can do it."

"Great," I reply with a slight smile and then return to my computer screen. I need to make at least twelve calls today to complete my marketing quota for the month, and I really need one new business to sign on with me. In spite of my lack of enthusiasm or dedication, I did well early in the month with residential clients, adding eight new installations; but I'm still down on my business numbers.

He stays where he is; I can feel him watching me, but I don't respond.

"Are you okay?" he asks.

"Sure," I answer, still scrolling through the list. "Perfect," I add.

There are several nail salons opening this month and a new restaurant on South Street. Both of these are potential customers, and I highlight them to copy onto my call sheet.

"I heard you were sick yesterday."

"It was just a twenty-four hour thing. I'm fine now," I say, and I glance up and smile, giving the appearance of confidence, hoping to confirm the prognosis.

"Okay," he says but lingers.

I see Kathryn come out of her office and stand at her door. She's glancing around, making sure all her staff is busy, I guess. She gets to the two of us, and when she catches my eye, she gives a big grin and waves.

I return the greeting and wave in her direction.

"Do you need to know when I'm going?" Bus says.

"Where?" He's lost me now.

"To call on Mrs. Lewis, for the tutorial."

"Oh, sure," I answer. I click off the business license page and navigate my way to the scheduling software.

"Monday," he says, stepping around the desk and moving behind me so he can see his schedule. "Monday after lunch."

I nod, type in the information. He has an installation scheduled, and I highlight it for him. "This is already booked," I explain and slide over in my chair when he leans down, his face close to mine. I notice the diamond stud in his ear, the strong chin.

"Oh." He seems disappointed or uncertain. I'm not sure of the tone.

"I can try and change it for the morning," I say, still leaning away from him. "I don't remember if they requested this time or if I just gave it to them."

"Nah, I'll just call her and see if I can go by during lunch." He stands up, but he remains close, and I notice he smells clean, like soap, the way Nathan smelled before he switched to a body wash. I close my eyes briefly while I take in a breath. I miss the soap smell.

"You don't even have to put it on the schedule. I'll just do it on my own time."

I open my eyes.

I turn to him and shrug. "Okay." And I click off the page and return to the business licenses I was reviewing.

"She said you were real nice to her when she called."

"I *am* a professional," I say, trying to sound funny, but I come off sounding agitated or proud. I never really do funny very well.

"She said you were kind, that it was like you seemed to understand, and she was grateful for that because she was having a hard day."

I nod. "She sounded troubled, like she could use a friendly voice."

"It was his birthday," he informs me, and for some reason, this causes me to stop studying my screen and glance up at Bus, who has taken his place beside my desk. "He would have been eighty-one. She had gone to visit his grave and just walked in the door when you returned her call."

I'm guessing he's buried at the city cemetery; that's where most of the old-timers from around here are laid to rest. It's about a mile and a half from the center of town, a nice, wide plot of land, a series of rolling hills, rows and rows of small, white headstones. I know the place well. I used to run a four-mile loop that included a few laps around the graves.

"Well, I'm glad I was helpful," I say.

Jon gets up from his desk and heads toward the break room. I assume our conversation is getting on his nerves. Our work stations are very close, and he told me once he has a difficult time concentrating when there's a lot of noise in the office.

"Kind," Bus replies.

"What?" I am watching Jon, wondering if I need to apologize later.

"She didn't say you were helpful. She said you were kind and seemed to understand." He seems to be waiting for something from me. I'm not sure what it is.

"Bus, I'm sorry, but I really need to get some of this work done before lunch; I'm so behind after missing yesterday."

"Oh, sure, I'm sorry," he says and appears to be genuine with his apology.

"It's okay," I reply, now wishing I hadn't said anything. He actually seems embarrassed.

"No, I need to head out on a call. So, thanks then." And he's gone before I can try to change his mind.

Jon returns, and I notice him watching Bus as he leaves.

"Why is he so concerned about an old widow?" he asks. "And how did he get a name like Bus?"

I decide against the apology, just shake my head, and keep working.

Chapter Ten

It's late when I get home because I stopped at the grocery store for milk. I used the last of it yesterday morning, cooling off my oatmeal and then drinking four cups of coffee. I knew my mother wouldn't run the errand, not after the way we left things between us, and I forgot to buy any on my way home from the beeyard.

I stand at the refrigerator and think about what happened yesterday morning, how it ended between us, how I got up from the table and left her here. I heard her leave, just as I had asked her to do, before I got into the shower. I'm sure she packed quickly, hurried out of the guest room. When I checked, the bed was made and the used towel from the guest bathroom was folded on top of the washing machine.

In the kitchen, my bowl was still in the sink; she had not even taken the time to wash it, and I know how she hates to leave dirty dishes. She had not turned off the coffee maker or put away the nuts and honey she had put in my oatmeal. This was not the typical departure of my mother. She was hurt by my reaction to her cleaning, and I suppose it will be a few weeks before I hear from her again. I guess I will call in a couple days and apologize.

The kitchen is the same as I left it, almost exactly the same as it was before my mother made the changes. The box of cups was in the pantry along with the cookbooks and the wine opener. I did throw out the rice and pinto beans, some of the cans of food that were out of date. I did allow those to be purged; but not the accessories, not the things that he used. I open the refrigerator and put the milk on the shelf. When I close the door, I see him sitting at the table, and I'm not startled at all.

"When did you come back?" I ask, taking off my coat. I walk to the entryway, hang it on the rack, slide out of my boots.

"Have a cup of tea," he says, and I study him. He looks better than he did a few months ago. There's slight color to his cheeks, his hair has grown, his eyes are not as dulled. "There's ginger and chamomile."

I know about the tea because I bought it last November, near the time of his birthday. I bought it as a kind of birthday gift we could share. He always liked ginger, and I always wanted chamomile. This was the first brand I had ever found with the combination of our favorites. I thought he would get a kick out of it, this blending of our passions.

I put the kettle on, turn up the stove, take out a bag, and find a cup. I stand in the kitchen but in a spot where we can still see each other.

"Tough day at the office?" he asks.

"Today was fine," I answer and then wait. "Before."

"Carla," he says knowingly. "Your mother."

I nod.

"And what was the fight about this time?" He folds his arms across his chest, and I think how skinny he is, but not bad—not sick, just thin.

I shrug. "The same."

He glances away. "Me."

I nod. "She tried to throw out the demitasse set."

"From Ronald."

I pull the string from the teabag and drop it in my cup.

"Well, it's not like we ever use it," he adds.

"She meddles."

"That's our Carla."

We are silent as we wait for the teapot whistle. A few cars pass on the street in front of the house. I hear a siren in the distance. When the water is ready, I take the kettle off the stove, pour it in my cup, and then hold it up, offering more to him. He shakes his head, and I take my cup and join him at the table.

"You look tired," he says to me. "Still not sleeping?"

"I always get a few hours," I answer, knowing he recognizes when I lie.

"And work?"

I wrap my hands around the cup. "It's work."

"And how is the state of security systems these days? Still able to make a living on the fears of the privileged?"

"Not just the privileged," I reply. "I got an order from the homeless shelter this morning. It seems someone keeps breaking in during the morning hours when they close up to clean. They jimmy the lock and come in and steal toilet paper and cans of black beans from the kitchen."

"Well, I suppose on the streets those are a valuable commodities."

"The black beans or the toilet paper?"

"Maybe they're sold together?"

"Lots of fiber, I suppose. I see the connection."

I smile, and then he smiles.

"It was fine," I say, answering his earlier question about work.

"But not fulfilling?" he adds.

"If you recall, I gave up that search a long time ago."

He glances down at the table, and I know this is a sore subject for the two of us. He's always wanted more for me.

"I went to the beeyard," I say, hoping this will bring a bit of cheer.

"And how are the mighty drones and workers?"

"Everybody seems okay." I take a sip of my tea. "There were a few tracks around the hives."

"Racoon?"

"Possum," I answer, remembering the openhanded print, the small, flat indentation of what looks like a thumb.

"Did he get any? Did he do any real damage?"

I shake my head. "Something must have scared him off. I didn't see any signs of dried body parts."

"Dirty little scoundrels."

"Now, now," I say, deciding to use his own words against him. "Everybody needs a bit of honey."

He smiles. "Yes, I know." And he nods.

I drink more of my tea and feel him watching me. I know he knows we need to talk. I know he knows we didn't finish the conversation from a few days ago, the last time I saw him, the morning after the big fight.

"What about you?" I ask, trying to avoid what I know is necessary. "What have you been doing?"

He shakes his head, drops his face. "Oh, not much."

"But you've been okay?" I never ask him where he goes when he leaves, what he does with himself while I'm at work. I don't know much about things for him anymore. I don't ask, and he doesn't volunteer. So, I have no idea. "I mean, you have a place to stay, right? You get something to eat at meal time?"

He shrugs. "I found a guy who keeps me in beans," he says and we both laugh. "You know ..."

And I don't want to do it. I don't want to have the conversation. "How about another cup of tea?" I ask and jump up from the table. I hurry to the stove, add water to mine, glance over in his direction for an answer.

"We should talk, Em," he says, and I return the kettle to the stove. "I'm sorry," I tell him as I put the cup on the counter and walk to the table. I kneel in front of him, my hands on his knees.

"I'm sorry I said all those things. I don't want you to go. I don't care what my mother thinks—the others either. I want you to stay. I want you to come home for good and stay."

And he reaches out and takes my hands, and for a moment, it feels like it always did.

Chapter Eleven

"I'll be there in a bit." I end the call and try to see the time on the clock by the bed.

"It's seven thirty in the morning, and it's Saturday," he tells me. I roll over, and he's lying beside me. It's like we never had the fight, like I never told him he had to leave. Like it was when he was healthy, himself—when we were so strong, so happy, so together.

"I have to go," I say, not wanting to explain.

"Emergency at Klocks?"

"K-Locks," I say. "You know I hate it when you call it that."

"Well, it's a ridiculous name for a security systems business. What was Kathryn thinking when she chose that classification? Didn't she realize that everyone was going to call it Klocks, that no one was going to get the clever hyphen?"

"A clever hyphen, that's cute," I say, throwing off the covers, getting my feet caught in the blanket. "But as an esteemed professor of the English language, is it right to claim that a punctuation mark might actually be clever? Aren't you making a very big leap with your anthropomorphizing? Isn't the grammatically correct way to say it, that a hyphen was cleverly placed?"

He rolls over and pulls all the linens with him, yanking me back because of my tangled feet. "You're too smart for your own good," he mumbles and then gets up, keeping the sheet and blanket wrapped around him and leaving me alone.

"Well, smart maybe, but am I as clever as a hyphen?" I make a move to get out of bed too, but I then sink down, my head on the pillow, my hand feeling for him, searching for the warm place on his side that I'm sure I will find, but it has already cooled.

"Who needs you this early?" I hear him calling from the bathroom.

"It was Bus." I say it softly because I don't want to fight about the new guy. I stay where I am; I don't want to get up.

He walks in with the sheet and blanket dragging behind him. It makes me laugh seeing him this way. His hair is sticking up all over his head. He's wearing bed linens.

"Bus?" he asks. "Why does an installation guy need an office worker?"

"That's how you think of my position?"

He holds out his hands. "Isn't that what you are? Don't you work in the office?"

I feel like I should argue, but the truth is he's right, in the most literal sense of course. I leave the bed, walk past him in the doorway to the bathroom; he stands aside, making room for me.

"He's out on a call," I respond. I close the bathroom door. I brush my teeth, flush the toilet, make a lot of noise so I don't have to hear if he's fussing or interrogating me. It is odd to get the call so early, but Bus knows about our bees. He's found hives at the site where he's making an installation—landowner out of town—and he doesn't want to bother the insects. He thought I might help, that I might know what to do with them. It's a perfectly legitimate request.

When I walk out of the bathroom, Nathan is sitting on the bed. He's still wearing the sheets.

"You slept late," I say, after thinking it.

"It was nice," he answers.

I smile. It was. It was better than nice. It was heavenly and divine and perfect, and as I think about it, I realize I should call Bus and tell him I can't come. I should crawl back in the bed with my husband, wrap us both up in the sheets and blankets with arms and legs all intertwined, and just stay there all day.

I can tell he is reading my thoughts, and he even stretches out his arm, pulling open the covers, an invitation.

"No," I say, waving a finger in front of him. "We did this before." I hurry over to the chest of drawers, pull out tights and underwear, and start taking off my pajamas.

"We did what before?" he asks, teasing me. He knows what I'm talking about.

"Nathan." It's all I say while I dress; but then when he pouts, I go on. "I promised Kathryn I wouldn't just drop off the face of the planet again. She was very kind to give me back this job." I yank on the tights.

"You're her best employee," he insists.

"I was out for a long time."

"You were taking care of me."

"I was out three months after your surgeries." I pause, remembering. "And then again later."

"You were taking care of me."

I walk over to the closet. "I can't," I tell him but I know I'm wavering. I know the temptation, and I am fighting it with all I have. I open the doors and pull out a sweater and a pair of jeans. "If you stay, it has to be different this time."

He sighs. "So what's the big emergency for a man named Bus? And what's his real name anyway, and how did he get such a ridiculous moniker?"

I button up my jeans, yank on the sweater. I don't turn around; I'm trying to decide if I'll wear my boots or just a pair of sneakers. I can't remember if they were calling for rain today or not.

"His first name is Buster. He was named for a movie star."

"Keaton?"

I shake my head. "Crabbe. Played Tarzan and Flash Gordon," I tell him. "He was an Olympic swimmer and designed pools. Apparently, Bus's mother had been taking swimming lessons in a Buster Crabbe pool when she went into labor and decided it was a good name for her firstborn." I'm thinking just the sneakers, but I didn't see the weather forecast.

"He died tripping over a wastebasket."

"What?" I turn to look at him now.

"He was seventy-five, tripped over a wastebasket in his house, had a heart attack, and died. Buster Crabbe."

"How do you know this?"

And then I remember, Nathan has always known the strangest facts about people, especially how they died. He's always fascinated with how a person dies. I just shake my head. "Never mind. I forgot it's what you do for entertainment."

"There is usually an interesting symmetry in a person's cause of death," he explains in his rough morning voice. He's still sitting on the side of the bed.

"So you say," I reply and decide on the boots. We may be outside in mud or old snow if there are bees. I make a quick search in the closet, and then I recall I left them at the door when I came in from work the day before.

"And Bus?" He's not letting this go. I don't understand why he keeps needling me about the new guy.

"And Bus was what his younger sister called him. Like Em for Emma and Nate for Nathan, it just became his name."

"But Buster is already a nickname. Why would you shorten a nickname, make a nickname out of a nickname? If I'm correct, Buster was not the actor's real name."

"No, it was Clarence," I reply, feeling slightly puffed up that I knew something he didn't.

"You researched that?"

And I notice a change in his voice, and I don't really know why. I turn to him. "Yeah, so?"

And he doesn't say a thing. He opens his arms and gives the sheet and blanket a big fluff, spreading the linens across the bed, and then he crawls underneath them.

I don't understand why he would be upset that I searched the internet for the man Bus was named for, but I check the clock and realize thirty minutes has passed since the call. I need to go. I walk out of the bedroom without saying goodbye.

Chapter Twelve

"Good morning," I say as I get out of the car. Bus is standing near the van. I glance around, not seeing anyone, not seeing any bees. "So, where are they?" I ask. I have arrived at the scene of the system installation. It's an old farmhouse not too far from where we keep our hives.

"Oh, hey, Emma. I'm glad you could make it."

I'm not sure if this is some passive-aggressive comment about my late arrival, and I'm about to make an excuse when I see his face. His blue eyes sparkle, and I see tiny lines at the corner of his lips. He's about my age, I think. Forty, maybe younger, and he isn't the least bit upset or troubled. I see nothing but sincerity. I check my watch. It's been more than an hour since we talked. I didn't write down the correct address and ended up on the other end of town, but I decide not to explain or apologize.

Bus smiles and then turns his attention behind the house. I follow his gaze. "They're over there," he says. "Behind the barn. Eight boxes stacked in groups, facing south. I knew they were bee boxes because I've seen them before."

"Hives," I tell him, and he turns to face me. "That's what we call the boxes and the parts where the bees live. Supers are the cases for the honeycomb frames and sit on top of them." I shake my head. "Never mind," I add, thinking I sound like Nathan telling all these bee facts, stuff most people find boring.

He nods, folds his arms across his chest. He's wearing a thick denim jacket, jeans, a ski hat, and work gloves. And unlike others with whom I have shared my bee trivia, he seems to be taking in what I've said.

"What are you doing working on a Saturday?" I don't remember setting up a weekend appointment. "Who owns this place?"

"The woman from South Carolina," he says as if that will jar my memory. "The daughter whose father lived here and died not too long ago."

I think about the week's calls. I shake my head; I don't recall.

He pulls out an order form from the pocket of his jacket. "Julie Pendleton. Her dad was Ray Mills." He studies the paper a minute and folds it up and stuffs it in his pocket. "Mills Farms." And he looks around at the place where we are standing.

I remember. There was a break-in just after the funeral. Somebody smashed a window and crawled in, took a television, a couple rifles, some old jewelry. The police caught the guy, found the loot; but Mr. Mills's daughter was concerned someone else might try again. She can't come up from Columbia and clean the place out until the spring. *Yes*, I think, *protecting an empty house*. It's our bread and butter.

"I thought you were doing this Monday," I say now that I know the customer and the situation.

"She called last night. A friend of her father—a neighbor— telephoned her yesterday because he saw a strange car in the driveway. She had the police come out here, but they said nothing appeared to be out of place." He shrugs. "She had my cell number, called me about eight o'clock last night, asked if I'd come out today." He zips up his jacket. A sharp wind picks up, and I tug my coat around me too. "Kathryn approved of the overtime and the weekend pay, and I didn't have anything else to do."

"What did she order? She still just asking for the outdoor monitor?" I think about the call and how we went over all the packages for home security.

He shakes his head. "Changed her mind; she wants the deluxe. That's why I need to get behind the barn, why I need to move the hives if I can." He glances over at me. "Anyway, I guess since you're the original sales person, you'll get the bonus points."

That'll be nice, I think.

Kathryn set up a sales contest for the office staff. We get points based on the packages we sell. Deluxe systems generate a lot more points than standards. This might help me make a few extra dollars at the end of the month, and I suppose I should thank him since he somehow talked her into an upgrade; but I don't.

"You got a key?" I ask, wondering how he'll get inside to install the system without one.

"Neighbor had it, met me here first thing."

I nod.

"So, what about the bees?" I ask. It's cold, and even though I don't mind talking to Bus, I'm not enjoying standing outside. Plus I'm curious, and I want this conversation to move along.

"Sure," he answers and starts walking toward the barn standing not far behind the house. I guess the daughter wants the barn monitored too. Otherwise I'm not sure I understand what he was even doing out here.

"She asked me to check out everything," he tells me as if he's read my mind. "She wants to make sure nothing outside was vandalized and stolen since she isn't exactly sure what the police checked."

We walk to the front of the barn, and I notice the barren fields around us, the strings of grapevines near the house, the pasture to our left.

"They're stacked over here." And I follow him around one side.

The barn is an old red one, not terribly big. There's a tractor parked on one side—looks new—and horse stalls on the other. A loft with bales of hay stacked across it. There are a few tools hanging on the walls, and piled in the corner are harnesses, straps of old leather, rope, horseshoes. Over at the rear entrance of the barn there's a wooden sign that reads Mills's Eggs, and when I get to the area where Bus found the bees, I realize that I have met Mr. Mills. He was a regular at the town farmer's market held every weekend in the spring and summer. Nathan and I used to buy our eggs from him. I glance around the property; another building I assume is the chicken house stands directly behind the main house. It's white, squatty, has windows lining it with a long, thick layer of plastic covering them.

"When did he die?" I ask Bus.

"What?" He's moving a rock with his foot trying to shove it right next to the barn, out of my path.

"Mr. Mills, when did he die?"

Bus stops, scratches his head like he's thinking. "Not long ago," he answers. "Thanksgiving maybe."

He was a kindly old man, friendly. He and Nathan always talked. Nathan wanted to know about the chickens—how many he had, what kind. At one time he was thinking about getting a couple to keep in our backyard, but eventually he decided he'd rather have a bee house than a chicken coop. Mr. Mills talked to him about that too. He was one of the farmers Nathan had sought for advice about beekeeping. Of course there are hives here. Mr. Mills also sold a few jars of honey at his booth, and if I'm not mistaken, he gave Nathan some tools, a smoker he said he didn't need anymore. He was less interested in keeping bees, I recall him telling Nathan last year.

"Here they are," Bus says, jolting me out of my memories. Still, I can't help but feel a little sad. I didn't realize Mr. Mills, the old farmer, had died.

He had fifteen hives, all of them white, placed neatly on stands and stacked against the southern wall of the barn, strategically placed beneath an overhang, sheltering the bees from rain and snow. They are pushed together; and at first sight, I can't tell if there are any bees inside the boxes or not. The entrances are covered, and there are no signs of opossum or mice having overtaken them. I walk over, place my ear near the frame, but it is quiet. I can't hear the shivering.

Bees have one important job in the winter and that is to keep the queen warm. They form clusters; and in the warmest part, the place where the queen resides, the temperature can rise to over eighty degrees. The worker bees take shifts, gathering around the queen, fluttering their wings, and making a kind of shiver that you can feel if you put your hand on the outside of the hives. It's this movement and this continuous use of energy that keeps the inside of the hives warm.

The concern for beekeepers, of course, is that in order to maintain the temperature and be able to keep the queen warm, the bees must have enough honey. This is their source of energy, and this was one of the first lessons Nathan taught me about beekeeping. You must make sure you don't take too much honey from the bees. What you leave in the hives must last the bees at least four months.

I check the outside of the hives, but I see no evidence that the bees have come out and defecated. Usually when there's snow on the ground like today, you'll see tiny spots of yellow near the entrances, giving proof that the bees have left their clean hives and come outside to relieve themselves of their wastes. I place my hand on the side and wait, but still, I hear and feel nothing from inside.

Carefully, I raise the metal, protective overcover of the hive in the center. It's not hard to lift and move. I place it beside the stack. And then I raise the telescoping cover and the inner cover. This last one is stubborn, but after a few gentle pulls, it loosens and lifts. I wait for a second just to make sure the bees won't swarm and sting, and then I look inside.

Chapter Thirteen

"They're gone." I return the inner cover, placing it on top, and reach down for the other two.

"Wow, all of them?" Bus is standing right behind me. He must be waiting for me to check and see, but I don't have too. It seems pretty clear that if this one is empty, they all are. There's no humming sound from any of them, no sign of bee glue sealing up the hives.

"I would say so." I place the protective overcover on top of the telescoping layer and place them both on the top box, and then I pull off the covers of the other two that are on top of their stacks.

Both of them are empty, just like I thought. I put the two covers on the ground and stand aside. I check to see if there might be other hives somewhere else.

"Maybe they're just extra ones he had and didn't use." I say this mostly to myself, but I know Bus is listening. Of course, empty hives don't necessarily mean that the bees died or lost their queen, disrupting the colony; Mr. Mills could have sold them before he got sick.

Still, I stand on an edge of sadness. An empty hive—it just makes me lonesome.

"Maybe," Bus says in agreement, but I can tell by his tone that he doesn't believe it.

I turn to him; he clearly has something else to say.

"Or maybe no one told them that Farmer Mills died."

I set the cover on the top of the first box. "What?" I wipe my hands on the front of my legs, knocking off the small splinters of wood and paint that had come off the hive.

"Maybe the bees weren't told that their beekeeper was dead."

"I'm not following," I say.

The sun has climbed above the tree line behind us, and I feel the morning rays warming my back. I face that direction.

"John Whittier's poem."

"About bees?" I ask.

He nods.

"I don't think I know it."

"But you know him, right?"

And I do. I remember him from the nineteenth-century poetry class I took. He was a Quaker, American, and known as much for his advocacy for the abolition of slavery as for his poetry.

"He was a Fireside Poet," I say, letting him know I recognize the name. "A lot of his poems were turned into hymns for the Quakers." And I recall a couple of his that we read and discussed in class: "Moll Pitcher" and "Barbara Frietchie." The last poem I remember best. It is said that Winston Churchill recited the poem when he was driving through Maryland with the president at the time and that F.D.R. later asked his staff for a copy of Whittier's verses because he was embarrassed the British leader knew more about American history than he did.

"Right." Bus smiles. "Did you know he had a poem published anonymously, and it was erroneously attributed to Ethan Allen for almost sixty years?"

I shake my head. "Nope, didn't know that."

"Yeah, 'The Song of the Vermonters, 1779.'"

I don't really see where this is going but would like it to hurry. Even with the reach of the sun, it's still cold. "And he wrote a poem about bees?"

I don't remember much more about Whittier. In school I was more drawn to the women of that time period. And truthfully, like Nathan, I prefer the British poets: Brontë, Browning, Rossetti.

"Stay at home, pretty bees, fly not hence!
Mistress Mary is dead and gone!"

I assume he's reciting a line from the poem, so I wait respectfully before trying to make my exit. I wish I had brought a thermos of coffee with me. I think about Nathan and wonder if he's still in bed.

Bus faces me, and it seems like he wants something from me, recognition, applause—I'm not sure. With my husband the professor, usually a touch on the arm or a smile will do. He just likes to know I'm listening. I drop my eyes away from my coworker, turn in the direction of the empty hives.

"'Telling the Bees,'" he goes on.

"Nice," I say, facing him again.

"You keep bees, and you never heard about this?"

"The Whittier poem?" I have not heard of this poem. Like I said, I only remember the patriotic one and the hymns.

"No, the practice of telling bees that their person is dead."

I shake my head. I haven't heard of that.

"I think it's been around a long time."

I wait. This is all news to me.

"I can't believe you don't know this." He thinks about it and then goes on. "They say that if you don't tell the bees about the death of their keeper, they'll fly away, swarm, leave in distress."

I pull back slightly. Nathan has never mentioned anything about this to me before, and I thought he told me everything, especially the weird and interesting facts he learns. He always likes that stuff most. I feel somehow betrayed not knowing this.

"I even read that in parts of England, a person must tap three times, making the report of the death with each tap." He reaches over and knocks softly on the side of the hive closest to him. "Mr. Mills is dead," he says, leaning into the top.

I watch him grin, but I am not amused.

"I guess we're too late here, though, huh?" He sticks his hands in the pockets of his jeans. He shifts his weight from side to side, and I realize how small he seems compared to Nathan, how simple, pedestrian.

"Do you need me to help you move the boxes?" I am eager to leave Mr. Mills's farm. I don't want to be here anymore.

"Nah, I can do it now that I know they're empty."

I nod and check the area around me again, thinking about the farmer's bees, wondering where they went, wondering if the old wives' tale is true.

"I'm sorry I called you out here for nothing," he says. "If I had known the bees left, I could have just stacked the boxes somewhere else myself." He kneels down in front of the hives, and I don't know if he's going to try and pick them up five at a time, or if he's going to keep knocking on them and making his announcement.

"It's fine," I reply.

"Is it true they need about sixty-five pounds of honey to get through the winter?"

I watch as he tries to remove the cover from an entrance on one of the supers. He's gentle as he pulls it away. He peeks inside.

"More like eighty," I answer, hoping we are done here.

"That much?" he says, sounding surprised. He stands up and faces me, and I feel warmth.

I nod and glance away.

"That's a lot of honey," he says as if I don't know it.

"I'm going to go now if you don't need anything else," I say, stepping away.

"You want these boxes?" he wants to know. "You can reuse them, right? I mean, even if the last beekeeper died and didn't tell his bees." He grins again. "I can ask the farmer's daughter if you can have them." And he reaches in his pocket and takes out his cell phone like he might call her.

I move over to stop him. "No." I say, a bit too loudly.

And he glances up as if this surprises him.

"No," I say, softer this time, and pull away my hand. "I don't want them."

"Okay," he replies, watching.

"Okay." And I can't explain what's come over me—why I want so badly to leave this place, why I reacted so strongly to the offer, why I need to get home. But I am sure about one thing. I'm sure I don't want this dead man's hives.

"That's it then, I guess," he notes, eyeing me.

"That's it," I repeat, and then to finish the conversation, I nod and step away.

Chapter Fourteen

"Of course I know about Whittier's poem." He sounds angry, like I'm accusing him of something, and I don't know, maybe I am.

He's still in his pajamas, which isn't like him. And right away I notice that something seems off. He's lost more weight when I thought he was becoming healthier. I wonder if this has just happened because I don't know how I didn't see it before—last night or this morning before I left. He looks like he was when he first got sick. His face is drawn, his shoulders hunched, his spine curved. I start to ask him what's going on, what's happening to him; but I don't. He's private about those things now. He doesn't like to talk about his condition.

"It's not a big deal," I say, waving off the question; but I can tell he's not letting it go.

"You think it's a big deal," he argues, "or you wouldn't have brought it up."

I shrug, head toward the bedroom to change clothes. He's sitting at the dining room table, his usual seat, and probably has been reading the paper or listening to music. I don't think he's eaten.

"So Buster reads?" I can still hear him. "Whittier," he says, and he makes a kind of huffing noise, I suppose, trying to sound amused; but it comes out as snobbish, and I know he's just trying to deflect my query about the bees, about the wives' tale.

"This is his girlfriend's influence, I suppose."

This gives me pause since I don't recall telling Nathan about the girlfriend and her work toward a PhD. I wonder if he's been poking around the university, returning to the department, checking on things when he's not been here. I wonder if he's even met her, but I imagine that would be impossible. As far as I know, he doesn't actually see or speak to anyone there.

"She likes the British writers," I say, but I don't think he hears me. I think Bus reads without influence—at least that's how he strikes me.

"He was a lobbyist, a magazine editor." He makes that noise again and I think he's talking about Bus. "He wrote church hymns, for Christ's sake." Nope, he's clearly still on Whittier.

"I suppose they were," I call in reply.

"What?" He's yelling at me now. "Oh." He got the pun.

"He wrote decent poems," I say before I go into the bathroom, not sure why I feel the need to defend the American poet, and I close the door.

He's saying more about Whittier, I suppose, but I don't hear him. I flush the toilet and wash my hands.

"He had a nervous breakdown," he is saying when I leave the bathroom and head in his direction.

"Well, that certainly doesn't hurt his reputation as a poet, do you think?"

He waves my comment away. "He was weak."

"I think he was brave for what he stood for. Abolition was not a popular stance to take in his time."

"His writing was stiff, pious, unmoving, even with his lofty subjects."

"This isn't about the poet." I throw on my old robe as I pass by the dining room table and walk into the kitchen. "This isn't about Whittier and his poem."

"No?" He sounds surprised, but I know he's just bluffing. He knows exactly what I'm talking about. He knows exactly where this is going.

"No," I answer.

I glance at the empty coffee maker, then note that his cup on the table is also empty.

"You didn't make any coffee for me?" I ask.

"I wasn't sure when you'd return," he says sheepishly. "I wasn't expecting you in time for morning coffee.

"Whatever," I say and head to the sink to rinse out the pot and add fresh water. There is a pause, and I catch a glimpse of things outside the window. The neighbor is picking up his paper, notices me, and waves. I wave in return and wonder what he sees from his view across the road, wonder if he knows what goes on in here.

"Have you eaten?" I'm thinking of scrambled eggs, toast, and some of that peach jam he likes.

I don't hear a reply, and I move to the doorway where I can see him.

"Breakfast?" he asks.

"Of course breakfast. What else would I be talking about at nine o'clock in the morning?"

"No," he replies. "I have not eaten. I have no appetite."

I watch him. I see how he's trying to blame things on me, how he's trying to make me feel guilty for leaving him this morning—for meeting with Bus, for making him go away before, for the way he appears, the way he's losing weight. I see what he's doing, but I'm not taking the bait.

"Fine," I say and retreat to the kitchen.

I open the refrigerator and take out the eggs. I locate the skillet, take a piece of bread from the plastic sleeve. I prepare my breakfast, and I don't hear him. I wonder if he's gone to the bedroom; but when my egg is done and the bread has popped out of the toaster and been put on my plate, I walk into the dining room, and he's still sitting right where he has been since I returned from the farm.

"You haven't told me about the bees," he says and waits.

"Mills must have sold them," I answer, spreading the peach jam on my toast. "There weren't any there," I add and take a bite.

"When did he die?"

The question stumps me, and I don't answer right away. I shake my head and take a sip of my coffee. I am hungrier than I thought. "About three months ago," I respond.

I had checked it out on my phone before I left the farm. Searched the internet for the obituaries from November. Bus was right; the old man died the Saturday after Thanksgiving. He was in the hospital—cause of death was listed as a "short illness." I don't mention this.

"He was a good man," Nathan says softly. "Loved his chickens. Sold good honey."

"He had goldenrod, wasn't it?" I ask, trying to remember what his bees took in their hives, where they got their nutrients.

He nods. "Had his field full of the blooms. You saw them, didn't you?"

I shake my head. I don't remember goldenrods. Alfalfa, corn stalks, several grape vines, old plots plowed in rows; but I didn't notice goldenrods. Of course, it is winter, and they wouldn't be growing now anyway.

"I went out there before I got my bees. He showed me around."

I didn't know this, but I don't know a lot of the places Nathan goes.

"You didn't know he died?" I ask, and he stares at me for a second and I shrug. "I just thought you'd probably know."

He glances away like the question bothers him and doesn't answer.

I take another bite of my toast and egg, and there is no more talk about Farmer Mills, his bees, or the poem by the Quaker poet.

Chapter Fifteen

By the end of the weekend, Nathan appeared more like himself. He seemed less agitated than he was Saturday morning, and by Sunday night he was eating. We stayed in, read to each other, watched an old Cary Grant movie. I was awake when the snow started late last night, had gotten up to use the bathroom and caught a glimpse of the first flakes falling. He got up when I didn't come back to bed and sat with me on the sofa. Inch by inch it fell and froze, building a white fortress around us.

We talked about the past, about our travels out west, the coast of Oregon, the lakes in Wyoming. He almost took a teaching job at a small college in Idaho, and we talked about how things might have been different for us if we had moved away from his hometown—if we had left the south and the stories about us that everyone knew, if he had been riding his bike in a place where people were used to cyclists, a place where drivers knew to share the road.

He seemed sad at times in the late-night conversation but tried hard to keep everything light. Neither one of us brought up my recent decision to have him move out, leave, and the more recent one to have him stay. But I'm glad he's still here. And I was glad Sunday night. I hate the snow when I'm alone. By Monday morning it was as if we had never had the fight that lingered for us both, and he is happy. I, however, still well understand the consequences of our reunion. I alone know the costs.

"Why don't you stop off at the Indian restaurant on your way home, pick up some chicken masala. We can have that great beer you like so much—Taj Mahal—such a magnificent name for a drink, don't you think?" he says.

I'm putting on mascara in the bathroom, getting ready for work. I don't wear much makeup but the mascara seems to help my looks a little, helps me feel slightly more girly, which I'm not even sure why it matters. My mother's voice in my head I guess. *"Wouldn't just a bit of blush make you feel better?"*

I check my watch. I think I'll actually be on time today, even though we didn't get three hours of sleep between us. He's in the dining room or the kitchen, I'm not sure, but Indian food does sound good. We used to go there or order takeout at least once a week, but then I remember that it's Kathryn's birthday, and the staff decided a couple weeks ago to take her out. We reserved the banquet room at the steak house in town. The owners have been customers forever; our systems have foiled at least three break-ins. The manager is a friend.

I remember we decided that spouses and significant others are invited, but I can't bring Nathan, and he's going to be angry that I won't be home.

He's still talking when I walk into the dining room. I already have on my boots, my coat around my shoulders.

"So what do you think?" he asks, and I assume he's referring to dinner. "Chicken masala or saag?"

"It's Kathryn's birthday," I tell him. "We're having a thing."

He waits a beat. "Oh" is all he says.

"I already agreed to go," I try to explain.

"Sure," he replies, but it's easy to see he's hurt. "Where are you going?"

"Black Angus," I answer. "It's not my first choice."

"Yeah, I remember." And he picks up a magazine and thumbs through it.

He took me to the village steak house only once. It was after the news broke about our relationship, and he had dealt with the fallout from the dean. He had finished his required suspension and just found out that he was not going to be fired.

Technically, he hadn't really violated the college ethics standards. I wasn't his student when we started dating, and he was divorced long before the affair was public. Of course we both knew a professor dating a student was frowned upon by the administration of the college. Elon is a small, private school. No one wanted a scandal. The dean, however, had his own ethical dilemma involving another professor, a new one he had been instrumental in hiring, and he was therefore lenient with Nathan. So when the suspension was lifted, we went to the Black Angus to celebrate our newfound freedom to be out and the fact he still maintained his job status.

A colleague was dining there, and it became awkward. I ended up getting food poisoning from the salad bar, and we just decided later that we didn't want to go there again. It was not the celebration we had anticipated. I only go to the restaurant when Kathryn chooses it for office parties or special dinners. I don't even like steak.

"I won't be long," I try to console him. "I can stop by and get you some Indian food," I offer.

He shakes his head without looking up.

"Nathan, if this is going to work, I can't isolate myself again. It just draws attention to this." I take off my coat and sit down at the table. There are things I need to say, boundaries that need to be drawn. We can't just return to the way it was before I made him leave.

"To *this?*" he asks. He peers up at me now.

"To us. You know what I mean," I say.

"Why do you even have to work?"

I'm holding my coat in my lap, and I lay it on the table beside me. We've had this conversation before. He thinks I should quit work, somehow believes we can afford to do so, even though I've shown him the bills, explained to him about the lack of insurance coverage.

"I need to work to pay off the mortgage," I say softly. "And besides, it's not good for me just to stay home all the time. I need to be out some; you've said that yourself."

"I don't feel that way anymore. I choose to withdraw that argument."

"It was a sound argument, and you were right. If I quit work or stay locked up in this house, people will notice." I hesitate. "You know that. It happened the last time."

"We'll do better," he says, and I feel his hands on top of mine. I watch him take in a sharp breath, recognize his needs, his desires. I feel him so close.

"We did as good as we could," I answer. "We were careful, and I was meticulous about everything; people still found out. I almost lost everything."

I think about the group coming over on a Thursday afternoon just after the holidays, just a few weeks ago—the "Intervention," as Nathan and I like to call it—the letters they had written and then read to me, the sincerity in their concern, the embarrassment of being discovered; the excuses I made, the lies I told, the way I spoke of sorrow.

"It was a close call. I can't have that happen again."

"You told your mother to leave you alone last week. You made it perfectly clear that she doesn't have the right to meddle in your decisions. And Emma," he is pleading now. "This is your decision."

I pull my hand away. "I know that, and that's why this has to be done like I say. Not like you say. You don't get a say anymore. I have the only say here. And this is the only way it's going to work. I have to keep my job, and I have to keep my social activities intact. I have to keep you out of the rest of my life."

His chest falls, and he lets out a long breath and nods. "Okay. We'll do it your way."

It's a small victory, but one that I'll take. I know I'm weak to let him in like this again, but I can show some strength with how things go.

"I know this is hard," he tells me. "I know it takes a lot."

"Just as long as you'll let me handle this my way"—and I slide my chair away from the table—"we'll be okay." I catch the time on the clock. I'm late again.

He follows my eyes. "You should go," he says, which surprises me. I expected him to push me to stay, maybe make me miss, not just the dinner after work, but the whole day too. Maybe he is going to listen to me this time.

I stand, grab my coat from the table. "I'll be home by nine."

"And I'll be here," he replies.

I take my keys from the bowl where I keep them and walk to the door without turning around, and I can't decide if his response is a source of comfort or discontent. I shake my head as I ponder the nagging question—*what have I done?*

Chapter Sixteen

"Emma, now that you're here, would you take this call?" Kathryn is standing in the doorway to her office. She is holding a piece of paper in her hand. I check the clock on the wall behind her; I'm only fifteen minutes late, but still, it's noticeable, and I hate being caught right when I walk in. It's like she's been waiting for this very moment.

Fifteen minutes isn't that bad, and I know I can make up that short span of time, but as I glance around, it seems like I'm a lot later than that. Everybody else is in their place like they've been here an hour or more, making me check the time again; but I was right, it's just fifteen minutes.

I nod. "Absolutely, happy to do so."

I decide not to make an attempt at explaining my tardiness. I don't really have an excuse, and the truth is I'm winded from walking so fast from the parking lot, so I don't want to talk because I know I'll sound breathy and desperate. Besides, I can see the look in her eyes; trying to rationalize wouldn't be helpful. I take the paper from her hand.

"It's the Presbyterian church on Fourth Street, the one that was broken into last week, the one in the news reports."

She waits while I read over her note. It says exactly what she's telling me—it's the Presbyterian Church on Fourth Street, but I don't know about the break-in. I don't read the local paper.

I glance up at her and smile like a dutiful employee. "Got it," I reply and turn toward the direction of my desk. I feel her eyes following me. Maybe she was expecting an explanation—I don't know.

"You're late." Jon leans over the divider, staring at me and stating the obvious that my boss did not. He eyes Kathryn like maybe he's spoken to her about my delayed start.

"Thank you," I reply, taking off my coat, dropping my purse on the floor beside my chair. I walk over and hang my coat on one of the hooks beside the kitchen. Since I'm there, I peek in to find out if anybody made coffee, but the pot is empty. I guess that means no one has taken on that responsibility, or everybody has already gotten a cup. I shouldn't waste any more time, but a pink box on the table catches my eye; somebody brought something from the bakery.

"You missed the meeting." Jon is still standing so I can see his face. I can only assume he was watching me while I stood at the kitchen door.

"There was a meeting?" Perhaps this explains why everyone else is here and seems to have been working for a while.

"The monthly staff meeting, remember? Fourth Monday of every month. Thirty minutes early, eight o'clock Boss brings doughnuts."

"What?" I know nothing about this, but now I know who went to the bakery.

"The monthly staff meeting," he says again, like this time it will mean something.

I shrug and wait.

"Oh right. You missed last month's because you were sick or something." He pauses, wrinkles his brow like he's trying to remember something from the past. "Did you come to the ones in December and November?"

"The monthly staff meeting," I mumble, and the light comes on. The monthly staff meeting that was announced last fall, followed by the complaints that were lodged about having to get to work early on a Monday. How Kathryn called us into her office to explain and tried making it sound like it was a special breakfast and that it would be fun. No one had believed her, and frankly, I hadn't taken her and her memo seriously. I wonder now how many staff meetings I've missed and the reason she hasn't yet called me out for not attending them.

"Why does she let you get away with being late all the time? What are you, like, a relative or something?"

I take my seat, turn away from Jon. I don't really have an answer as to why Kathryn goes easy on me, and I see no reason to engage with my colleague. I do wonder if I should jump up right now and apologize to her; but when I check out her office, Kathryn is making an exit. She puts on her coat and pulls the door closed. She's leaving. It's clearly not the best time to approach her.

"We didn't really talk about anything," Jon explains. "She just wanted to give us a sales report and a kind of pep talk."

I spin my chair around when she's left the building. "Why do we need a pep talk?"

"You don't know?" he's asking me.

I shake my head. I haven't heard anything new about K-Locks Security Systems. As far as I know, nothing's changed for Kathryn's small business. We're still managing quota, and she's still making a profit.

"CPI is opening a regional office here."

"CPI? When?"

I know we've been taking hits from the national companies for a while. With internet capabilities and the ease with which businesses have to streamline and globalize services, small security companies like Kathryn's are being forced to close their doors across the country. We're like any mom-and-pop operation—we can't compete with the big guys.

"Do you even read the memos she sends out?"

"Yes, Jon, I read the memos." Although the truth is that I haven't checked anything in my company inbox for a while. Kathryn sends out lots of emails with pithy quotes and motivational ideas. I quit opening her notes some time ago, probably about the time we got that first one about the monthly staff meetings. I figure if it's important she'll tell us; we're not that big of an organization, and I thought our boss's policy was to always tell us what's urgent. I guess I've been wrong, and this makes me wonder what else I don't know.

"Check your files," he says. "I've got work to do." And he sits down, clearly tired of trying to catch me up on the happenings at the office.

I turn on my computer, log in, and go right to my inbox. There must be twenty emails from Kathryn marked Memos and Reminders. I open them up, read and discard them since most of them are old and not all that important, until I open the one from two weeks ago.

It reads: "With the expansion of CPI in our territory, we need to accelerate the volume of our customer base. Let's work hard to increase our sales before this competitor arrives. If we can lock in new customers before they set up shop, we can halt the damage that can be done by this national chain. Those of you focusing on businesses now need to work on finding domestic clients as well. Please plan to come to our next monthly staff meeting with ideas on how we can keep K-Locks the number one security system in the Triad Region!"

And it was signed "Kathryn."

Four more memos like this one followed. It appears the monthly meeting held today was an important one after all.

I'll need to talk to Kathryn. I have to make some excuse. I check the piece of paper she handed me when I walked in the door and think that signing a new customer would be great news to start with before I try to make amends.

I close the computer files and pick up my phone and start to dial the number on the paper, but before I can punch in the numbers,

Bus has come in from the rear of the office and is standing in front of my desk. It seems he has something to say so I put down the receiver to greet him.

Chapter Seventeen

"Hey," he says. "I need to talk to you."

Seeing no one else around, I realize he is in fact, asking me to give him my attention. "Okay," I answer.

He takes in a breath like what he is going to say has been rehearsed.

"I'm sorry again about calling you out Saturday." He has a cup of coffee in his hand, and it makes me think I will go and make a pot now that Kathryn is gone. It certainly doesn't matter at this point if I make this sales call right away or in fifteen minutes.

"It's not a problem," I say, starting to get up. I hope there's milk in the refrigerator, and I wonder if there are any doughnuts left.

"Yeah, it was stupid of me." He stays where he is, and because he's so close, it makes it awkward for me to leave.

I keep my seat and think that I probably don't need a doughnut anyway, but I would like some coffee.

"Seriously, it wasn't stupid at all, Bus," I say, trying to help him let this go, but it's easy to see he needs to speak his piece. I wonder just how long he's been worrying about this. It truly wasn't this big of a deal to get the call.

"It's just that I knew you had that experience."

"Right."

"With the bees."

"Yep."

I hear a sigh behind me—a sure sign of my coworker's discontent. I figure Jon is already searching for another job. Monthly staff meetings at eight o'clock on a Monday morning when some staff members are obviously excused; a push from the boss for more sales; a competitor moving in—yeah, he's searching, which means I'll have to train someone new while trying to meet my quota.

"It was dumb of me."

"Bus, it's fine. I didn't mind. Really."

"If I had known the boxes were empty and that the bees were gone, I wouldn't have called."

I don't understand the point of all this. *Why is he going on and on with it?* I thought we went over his apology already, and it really is of no matter to me. I start to wave it off one more time since I know I need to make this call to the new customer and because I also want a cup of coffee, but when I glance up at him, I get an odd feeling that there is something different about this bit of nicety happening now, two days after the call, after our brief meeting at the farm early Saturday.

I can tell that there is something more to this Monday morning confession, and although I'm not sure why, I start to feel slightly anxious.

"Bus, I told you I didn't mind going out there, so just let it go, okay?" My voice tightens, so I smile and start rifling through the folders on my desk. I'm trying to be polite, but I also want to give the clear sign that it's all fine between us and that he needs to walk away.

I sense him standing there. He hasn't moved.

"I just feel bad that I ... you know."

I hold the folders in my hand and look at him. I sit up tall in my chair. I clear my throat, feel the skin on my neck tingle and grow hot.

"Bus, I went home and went right back to bed, slept until noon. It was fine."

I can only assume that he's sorry for waking me—that he's talking about the early hour that he called, the inconvenience he assumes about me, of having gotten up and dressed and driven out there for nothing. And I just want him to go. I feel as if he's drawing attention to my small, confined area, to my late workday start, to me.

I really need him to leave. I need to have an ordinary day at work. I need to call this lead. I need to make a sale.

He's leaning in now, close, like what he has to say is private; his head is down, his shoulders rounded and hunched. His eyes are soft, and he seems as if he needs something from me, some response or absolution. And suddenly for the second time this morning, a light goes on, a light I had not expected or prepared for. *How is it that I can miss so much?*

He knows.

I don't know how he found out; but it's clear. He knows.

"I feel bad."

"Let it go, Bus." *Please, just let this go.*

"I feel bad that I made the joke about dead beekeepers, that I wasn't sensitive to ... that I spoke out of turn."

I feel my face flush, my throat start to close, and I hear my heart beating. I need to leave. I need to get out of here or away from him. I need to stand up, get my coat, walk out; but I can't. I'm stuck having to hear this confession, his pity.

"I'm sorry I mentioned the Whittier poem," he goes on.

He pulls away now. He's holding the coffee in one hand, but he doesn't seem to know what to do with the other. He shifts his weight from side to side. He's clumsy. If he practiced this in his head, he hadn't anticipated how it is to be saying it to the person he thinks he wronged.

"If I had known about your husband ..."

He hesitates, and that's when I finally make my move. I take in a breath and stand up. My hand whips across my desk, searching for my purse or just moving somehow, and I knock over the files I had set out.

I feel Jon stand up from his desk. "You okay?" he asks, but I don't answer.

There's a pause, and then I watch as he walks away in the direction of the break room, but then turn around and stare. Now a couple of others who were chatting or working on their computers, just doing their jobs, have heard what's going on, and I feel them all peering in my direction. Dexter steps closer.

And Bus just keeps talking, like he can't stop, like he's on this roll and has to say these things, has to say *it*.

"I mean, if I had known that he was the primary beekeeper, not you, not the both of you, I wouldn't have brought up that poem or that old wives' tale about telling the bees."

I quickly drop from my standing position and bend down to pick up the files from the floor, and I hear the loud thud of blood rushing to my head.

"If I had realized that you inherited the bees, that you took over because he ..."

I stay down on the floor, kneeling by my chair, the folders spilled and strewn around me. I feel my right hand clutching my chest.

"I just wouldn't have said anything as stupid as that if ..."

The office has gone silent, and his next line echoes all around me.

"If I had known he was dead—"

I breathe in sharply; it's practically a gasp, and I quickly stand up with some of the files in my hand.

"Just forget it, Bus," I say too loudly, and I hear Jon moving behind me. He's returned from the break room, and I think he's coming around his desk, coming to my rescue perhaps, but he doesn't appear.

I stand alone.

Everyone has stopped what they were doing. All eyes are on me.

"I need to go out for this call ... I need to go out ... I need to go."

And I spin, throwing the files on the desk and reaching for the piece of paper Kathryn gave me. I grab my purse and somehow get to the hooks where my coat is hanging, find mine, and yank it hard, causing the collar to rip so that it hangs loosely from the rest of the garment. I stuff it under my arm, moving as fast as I can out the door.

Chapter Eighteen

I have not fed the bees this winter. Nathan made that recommendation to me when he turned over the hives. He said that he learned this lesson the hard way a couple years ago when he first tried to use feeders. He had become worried about the honeybees, worried that their boxes seemed too light when he tried to get a feel for how much honey there was left in the hives; and like a lot of novice beekeepers, he thought he needed to feed them.

He researched as best he could and bought feeders from a beekeeping supply house he found online. He followed the instructions and placed the small plastic containers close to the beeyard. Experts explained that this method would be easier that using frames of honey from other hives. Feeding them that way, he read, by opening the hives of two colonies, breaks the seals the bees have worked so diligently to create—seals made out of the bee glue that protects them from the cold. Taking honey from one hive to give to another often causes stress for both groups, and Nathan thought the feeders would be less intrusive.

So he bought a couple and made a concoction of sugary syrup and hung them near the hives. For a few weeks it appeared as if it worked. The bees seemed to be fine. But it was unusually cold late in the season that year, and when he came out to the hives getting ready for spring, he discovered that his bees were dead. They had drowned in the feeders, and he had to start all over again with new bees.

From that point on he made sure he left enough stores of honey, about seventy or eighty pounds, and did not harvest all of it in summer but rather allowed them to feed on what they made, and when he explained it all to me, I agreed with his reasoning. We weren't really ever in the beekeeping experience to make money or turn a profit. He started it as a hobby, and that's pretty much the way I have continued to think of it.

Some beekeepers in very cold places like the northeastern part of the country and in Canada, he told me with a depth of sadness in his voice, kill their bees, gassing them at the end of each harvesting season. They take all the honey they produced in the summer and then just get rid of the bees as if they never mattered, as if they were only as good as their honey.

I think of him now, explaining this practice to me, sharing what he thought to be this ugly side of beekeeping. We were standing by the hives, and he held out his arm where a honeybee landed, and we both watched as it walked from his hand to his elbow.

"*I do not fully comprehend these mortal ways,*" he said, quoting some obscure poet but speaking from his own truth.

Like Kathryn had noted, it's true that there isn't much to do in the winter for bees, but that doesn't mean there aren't a number of challenges they face during the cold months. They have to struggle with the threat of starvation, mite overload, beetle overtake, and the severe winter storms that sometimes occur.

There are the hungry and destructive animals—the opossum and raccoons—that arrive ready to steal the honey and destroy the bees' homes. There are mice that try to move in, chew up the combs, and make their nests. And there are the roaches, which nobody in the animal kingdom seems to like.

There are always dangers in nature for the bees, so that even though Nathan didn't actually pull off the tops of the hives and see the bees for a few months, he liked to come out here, liked to know that at least from the outside, everything appears to be in good working order. I have found I have the same protective tendency. After all, no one ever knows when trouble might strike.

I pull into the driveway, park the car, and turn off the engine. I just stay as I am for a few minutes, knowing that I've come to the farm because I couldn't think of anywhere else to go. Flying out of the office like I did, I had to go somewhere, and I didn't want to be at home or sitting in some booth at a restaurant. I'm not quite ready to make a sales call, so I've just come out here—like I did after the recent fight with Carla, like I do a lot when I feel overwhelmed. I drove the twenty miles out of town and am now just sitting in my car at the beginning of the dirt path that goes out to the hives and the line of trees where we keep our bees.

I pull out the key and get out of the car and stand by the door for a few minutes. It's warm this morning, the sun bright and high, and I lift up my face, close my eyes, and I feel better able to breathe than I did just a few minutes ago. As I anticipated and needed, there is comfort to find when I come out here, even though I'm not sure exactly why.

I take in a long, deep breath and start walking. It's about a quarter mile up to the hives, and I'm glad I wore my boots, have a coat, even though it's now torn. I know that I could easily drive closer to our row of stacked boxes, but the sun is so warm, and I'm so clearly in need of getting myself together, I can use the walk.

There is very little traffic on this county road, not many houses, and I feel alone out here. I suspect it won't always be this way. Sooner or later the development will keep reaching east from Greensboro and west from Mebane and Hillsborough so that the farms will be subdivisions, and the chicken houses and barns will be strip malls. I've seen the landscape change over the years, and I'm sure it will just keep growing. Still, for now, this remains rural and peaceful territory.

I walk, and because the pain is so fresh, the event so recent, I cannot help but think about what just happened at the office—how abruptly I left, how the walls started to hem me in, how much strain and pity Bus's eyes held as he tried to make his apology, tried to explain what he didn't know when he said what he said. How it appeared that he was trying to put things right but proceeded only to dig the hole deeper for himself. I think about how awkward our next conversation will likely be and how I dread seeing him again, facing him once more.

I assume it had to be Kathryn; she's the one who told him; it had to be. Jon never talks to Bus, and I'm not even sure what he knows about my marriage and dead husband. Margaret never tells what she's heard, never participates in office chatter, and the other installation guys, Dexter, their manager, don't really ever hang around at the office. They don't usually even see each other; so it has to be Kathryn. A light breeze blows, and I tug my coat around me.

I get to the hives, and I place my hand on the top of each box. I wait for the feeling of vibration, the bees in their brood nest, generating heat, metabolizing energy; and as antsy as I am, I try to be very still and quiet.

That's when I feel it. I know they are in there even without lifting the box to feel the weight. I sense their presence, the vibrating ball of bees inside.

I notice also that a few bees have left the hive since it isn't that cold outside, the temperature warm enough to let them go out to eliminate their wastes, clean out their little habitats, and I stand and watch as they fly in and out the entrances. I am careful not to get too close, however, because I'm not protected. I'm not wearing a suit or helmet. My heart is beating too fast, my breathing still ragged and loose.

I think about Farmer Mills and wonder if his bees died, or if he gave them away, sold them to another keeper. I think about the poem, about what Bus said on Saturday—how easily he had mentioned Whittier and made a joke about telling the farmer's bees that Mr. Mills had died. He had been careless with his words, but they had not been hurtful. If anything, they opened up a channel for Nathan and me to talk—one that hadn't really opened for us since he died but didn't leave.

I kneel close to the last hive, my ear to the wood. I hear their tiny movements, their work and devotion to keeping their queen safe and warm; but I do not speak to them since I have nothing to say. I simply close my eyes and listen, relieved that most of them are still inside and that not many have left their hive.

My pulse still racing, my mind bent with trouble, I know that if they noticed me today, I would surely be stung.

Chapter Nineteen

"Hello, I'm in here." The voice is male.

I left the hives in better spirits, but not so good that I can return to the office, so I decided to make my calls. I met a guy at the side door who sent me to the rear of the church, to the door nearest the parking lot. He told me that door would be open, and he was right. I checked the doorknob, which was unlocked, turned it, and pushed it open a bit. I had just called out a hello.

I clear my throat and walk in. "I'm Emma," I say as a way of announcing myself. "I'm from K-Locks Security."

From the office near the door I hear what sounds like a drawer close, a chair squeak, followed by footsteps coming in my direction.

"Hey there, hi." He stands in front of me, holding up his hand, like a wave or maybe it's some church sign or blessing for visitors—I'm not quite sure. He looks to be about fifty, still youngish, a sort of twinkle in his eyes, brown hair tousled with touches of gray.

I stand in the doorway. "You called us?" I surprise myself with just how calm I seem, how unordinary this visit is.

He seems to be thinking. His hand is still up. And then he drops it to his side, the greeting and blessing completed. "Hmm," he says, like he's forgotten. "Well, come on in." And he steps aside so I can walk through the office door.

I assume he's the pastor and this is his study. He's not wearing a clerical collar, but he seems at home here. There is a large desk facing the door, cluttered with folders and papers and books. There is also a laptop open and a printer on another table situated next to the desk. Two large chairs are in the corner where I am standing, a small table between them. He walks around me, heading toward the desk.

"Let me just save what I was working on. I'm Dillard, by the way, Dillard Brady."

"Emma," I answer him. "Emma Troxler, and please take your time."

"Have a seat." He's kneeling over his desk, tapping keys on the keyboard.

I glance around and think he must mean for me to sit in one of the chairs over in the corner, since besides the tall one behind his desk, they are the only others in the office. I take one step behind me to the one closest to the door and have a seat.

The small table next to me has a few items arranged on top. There's a candle, a box of tissues, a feather, and a few seashells and smooth round rocks. I have my book bag with information on our K-Locks systems, and I hold it in my lap.

"Once I lost an entire sermon on a Saturday night," he tells me as I watch him close the laptop. "I actually wept, if you can believe that."

I actually can, I think but don't say. He's still talking, but I think about the time I lost a term paper the night before it was due. I was suicidal for about an hour, so I totally understand.

"You heard the joke about Buddha and Jesus having a writing contest to see who could write the best mission statement?"

I shake my head since this isn't a joke I know.

He grins, shuffles a few papers around. "Buddha wrote this beautiful piece about his religion, all these wonderful notes about compassion and an intention for detachment, about the merits of meditation; it was over twenty pages. Jesus, however, sat a long time until he finally typed out one sentence about loving one's neighbor as oneself, not anything as intricate and lovely as his competitor had penned. After they finished, there was a power outage, and when the electricity was restored, God immediately declared the winner of the contest to be none other than His Son. When Buddha asked how it was that he lost the contest when he had written so much more detailed information, God answered, 'Buddha, my dear, your statement was quite lovely and complex, but in the end, his was better because, well, your work was lost in the outage, and as we all know, Jesus saves.'"

He sits down in the seat across from me, and I smile. Now that it's finished I think I have heard a similar joke and have to say I didn't really think it was that funny the first time. He lets out a laugh. I just keep smiling, ever the good sport until finally I clear my throat for the second time.

"Okay, so you have heard it." He watches me closely. "So, Emma from K-Locks, what can I do for you today?"

"I believe you called us this morning. Maybe you have security questions, need some assistance?"

He doesn't answer, his face a question mark.

"There was a break-in?" I add. "It was in the paper."

"Oh, yes, that is right," he answers, nodding like the mystery is now solved. "Last week. They came in through the rear door, no evidence of breaking in actually, had a key or the door was unlocked. And they didn't take much—a couple blankets from the quilters' room, food from the pantry, money in a collection jar for the soup kitchen." He turns away, watches a car drive through the parking lot. "Seemed to me that it was just somebody down on their luck. Just took what they needed."

"But you called the police?"

He lets out a sigh. "The chair of the maintenance committee did, Dwayne Jessup, the one who found the door unlocked the next morning. He was here to check the furnace since we had a few complaints after Sunday's service. The members of the older women's Sunday school class claimed they couldn't do their lesson because the room felt like a meat locker, claimed we were trying to kill them. He's on the premises somewhere today." And he rolls his eyes like he doesn't care for Dwayne.

I assume the maintenance committee is likely headed by the man I met at the side door, but I don't interrupt.

"Anyway, he noticed the collection jar emptied and the pantry doors open. He called me first and then the police. We arrived about the same time. And I'm guessing that's who phoned you since I haven't called anyone about a security system."

I don't respond because it seems like he has more to say, but he doesn't, and I realize the name Dwayne Jessup was in fact the name on the piece of paper that was handed to me this morning.

He appears to be waiting for something from me at this point.

"Do you want to hear about our business packages?"

He slides his hands down the front of his pants, drops slightly lower in his seat, stretching out his legs, crossing them at his ankles. "Sure, let's hear it," he replies, trying to sound interested or maybe just polite—I'm not sure. He folds his hands together.

I open my book bag and hand him a packet. It is the information about the most expensive package we sell, and Kathryn has asked us to always start with that one. I do this reluctantly because I don't really think a church needs in-touch platforms and heat sensors. My guess is, all they need to do is install a few dead bolt locks, maybe cut bushes near the windows in the back, add some outdoor lights. They don't really need a deluxe package, but I do as I am told and give the options.

"We can put cameras at every exterior entrance, others inside. We have a new smartphone app that can be used to engage and disengage the system by remote. We have secure locks we can install and even help you with your temperature-control problem. There's round-the-clock monitoring and twenty-four-hour customer care."

He flips through the material in the folder. He is not drawn to any of it. He just turns the pages, tries to stifle a yawn. This may have kept me out of the office, but it's clearly a waste of time. He closes the folder, and I prepare to be dismissed. I fold the top of my book bag over, still holding it on my lap.

"Emma, I really do appreciate you driving all the way over here. Truly I do." He taps the folder on his leg and then places it on the floor beside him. "I figured Dwayne and the committee would eventually want to take it this way." He scratches the side of his head. "There have been a few things missing of late, and that's starting to make people nervous. We should've changed the locks years ago. I heard that the pastor before me gave out a key to every member."

I feel my eyebrows lift. Hearing this makes me surprised they haven't had more things missing at the church. There's bound to be a lot of keys floating around town.

"I did at least stop that practice." He sits up in his chair, raises his arms, placing them on his knees, and leans toward me like he's about to say something personal. His face is flushed, his neck a little splotchy, but the twinkle is still there in his eyes. He seems kind, smiles slightly before he speaks again.

"The truth is I know who broke in last week, and it actually doesn't really qualify as a break-in since I sort of gave my permission for it to happen. Well"—he pulls away from me, leans in his chair—"I didn't tell him to take the money from the collection jar, but in his condition, who would blame him?"

I don't answer since I'm not sure what there is for me to say. I don't know who had the key or what condition he was in. I'm not quite sure what the pastor's confession means.

"I suppose I need to just tell the truth to Dwayne." He blows out a tired breath. "He'll have everyone here scared to death that all their fears have come to fruition. There are folks here who wanted to have self-defense classes when they found out a falafel place was opening near the college."

And thinking the pastor is telling another joke, I actually laugh out loud.

Chapter Twenty

Instantly, I realize my blunder. "That's not really a joke, is it?" I clear my throat, push the sides of my hair behind my ears. It's warm in the church, and I wish I had taken off my coat before sitting down. To do so at this point would make it seem like I plan to stay, which seems pushy now that I understand the pastor doesn't really want a security system.

"Unfortunately not, but I like that it sounds humorous and not completely horrible. I hate saying those kinds of things about the congregation I serve."

"Just because a person sits in church doesn't mean they don't have their demons," I say, thinking about Nathan's distaste of organized religion and his complaints about the hypocrisy. He would never go to church except for weddings and funerals, and even then he fidgeted and squirmed, wanting to sit at the end of the pew, always the first one out the door when the services were over.

He told me once his grandmother used to make him go to church with her, pull him too close, wrap her long, fleshy arm around his shoulders. He hated how he felt pinned in both by his grandmother's clutch and the fire and brimstone leveled at him from the pulpit.

"I'm sorry to say, but it's my experience that those who choose to be in church actually have more demons." And there is a hint of sadness in his voice.

"So who came in last week and took the food and blankets?" I'm trying to lighten the mood.

"And cash," he adds.

"And cash."

Pastor Dillard sighs. "Travis Beasley is his name. He hangs out at the college—homeless, lives in a cardboard box when he can't stay at the shelter. He stops by here a lot."

I suppose dealing with transients is one of the things ministers have to do.

"He's harmless, has a bit of a drinking problem. I let him sleep in the fellowship hall from time to time, getting him out before anybody might find him. One day last week he saw me out at a meeting, said he was hungry. I gave him my key, told him to leave it in the mailbox." He reaches in his pocket and pulls out a single key and places it on the table between us. "This key," he adds. "Which he did leave in the mailbox, just forgot to lock the door on his way out."

There is a softness to Pastor Dillard, an ease to him. He's tall, slender, looks like a man who's either uncomfortable with his height or just trying to hide. He's wearing khaki pants, a blue shirt, and navy sweater. You can tell he wants to be inviting. There isn't a wedding ring on his finger, but there are pictures of a couple children on the shelves near his desk. He has a narrow face, thin nose—and up close I can tell his thick, curly hair is just a couple inches too long.

I don't know the man, but sizing him up, even with the open way he talks, the kind eyes, he seems a bit tired or gloomy, and this makes me wonder how long he's been the pastor of the Fourth Street Presbyterian Church and if he's stuck in a job or a place that he cannot seem to leave. I wonder if pastors struggle with professional malaise like college professors or security system salespeople. I wonder if he wishes he had just learned a trade and spends his days pouring concrete or driving long hauls, sorting mail or laying pipe. I wonder how this call to serve a flock with demons is working out for him.

There is a lull in our conversation, and I suppose he's trying to figure out how he's going to confess to his parishioners that he gave the key to the thief. I take the opportunity to study my surroundings.

The shelves are stacked with books. Most of them are of a religious nature, but there is also a good collection of fiction. A couple of certificates and diplomas hang on the wall, a large watercolor of trees in autumn, a boy walking along a path. He has lots of crosses and angels on the shelves and file cabinets, various sizes, likely gifts from parishioners, I assume; and there's a big jar of candy—cinnamon fireballs—situated on the corner of his desk.

There are the personal photographs I had already seen—two children, towheaded both of them, eight or ten years of age, I guess, and a few others of the pastor on a ski slope and standing at the ocean. There's a wedding picture of him standing between the bride and groom, smiling like he's pleased at being part of the snapped shot.

It's a good office, bigger than Nathan's at the university, and it's easy to see that he's made it his own, created a personal work space that is roomy and comfortable. I turn my attention once again to my customer.

"You don't really need a security system," I say, acknowledging what we both know to be true.

He nods his head. He knows this.

"I'm not really a security consultant," I tell him. "But I think you could just do a few things to make the church less of a target for break-ins, maybe ease the anxiety of your maintenance committee."

He crosses his long arms, tilts his head, listens.

"The shrubbery is a bit high around the rear entrance," I inform him. "I'd change the locks since there are so many keys out there, and you should probably make the policy to do that every couple years anyway. Too many keys can always make for security problems. Make sure the lights are working at the exterior doors; you could put a motion detector on them to save on electricity. We can do that for you, or you can just ask Dwayne—I get the feeling he'd know how to install them." I pause. "And I wouldn't tell anybody about Travis."

He lifts his eyebrows.

"It was a couple of blankets and some canned food, a small amount of cash stuck in a jar. The police won't spend a lot of time on it, so just tell Dwayne and the church council that you spoke to a security firm, and the first suggestion they gave is the new locks."

He smiles. His features soften.

"Maybe this will just blow over."

"Maybe." He sounds slightly buoyed.

I figure this is my opportunity to leave.

He stops me. "I think we may have met somewhere before," he says, keeping me in my seat across from him.

I shake my head. Pastor Dillard doesn't appear familiar, and I know I've never come to his church.

He sits up, studying me.

"Did you graduate from the university?"

I nod. "1994."

"For me, 1992. But you didn't major in religion, I'm thinking." He smiles.

"English," I answer.

"Did you play tennis or sing in the university choir?" He continues to try and place me somewhere in his past.

I shake my head and start to feel slightly uncomfortable. After what happened at the office earlier in the day, I don't like any extra attention on me.

He stays where he is, elbows on knees, eyes on me. I glance away.

"Did you work in the cafeteria?"

"No. I guess that means you did?"

"Line cook all four years."

"So you're responsible for the freshman fifteen I never got rid of." I'm trying to break the stare or stop this query. I fidget in my chair, pull my bag closer to my chest.

"Guilty as charged." He peers at me a few seconds more, then seems to sense my discomfort and sits back in his chair, runs his fingers through his hair. It appears he's giving up the interview. He nods like he's made a decision.

"So your professional suggestion is that I do not confess my participation in the break-in and throw poor Travis under the bus?"

I am glad for the change of subject.

"That is my professional advice, yes."

He picks up the folder he had placed on the floor beside his chair. "I will pass along this information to the chair of our maintenance committee, let him know I was proactive in searching out available security systems, and I will inform him of your good tips."

I stand up, place my bag across my shoulder, and hold out my hand. He does the same.

"Thank you for seeing me today, Pastor," I say.

"Thank you for the information."

And as he shakes my hand, he stares at me and then quickly glances away, and I can't say for sure, but I think he has just figured out where he's seen me before. He squeezes my hand and then lets go. He steps aside, and I walk around him to the door, making my exit.

Chapter Twenty-One

"I thought you had a thing at work."

And just like that I remember the birthday dinner. The steak house. The hard way I had to tell him he couldn't go. Stopping by later to get him saag, maybe extra naan. I put down the bags of Chinese takeout I picked up when I drove into town, and I lean against the counter. *How did I forget this?*

"You forgot?"

I feel him behind me.

"I went to see the bees." I close my eyes, deciding not to tell him about Bus and the fact that he now knows my husband is dead.

"And you got Chinese?"

I hear him take a whiff, trying to detect what I brought home.

"Duck? That's better than saag."

"I've got to go."

"It's kind of late now," he lets me know.

I glance at the clock on the stove and he's right. It's after six. They would have already ordered. Now it would just be an embarrassment for me to show up. Still. I could be there in time for cake. I could say I got caught up with the last customer. I could make excuses. I think about the decision, about seeing Bus again, about seeing everyone again.

"How were they?"

"Who?"

"The bees?" It's clear that he doesn't want me to go to the office dinner. He's trying to keep me distracted, trying to keep me home. This is what he does.

"They're fine, Nathan. I really should go." I turn to face him, and he walks into the dining room. He's wearing a bathrobe, the flannel one he kept from years ago. He looks old shuffling away.

"Then go. Make your appearance, do your duty. Show up and celebrate Kathryn's great day of birth. Party on."

"Nathan," I start to explain, but it's no use. It's an argument I will never win.

"No, really," he says as he takes his seat, trying to soften his tone. "Go. I understand. It's important." He rests his elbows on the table, clasps his hands in front of him.

I take in a breath. I can wait a few more minutes now that I'm this late anyway. I go to the table, pull out the chair across from him.

I study him, reach out for his hand.

"How was your day?" I ask.

He does not lean in or stretch out his arm so that I'm able to touch him.

"I'm a dead man, Emma. All my days are pretty much the same." I nod.

"And yours?" He is trying to act interested, but it comes off sounding pretentious.

"It was fine," I answer, deciding not to bring up his tone.

"I was out, making calls in the field today. Met a couple new business owners but didn't sell anything, though."

He nods, looks down

"Oh, and I went to a church. Talked to the minister. Nice guy actually."

Another nod, still not meeting my eyes.

"There was a break-in. Well, technically there wasn't, but that's why we got the call."

"Which church?" he asks, showing a certain amount of interest I hadn't expected. He's looking at me now.

"Presbyterian, the one on Fourth Street."

He nods because he knows the one.

"He thinks he met me somewhere before; he graduated from the university but I don't remember him."

"You tell him about Lorenzo Langstroth?"

I shake my head. I had not mentioned the old minister who kept bees.

Nathan told me about Reverend Langstroth a long time ago, when he first took up beekeeping. He says the minister from the 1800s wrote what he called a beekeeper's bible that would be required reading for any novice in harvesting honey.

The book is entitled *The Hive and the Honeybee*. Turns out, Pastor Lanstroth is also credited with having invented the beehive as we know it today and even was said to have imported and developed the strain of bees still used by most beekeepers, the Italian strand, *Apis mellifera*, more commonly known as the western or European honeybee.

The sweet bee, or common honeybee, is said to be one of the first domesticated insects and now occupies every continent except Antarctica.

Padre Langstroth is a rock star in the world of beekeeping.

Like Reverend Brady, Lorenzo Langstroth received theological training with an expectation that he was called to and would thereby serve as a parish minister. The word about Langstroth was, however, that the young pastor struggled with panic attacks while trying to deliver his first sermon, so anxious and afraid that he was rendered unable to speak. He went on to finish his studies and even pastored a few churches, served as principal in a girls' school. But he eventually turned to beekeeping as a means to deal with his depression and issues with anxiety.

He claimed the hobby, which later became a passion, helped him with his "head trouble," as he liked to call his condition, and he soon became a prolific writer and researcher in the field of beekeeping. Nathan told me once that he thought the bees must have brought him a certain measure of comfort the young and anxious clergyman could never seem to find in the pews or at the altar of a church.

I think about Pastor Brady and wonder if he'd like to know about Reverend Langstroth. I even consider getting him a copy of the book so he can know there is another life waiting for him beyond the stained glass windows and the locked church doors. I think he might like the idea.

"So that was it? You went to the office this morning and then went out to make calls in the afternoon?"

I'm pulled back into the present conversation. "That's it," I answer.

He sighs and I face him, notice the way he's still losing weight, the unsettled nature he has demonstrated since he followed me home from the dead.

"Why are you still here?" The question falls out of my mouth like something rotten—a bad grape or sour milk.

He peers at me, doesn't answer for a few minutes. "You don't know?"

I shake my head. I don't.

There is the slightest sound of breath exhaled.

"Because you asked," he tells me, still watching me closely.

I wait.

He obliges. "You asked me to stay. The natural order of things had me leaving, and that was what I was going to do, but you changed that order. You messed with it. You did this—you."

I wait for the rest of it, the part I am so familiar with, the part I remember as clearly as he.

He doesn't disappoint, and I see the color come into his cheeks.

"You came into that sterile, curtained-off spot in the emergency room and asked—begged actually. You held my head against your chest and begged me not to go, said you could not live without me."

I glance away without responding, without affirmation, but he knows I recognize the truth. The night is clear for us both.

Nathan was in a bicycle accident two years ago. He was hit by a van that turned right without paying attention to what or who was crossing in the crosswalk. Nathan was thrown from his bike, landed on his head and cracked his helmet, causing a concussion. He broke bones, suffered damage to his spleen and kidneys. The van even ran over his foot, which is why his mobility was affected, why he shuffles. There were weeks of surgeries, a three-month-long hospital stay, rehab, months of physical therapy. He became depressed, sullen, querulous, withdrawn; it was hard to stay with him all the time, which was when my mother made me get a sitter, made me get out of the house and return to work.

And then, with some med changes, graduation from physical therapy, and some sessions with a meditation teacher, he was better for a long time. Though it took him longer with the physical consequences from the accident, he was able to tend his bees. He learned to cook, seemed to like it, and walked a mile every day. We read to each other, watched old movies, went on picnics, shopped at garage sales, put up new curtains in the bedroom; and things felt like they did when we first fell in love. It was sweet, perfect.

And I never thought he would die. I thought we had made it through the worst possible thing, that the suffering somehow made us both stronger, that he was lucky to be alive and was even luckier that he was able and willing to work through the pain, the physical therapy, the neurological scars, the despair, and come back to me. I thought the worst was over and I relaxed. I was easy. Light.

The pneumonia was a fluke, not anticipated or worrisome, and even his doctor thought it would clear up with one round of antibiotics. But after five days and no improvement, his temperature spiked, and we returned to the emergency room at the hospital. One of the nurses who cared for him after the accident even remembered him and joked that he returned to the department because he missed them so much.

And then after that, I don't even really know what happened. I stepped out of the room while they did a chest X-ray to go down to the bathroom, and when I came out, people were running from the nurses' station, a doctor flying past me almost knocked me over, and then I got to his room and they were shocking him with the defibrillator, yelling out instructions to each other about meds to administer and screaming for everyone to stand clear. A nurse saw me and ran in my direction, picking me up by the elbow, and leading me to a small room, where I sat by myself for what seemed like hours.

Until all of a sudden I wasn't alone anymore. Someone came in to sit with me, a representative from the hospital. And I realize that I had completely forgotten this part, this person next to me while I waited and my husband died. It was a man, a man with a white coat and badge, but not a doctor or nurse. He was the on-call chaplain, a local minister who volunteered one night a month; and he stayed with me until my mother came.

He sat there next to me, seeming as white-knuckled and afraid as I, trying to bring me some comfort, trying to give me water and tissues and keep me up-to-date on what was happening. After the doctor came to say those dreaded horrible words about death and having done "everything they could do," this man walked with me, a few steps behind me actually, as I was permitted to say my goodbyes.

He stopped when I went to the gurney and pulled the curtain behind me, separating himself from me so I could have my privacy, be with my husband, like there might be a few last things for us to say.

And just like that, I remember how Reverend Brady knows me. Without the white coat and the grave look of helplessness, I had not recognized him.

"Do you want rice or just the duck?" I stand up from the table. "I think I'll warm mine."

Nathan doesn't respond, and I know he's waiting for an explanation for my silence, for why I've changed my mind and am not going to the birthday dinner. I can see he wants to know where I disappeared during the long pause that stretched between us; but I don't explain.

I put my dinner on a plate, stick it in the microwave, turn it on.

"I'll just make a scene if I show up now," I say softly, noting why I'm not going to join the others, why I've decided to eat Chinese with my dead husband.

"No one likes a scene," I hear him say, his face turned away, and the microwave dings, signaling our food is now ready.

Chapter Twenty-Two

He is gone by the time I wake up. I call for him, but he doesn't answer. I slide my hand over to his side of the bed like I always do, but it's cold. I reach for his pillow, hold it to my face, trying to smell him—Irish Spring soap, that smell of citus and bergamot, the floral and woodsy smell of love, trying to feel him near me again; but even that smell of him is becoming harder and harder to maintain. I let the pillow stay on my face, hiding from the light.

I know I have to go to work; I cannot keep missing meetings and birthday dinners and showing up late. I know I have to call my mother, make amends, tell her I'm better, calm her nerves. I know she's worried, and I think that maybe I'll tell her about the pastor, make her think I'm reaching out to a professional, that I reconnected with the chaplain who was with me when Nathan died. That will bring her comfort, I decide, keep her from contacting her friend—that shrink in Raleigh she's threatened me with in the past—or calling Violet, my sister, and getting her all worked up again, trying to arrange for another intervention like she did when she finally figured it all out.

I let Nathan's pillow fall to the side and close my eyes, remembering the conversation from last night—how he told me that I am the one who kept him here, that I am the one who will not let him leave. And then I think about the gathering at my house not so many weeks ago, the night they all showed up to confront me, to take me to task for not dealing appropriately or effectively with my grief.

It's funny to me that my mother did not catch on right away, that she was oblivious to my complicated grief or whatever the bereavement experts have decided to call this. For months my mother simply believed I was dealing with my sorrow like any other widow, that I was in shock and perhaps depressed and then maybe quarrelsome, unpleasant, dull-witted, but she never suspected a denial this relentless. She never considered that I had refused to let my husband go. She never thought I had that much power, never believed I could actually keep Nathan from leaving me.

Even at that gathering she arranged in my living room not long after the holidays, she refused to call what I'm doing delusional—it was Violet who used that word. My mother spoke more about my lack of sleeping and my poor diet, my unhealthy habits, my short attention span, my belligerence, my lack of social interaction, my inability to go on with my life; but she never named this for what it is.

I roll over, pull the covers around me, and think about that night, the one when they all showed up "to help." Violet, out of uniform and uncomfortable in civilian clothes, wearing new jeans and a men's sweatshirt, sitting so tall and stiff in the dining room chair, her arms folded tightly across her chest, her hair pulled back in a severe bun, so clearly wanting to be somewhere else, anywhere else; Jocylin Edgar, the young social worker from the local hospice, the one who had suggested the gathering, the one who kept smiling and holding her hand to her heart, making these humming sounds after every sentence I spoke; Kathryn, still dressed from work, who never said a word and wouldn't meet my eyes; and Mrs. Hinshaw, Mama's friend from the Garden Club who for some unknown reason joined this intimate group and kept wanting to serve refreshments.

They all came with Mama, who ended up being the most uncomfortable of them all, who opted for tenderness over confrontation, and who tried to keep it light, as if she realized that once she had arrived and had the group assembled, she suddenly decided it was a bad idea. That once they were all seated and staring at me, with that old ratty blanket wrapped around my shoulders, my hair dirty and unkempt, my clothes unwashed, she wished she hadn't called for the intervention. I think if Mrs. Hinshaw had suggested they come another time, she would have jumped up and run. She was easy to wear down and I pushed. But Violet knew what I was doing right away and called me on it, made me shut up and listen to their concerns.

So I sat and listened as they read their letters to me—pages of what they had seen in my behavior, what they had noticed about me, my lack of communication with any of them, my failure to return calls or engage with them in conversation, my repeated absences from work, my lack of interest in anything and how I seemed not to eat anything other than popcorn and bread with honey, the way I refused their invitations to join them for dinner or a movie. The way, they all said, I had chosen death—chosen death over life, that's what they said, the exact words, "death over life" —the way I could not accept reality, could not accept what was real and factual and would not be disputed.

And they were right. And they knew they were right. And I knew they were right.

My husband died.

My husband died May 25, 2019, on a Saturday—the Saturday of Memorial Day Weekend. We were planning a barbeque on Sunday, a get-together with a retired American literature professor—one who Nathan liked and had stayed in touch with, a woman whose office was just down the hall from his—and her boyfriend, another professor. Chemistry, I think. We were grilling steaks; they were bringing dessert and red wine, a light-bodied variety, something that would enhance the flavors of the meat. We were going to talk about traveling together in the fall, San Francisco maybe, New York. Nathan thought it was a good idea, thought it would be fun exploring the museums with another couple, taking in a Broadway show. He was finally ready to branch out, and I was open to the new possibilities.

We canceled when we knew he was sick, when he had the chest X-rays in the middle of the week and they found the pneumonia. Our invited guests were kind and understanding, even brought by the bottle of wine that Friday night, stood at the door so as not to bother Nathan, who was resting. I had placed the bottle on the counter near the sink, and I drank it when I got home from the hospital.

I drank the whole bottle.

Kosta Browne Pinot Noir, a lovely red variety from the Sonoma Coast. I hadn't eaten all day, and I still drank it all. And then I got sick and threw up and sat at the toilet, my hair wet with sweat, my mouth dry, my stomach empty. And I lay down on the cool tile floor and made the decision, told myself what I would do. It was bold but simple.

I would not let him go.

I pretended to plan the memorial service in earnest—asked my mother to go with me when I picked up the ashes from the funeral home, put his obituary in the paper, answered questions for the college alumni paper, scheduled the service on a Wednesday, collected photographs from books and albums, did a slideshow, pretended to mean the words I read, the poem by W.H. Auden, wept when his graduate assistant spoke, smiled when the dean shared his light-hearted stories; I acted out the part of the brokenhearted widow to perfection.

Afterward, I was present for the reception given at the faculty club. I received everyone, shook hands, attended to their sympathetic gestures, thanked them, drank small sips of water, ate the meager appetizers, dressed appropriately—a tasteful, black pantsuit, a soft linen blouse—fixed my hair, and wore makeup that wouldn't run, not a lot, not too much, just enough to cover the dark circles under my eyes, to give myself a little color. I held my sister's hand, placed my head on her shoulder, wept a few tears so as to appear appropriate in my grief and bereavement. But it was just an act because I would not let him go.

When it was all over, the service and the reception, the great show, I came home alone, refusing the offers of company, asserting myself as no longer in need of a sitter or companion or sympathizer at my side, and I raised my husband from the dead. I called him out and forth, no less than Jesus Christ himself was called up by ghosts and God from the grave. I called Nathan Troxler out of his state of death, and I would not let him go.

It took more than seven months before anyone decided to do something about it; almost eight months before my mother "could bear it no longer" as she read from her tear-stained letter; seven months and a couple weeks before my sister claimed I was too close to being "mental" and took a leave from her military operations to buy new jeans and a sweatshirt and write a letter to me that she read without looking at me; and almost nine months before I finally did what they asked and told my dead husband it was time to go.

Only I guess I didn't mean it, since as of last night, he was still here. He has not yet been put out. My spouse, the one everyone else has released and probably even forgotten, remains.

I roll out of bed, sit for a minute—thinking about being a no-show at work once again—stand up, and walk to the bathroom. I do what I need to do: find clothes in the closet, dress, comb my hair, dab on a little lipstick, brush on a bit of mascara, make myself a cup of coffee, and grab my coat.

As I'm walking out the door, I turn and focus on the kitchen table where he's always been, even after his death, and I smile.

He glances up at me from the paper. "See you when you get home," he tells me, his cheekbones now prominent, his skinny wrists and bony hands protruding from his robe. "We can read those books we bought and didn't get to."

I nod, open the door, and content once again, head off to work.

Chapter Twenty-Three

"Wow, you're here before me." It's Jon and he's right. For the first time since he started working here, I am at my desk before he is sitting at his.

"I hope you have a good excuse." I don't even glance up, but he knows I'm messing with him. I don't need to know why he's ten minutes late. But I notice that Kathryn is watching. She is staring at her watch.

"You stayed out all day," he says, like I didn't know my whereabouts. "And you didn't come to the party."

"I was out making Elon a safer community for us all."

"And what about dinner? Where were you then?" He places his coat on a hook near me and falls in his chair behind the divider between us.

"Just didn't get finished in time." I have my head in my files.

"You just didn't want to face Buster." I hear him stand up again and lean in my direction. "What happened between the two of you?"

I shrug and don't look up.

"I heard him trying to apologize or something, and the next thing I know you've flown out the door." He pauses and lowers his voice. "Ya'll have a lovers' spat or something?" And he laughs as he plops down in his chair.

A lovers' spat? Is that what people thought yesterday? Is that how it looked?

I stand up, push the chair behind me, and peer at Jon, who has taken out a protein bar and is eating it. He glances up.

"Why would you think that?" I ask.

His mouth is full, and he doesn't answer but lifts his eyebrows, raises his shoulders. When he swallows, he clears his throat. "Cause it was intense, man." He takes another bite, puts his breakfast down. "And then you fly out and don't come to the party." He studies me closely as he asks his last question. "What was he apologizing for anyway?"

I shake my head and wave the question away, surprised he hadn't heard the whole conversation; but I don't answer. I don't need to start my day like this.

"I think he was going to follow you." He pauses, watching me. I wait.

"But then Kathryn had gotten back by that time and called him in her office, and they talked for like, I don't know, an hour or something. He wasn't there last night either."

I take my seat. I can only imagine what she told him, and I can only imagine what he thinks of me.

I hear Jon smacking and turn; Kathryn is sitting at her desk. She's talking on the phone, laughing. She appears animated, happy. I assume she's caught a big fish as a new customer, or she's talking to a friend from the police force. She still hangs out with those guys.

I click on my email to check and see if I have any messages. I wasn't really working when Jon came in. I was just trying to straighten up my desk, file some papers, discard some of the trash that had accumulated.

I delete most of the emails after reading them, sales reports and advertisements, all the usual junk that Kathryn sends to everyone. There's a recap of the meeting I missed, so I read that a little more closely. There's nothing too important except confirming what

Jon told me yesterday. Kathryn is concerned about the lack of new customers beginning this first quarter and makes mention in this letter of the new CPI office opening up in Burlington—the west side, not far from where we are. Everybody at K-Locks knows the aggressive sales and marketing they do, and I agree, Kathryn has real reason to worry.

I glance at her again, wondering how I'll apologize for missing her birthday party. She's twirling a strand of hair around her finger. She's definitely talking to a cop. She gets all girly and flirty when she sees one or is on the phone with one. I imagine she was a good police officer, but it wouldn't surprise me if there also were a number of inappropriate relationships when she worked at the police station. She's attractive, never married, carries herself strong and confident but still with a softness that makes her seem available. Plus she confessed once that she has a thing for men in those uniforms.

I finish reading the office email and hit delete, scroll down. I notice that Pastor Brady filled out a survey regarding my sales call yesterday, and I open that email.

For about a year, we've been asked to send email addresses of new or potential customers to an online survey system that Kathryn set up. The system then sends a survey to the customer we have contacted. It's only a few questions, but it gives Kathryn a good measuring tool for her employees. Most of the people I talk to and am able to get an email address from never respond. I guess the Presbyterian minister decided to help make my sales call worthwhile. I read over his responses:

"The sales representative from K-Locks was professional, courteous, and informative." He gave me a five out of five.

"The sales representative from K-Locks heard my questions and answered them in a way I fully understand." Again, five out of five.

"The sales representative from K-Locks knew the K-Locks security options and presented them to me in a professional manner." Five again.

And the final question: "If I was hiring a sales representative for my business or organization, I would consider this K-Locks staff member to be a good candidate." Five was his answer.

And he added a comment:

"Mrs. Troxler was informative and professional. She presented several options for the security issues at Fourth Presbyterian Church. We are presently considering implementing a security system, and when the time comes to make a decision, we will certainly look at your organization." And he signed it, "Dr. Dillard Brady."

It was a nice thing he did, and as I save the results in my inbox, I wonder if he did it because he really believed I'm a good salesperson or because he does it for everyone who makes him a sales pitch. Of course, it could just be an act of pity because he remembered me from the emergency department of the hospital last spring, and he feels bad that he kept pushing me to try and figure out how he knew me, and when he suddenly remembered me, remembered seeing me in that embarrassing light, seeing me in my broken, fragile state, he was trying to make up for the undue pressure he put me under.

Still, it was a nice gesture, and I can use a little positive feedback with my boss.

I hear the rear door open, turn around, and see Dexter, the installation manager, coming in. I return to my screen and finish scrolling through my messages.

There are just a few more, and I hit delete and delete and delete until I reach one of the last ones, sent yesterday morning. It's from another K-Locks employee—I recognize the last part of the address we all have.

It's from Bus. I click it open:

"Dear Emma,

I just wanted to say how sorry I am that I caused you such discomfort yesterday. I realize now that I shouldn't have spoken to you about your loss while you are at work. It was selfish of me, and I hope you will forgive me.

—Bus"

I click delete. When I look up, Kathryn is standing in front of my desk.

Chapter Twenty-Four

"Emma, could you come to my office for a sec?" She turns on her heels, and I let out a breath.

Jon has stood up, and I feel his eyes burning holes through me, but I'm not turning around to show my concern.

"Sure, what's up?" I follow her in and take a seat across from her desk.

"Could you get the door?" She motions with her chin, and I pause.

"Oh." I stand up and close the door, finally getting a glance at Jon, who is holding up his hand, like a wave or sign of surrender. He drops it, and I turn to Kathryn, take my seat again.

"You got some nice feedback from your sales call at the church." She has on her glasses and is staring at her laptop.

I assume she's reading the results of the pastor's survey.

"Yes, I just saw that," I reply.

She scrolls down and then glances up, smiles. She's studying me, sizing me up. I have become accustomed to this way she measures and tends.

"You'll follow up with him this week, right?"

"Sure," I answer, thinking I hadn't really planned on making another call to the Presbyterian church.

"Did he think they might buy a system?"

I decide not to tell her that his nice feedback does not equal a good sale.

"I think he has to run all purchases like security packages through committees, so it might be a while until we hear from him again."

"Right, I imagine that's protocol for a church." She nods. "Still, it could be a new source of revenue for us."

"Yes, that's right," I agree.

"Maybe a new niche for marketing? Protecting houses of worship?"

"Could be."

She writes herself a note.

She puts down her pen, her laptop still open in front of her. There's a lull.

"Emma, how are you doing?"

I drop my hands in my lap. "I'm doing okay," I answer, nodding.

"Really?"

I shrug. "Really."

She closes the laptop and is staring at me, and I think of her sitting in my intervention wearing the same look. It's pity, I guess.

"You missed a meeting yesterday."

"I know, and I apologize for that. I completely forgot."

"You haven't been to any of the staff meetings."

I just nod since I don't have an excuse.

"And you're still having some trouble getting here on time in the morning."

"But not today," I answer, happy to have that to brag about.

"Not today," she repeats. She hesitates. "Still."

"I am doing better, Kathryn," I say, trying to sound as convincing as I know how to be. "I am."

She clears her throat. "I know it's been hard for you," she says softly. "And I hope you know I've got the greatest respect for you and what you've been through. We all do."

I feel slightly out of breath because of how this is starting to sound. I feel my face start to flush.

"You've been more than kind," I respond. "And I'm sorry for yesterday. I'm sorry I missed the birthday celebration. I just got caught up in things and lost track of time."

She doesn't reply, doesn't change her position.

"I hope you had a nice time."

She nods, clears her throat again. It's a habit she has. "I hope you don't think this is about you missing my birthday dinner. I just feel like the others—" She pauses, carefully choosing her words. "The other employees are watching, and I think they ... well, it doesn't really matter what they think."

She stops and starts again. "I need you to set a better example." There's a slight smile. "You have tenure here, longevity. I'd like it if you become more of a leader."

"Sure," I answer, without knowing exactly what she has in mind. "I will make a point not to miss the future meetings, and I will keep working on getting here on time."

"I think it would be good for you to go out more, get in the field. You're obviously good at it." She points her thumb at the laptop, referring to the survey results from Pastor Brady. "Maybe go on a few of the calls to install the systems."

"Oh."

"I've assigned you to go out with Bus tomorrow."

"Why would you do that?"

"Because, as I just said, I think it would be good for you to go out more."

"I could go with Joey," I say, bringing up the name of the other employee who does the installations. Joey's been with the company about five years. He's quiet, unassuming, and he knows nothing about dead poets or bees or Nathan and me. I should go with him.

"Joey's taking Jon out. I figure I'd mix it up. Put you with a team member who hasn't been here long and put Joey with the sales guy who's only been here a short time. Give you all the chance to teach each other. Margaret is going to stay in the office—she's going to do more of the administrative part—and Pat and Dexter will go out as a team."

That's everybody at K-Locks except the graveyard shifts and the security officers; she's worked it all out.

"Is this about yesterday?" I ask, thinking it must be about— or somehow connected to—my quick exit, about Bus's newfound knowledge about Nathan. But I'm not sure what the two of us working together will accomplish.

"What about yesterday?" she asks, appearing clueless.

I shake my head. "Never mind." I'll play along. Besides I'd rather not talk about it again.

"I think this will give us new energy, help the sales team really see what's happening out in the field, give the installation guys a better sense of how we follow leads. I see it as a win-win, a great opportunity for us to increase our sales volume, maybe help installation know more about the packages we offer."

"Win-win," I repeat, wishing I had just gone to the birthday party, thinking that if I had just shown up, even for cake, we might not be having this conversation.

"Yes, it will broaden everyone's understanding of the business we're trying to run and maybe give us a good kick-start for the new quarter."

"I think that's a great idea, Kathryn."

She smiles and lets out a breath.

"So, is that all?" I ask, wanting to make an exit before she gives me something else to do, some other new assignment.

"I guess so, Emma. I thank you again for your work here at K-Locks, and I look forward to many more good days together."

"Me too," I say as I stand up, force a smile on my face, and walk out of her office. I pull the door closed, and it slams harder than I intended. I hold up a hand as a means of apology.

Chapter Twenty-Five

"Well, this is a nice surprise," my mother says as she sits across from me.

I've asked her to meet me for dinner, to make an attempt at reconciliation, to help sell the appearance that I am doing okay. Nathan and I agreed that we need Carla not to get suspicious, so I must apologize for the way I behaved when she cleaned out the pantry and keep the red flags to a minimum.

"You're dressed nice," she tells me.

I glance down at what I'm wearing. It's an old, red sweater and a pair of black slacks; she's seen the outfit a hundred times, and I get it that she's trying to be positive, give me a compliment.

"I haven't been here since they changed the menu," she comments as she takes a long gaze around the place.

I've asked her to meet me at the diner near the interstate. She used to enjoy eating here, and I thought she'd like coming again.

"You get a haircut?" I ask.

"Just a trim," she answers, touching both sides of her hair. "I thought I'd try a new place since James is gone." She then drops her hand to her neck. "I just can't get used to that girl who took his place."

Mama thinks having a man fix her hair keeps her current. She found James when he was just out of hair school, or whatever you call it, and she considered it a great loss when he told her he was moving out of state and quitting the business. She said that she was just going to cut her own hair, but one could see that wasn't going to hold up. Mama needs her style.

"Yours still looks great; I don't know how you do it."

She's really laying it on thick now. She has never approved of my hair—the nonchalant way I grab a handful and cut, the way I usually just keep it up in a ponytail if it gets too long. She has always wanted more for me and Violet when it comes to our appearances. Neither of her daughters can manage fashion like she can.

I nod, glance down at the menu. "You like the meatloaf here, don't you?" I ask.

She does the same, only she wipes her menu off with her napkin before she opens it. "I think I'll just get a vegetable plate tonight."

I notice the daily specials, read off the vegetables they are serving. I'd rather have a sandwich—club or turkey, I'm not sure— and I wonder if I need to take home something for Nathan. That would be a red flag, however.

I close the menu and wait.

A server comes by, gives us both glasses of iced tea, and my mother finally decides on butter beans and corn, cole slaw and fried squash. I pick turkey and avocado on whole wheat, thinking I can just eat half and take the other home.

"So, thank you for coming to meet me," I say.

She places her hands in her lap. "I am always happy to meet you for dinner."

"Yes," I respond and clear my throat. "I just wanted to apologize."

"For what?" she asks innocently, as if she doesn't know exactly what offended her.

I play along. "For the last time you were at the house, for making you return the things you took from the pantry."

"Nathan's things."

I nod. "Yes, Nathan's things."

"Well, I'm sure you have your reasons, and I will respect your desire to keep things like they were."

I don't respond, knowing she can't just stop at that.

"Even though they aren't."

And here we go.

She reaches for my hand. "You know that, right? You aren't still pretending your husband didn't die, are you?"

I glance away, hoping no one can hear us. I pull my hand away and place it in my lap.

"I'm not pretending that he didn't die." I know it's just semantics, but to state this feels like it gives me an out. I'm not pretending he didn't die; I believe he did die, but he came back. There is a difference, as small as it might be.

She doesn't push, but I know she has more she wants to say. She's seen the small way I live, the way I refuse to get rid of his things, being unwilling to clean out his closet, the way I still talk using the pronoun "we," as in, "We just had dinner. We slept late." This was what got her attention before.

"I've heard you can think of this as a new normal," she reports, making me believe she's still reading everything she can find about grief, especially the kind she thinks I suffer from, the kind she enjoys describing as complicated.

"A what?"

"A new normal," she repeats herself. "*Your new normal.*" She draws out every syllable like these are unfamiliar words for her to be saying. "I once heard a widow explain that she used to be an apple when her husband was living, but now she's an orange. Nothing is the same for her. It's a new existence. Your life is completely different now that Nathan is gone, and what you used to consider as normal isn't so anymore."

"Right," I reply, trying not to swing at her pitch, trying to keep the sharpness from my tone.

"But all the experts say you have to clean things up, let your surroundings reflect what is your truth, that there is no longer a 'we' but only an 'I.' Decide what you want your life to be about and recreate yourself."

"Into an orange," I note.

She sighs. "It's just a metaphor. It's just a way to say you're not the same anymore."

I glance away.

"He's dead, Em. I think it's time for you to accept it." She waits a few seconds. It's clear my mother prepared for this get-together. "I brought something for you."

Great, I think. Another brochure she picked up from hospice or ordered from that bereavement center where she sends donations. She reaches into her purse and takes out a pamphlet.

"It's about the stages of grief but a fresh way of understanding the bargaining, the anger, the depression, the acceptance ..." She pauses, taps her finger on her chin. "What is that other stage? There's five, right?"

"Let's talk about something else," I interject, taking the brochure from her and sticking it in my pocket. "How's Violet? Is she still stateside?"

She doesn't answer at first. She's not finished; but she can see that I am.

"Denial," she remembers.

Of course it is.

I pull out a napkin from the holder between us and wipe a few crumbs from the table, then I rearrange the salt and pepper shakers, start restacking the packs of sugar and replacing them in the plastic container.

"As far as I know," she answers, her voice not hiding her disappointment at my responses, or lack thereof. And yet, she chooses to stay with my deflection and let this go for now. "You know your sister doesn't talk much about her assignments."

I nod. It's true. My sister is very secretive about her work in the military. I figured a long time ago she was in some secret branch of the army, but I've never had that confirmed.

"How's work?" she asks.

It's a relief to have moved on, and I relax a bit, settle in my chair, stretch out my legs. "About the same," I reply, deciding not to mention Kathryn's new ideas. Bus's face pops in my mind, and I dread what next week will have in store for me.

"You're coming over for your birthday, aren't you?"

I had forgotten the invitation. "Sure," I say.

"It's Friday night, next week."

"I remember when my birthday is," I reply, knowing I sound perturbed. "Thank you for reminding me," I add softly.

She touches the sides of her hair again. She seems nervous. "I just worry about you," she explains.

"I know, Mom, and I'm here because I want you to see that I'm fine."

The server comes to the table and delivers our plates of food.

"I'm going to need a to-go box," I announce as I pick up half of my sandwich. When I glance up at my mom, she is shaking her head.

"What?" I ask, but it's insincere.

She clearly knows what she sees.

Chapter Twenty-Six

"You're going out in the field with a coworker?"

Nathan is waiting for me when I get home from dinner with my mother. I have just walked in, and I glance around, trying to make sure nobody else is there, but he's alone. I go back and hang my coat on the hall tree, drape my scarf over the top of it, and drop the keys in the bowl by the door.

"Do ghosts have some extrasensory skills you haven't told me about?"

He doesn't answer.

"Hello to you too," I say, trying to lighten the heaviness I feel in the room. I walk over and kiss him on the forehead. It tastes salty, like it did when he used to work outside. He doesn't move.

"How did you find out?" I stand up and watch for the truth. I have always had a good eye for his lies. Some things never change.

"There's a message on the phone. I listened to it."

"Because you're nosy and like to snoop?"

"Because I thought it might be you calling."

I nod but don't reply to his opening question. I walk into the kitchen.

"I brought you half my sandwich." I get a plate from the cabinet and place the leftovers on it, pull off a piece of paper towel, walk them over to the table where he's sitting. "You want something to drink?" I stand across from him.

He shakes his head, takes a gander at the meal I am offering him. "Carla think you're just not eating, or does she know you've got company?"

I shrug. "I don't really know what she thinks. I know what she suspects."

"That you haven't changed your ways."

I pull out the brochure from my pants pocket. "That I'm not adjusting very well to my 'new normal,'" I say, using air quotes. "And I'm now an orange."

I can see how this stumps him, I slide the pamphlet over to him and he opens it.

He turns it over to view the back cover. "The Grief Institute?" He peeks over the top of it.

I smile.

"There's an institute for grief?"

"Apparently."

He puts down the brochure and picks up the sandwich. He lifts up the top piece of bread. "Is this avocado?"

"Yep." And then I remember that he doesn't like avocado, and we both look up at the same time. "I'm sorry," I say, wondering how I could forget something like that.

He puts the sandwich down and picks up a pickle.

"So, you and Carla, everything okay?"

"Well, that's slightly overstated, but she's still talking to me, and she didn't bring a straitjacket or a shrink with her; so, yes, I suppose mother and daughter are still engaged in a respectable relationship."

"Thrilled to hear it."

"She wants me to come over for my birthday," I answer, staring at the half sandwich I didn't want an hour ago but now feel like I could eat.

He nods. "Well, with your *new normal* and all, I suppose that makes sense." He catches me eyeing the plate of food.

"So, who called?" I ask, curious about the message.

"Kathryn."

I wait. *You did listen,* I think.

"She just wanted to remind you that you'll meet your colleague at the office and go out with him on his assigned calls." He pauses. "Sounded like she might be worried you wouldn't show up."

"On time," I add. "She's worried I won't show up on time and that would mess things up."

"For your colleague," he says, fishing.

"For Bus," I say, taking the hook, thinking it will do no good to deny his suspicions. I might not be able to be honest with my mother, but there is no reason not for me to be honest with him.

"So, just what project will the two of you be working on?"

I steady myself and fold my arms across my chest, pull out the chair and sit. As prepared as I am to tell the truth, it still feels like I just emerged from one interrogation to now another.

"Never mind," he adds, sensing my displeasure, and picks up the brochure again.

"She thinks it will help business," I tell him. "Kathryn thinks that sending out members of the sales staff with the installation technicians will help us more clearly understand their role, and it will help them learn more about the work we do. It provides follow-up with the customer, because we'd likely meet them at the installation." I sigh. "She's watched some sales and marketing webcast, learned some new techniques, wants to shake things up; we'll just be working together for a couple days."

He doesn't respond.

"Oh come on, you can't be mad at me for this."

He opens up the brochure, keeps reading.

"What have you been doing while I was gone?" I slide down in my chair, cross my legs at my ankles.

He puts the pamphlet down. He seems old and unhappy, and I turn away. It's hard to see him this way.

"I practiced levitating and going through walls."

I roll my eyes, shake my head. "If you could do that, you would have already shown off. You would have already demonstrated that action."

And then I see the sadness again, settling on him like an old coat, and just like that, I realize how alone he has been feeling.

"You okay?" I don't know why I ask. Even if he isn't, there's nothing I can do.

He nods slowly, trying to appear convincing.

A truck passes on the road in front of the house, and we both wait.

"You want me to fix you something else to eat? You want pasta or an egg or something?"

He shakes his head.

"Maybe you should read the brochure," he says. "Maybe you should go to the grief institute. Maybe they can help you."

"Or maybe I should just bring home a sandwich you like. Maybe I should order roast beef next time."

"You don't like roast beef; Carla knows that."

"Yeah?"

"Yeah."

I eye my leftovers.

"Take it," he tells me, but I just look away.

Chapter Twenty-Seven

"So you've heard it?"

Bus and I are in a work van. We arrived at the office at about the same time, had a cup of coffee with the other teams, and are now driving to our first appointment. It's a small used bookstore on the edge of town. I sold them a package more than a year ago, but just last week the owner wanted to upgrade. Bus is installing cameras at the front and rear doors. There have been a few break-ins close to the store, and apparently, the client is feeling a bit vulnerable. Kathryn talked to him last week.

"Of course," I answer. He's just recited the rhyme found in *The Reformed Commonwealth of Bees* from the 1600s. It's familiar to most beekeepers.

"A swarm of bees in May is worth a cow and a bottle of hay. A swarm of bees in July is not worth a fly."

"So what's it talking about?" he asks. "What does it mean?"

"It means that a swarm of bees in spring are worth a lot of money, whereas bees swarming late in the summer aren't very valuable."

"Because late-summer swarms include bees that are older, not as healthy as bees in spring?"

I shake my head, pull down the visor to block the morning sun. "Because late-summer swarms have left their hives and don't have honey stored, and there's no way they'll be able to produce enough to last during the winter. A keeper would have to feed them or they'll starve."

"What makes them swarm anyway?"

Bus is quite the chatty one today. I assume he's just trying to act interested in my hobby, trying to make up for his blunder the last time we were together. Still, it's too early for me to have this kind of conversation. I stifle a yawn.

"I'm sorry." He noticed. "It's just I've been doing some reading." He pauses. "I think I might like to do it too."

"No, it's fine." And then I think about his last comment. "You want to keep bees?"

He shrugs, makes the turn onto the street where the business we have an appointment is located. "Maybe." He glances over. "Is it very expensive to get started?"

"I really don't know," I reply. "Nathan was on his own with the work at first. I could ask—" And I catch myself. "I could check our records and let you know."

He nods and doesn't face me, and I feel my face flush. Like all secrets, this one sometimes shows its teeth, biting you when you least expect.

"They swarm because the colony has gotten too large, and so they divide up and some of the colony leaves to find a new home."

"Does the queen leave too?" He checks the GPS mounted on the inside of the windshield.

"Sometimes," I say. "Usually, I think." He's asking questions I have only begun to ask myself, but I don't tell him this. I like being the expert; I like Bus wanting to know things and believing that I can supply the answers.

He pulls into the lot, finds a space, and puts the gear in park. He slides over in his seat, his back against his door, to face me. "Would you show me yours sometime?" Then because of the phrasing of his question, he blushes, turns away, clears his throat.

This makes me smile. I unbuckle my seat belt. "I will be happy to take you to the hives," I say. "But it would make more sense to wait until it warms up."

He listens.

"There's not much going on this time of the year. They're more active when the flowers bloom, when they start going out to work."

He nods. "Do you get stung a lot?" He's watching me now.

I face ahead to the front of the bookstore and wonder if the owner has arrived. I imagine that it's still about thirty minutes before he opens for customers. I try to see if the lights are on and if anyone's in the shop.

"I did at first; that's why I wouldn't go out there when Nathan first bought them. I hated the stings. I hated thinking about getting stung. Nathan—" And I turn to Bus to explain. "My husband," I say softly and wait as he nods to show me he recognizes his name. "Nathan said that the bees pick up on nervous energy; they can sense jumpiness."

"You can wear a suit, though, right?"

"Yeah, you can. In fact, you should. But I think after a while they get used to you and your energy, even if it's slightly, I don't know, frenetic."

He smiles. "You like it then?" He rests his elbow on the door. "It seems as if you like them."

"I guess." I think about his observation. "I didn't at first. It was just Nathan's thing, and I didn't really have much to do with it; but after he couldn't go out there, I don't know, it just became this place where I like to hang out. Bees seem better company than humans." I realize what I've said. "I mean, not all humans."

"It's okay," he says, excusing my outed view on humanity. "I totally understand. Animals in general, I think, are better company than we are."

He checks his watch and glances ahead at the store. "I'm not sure the owner is here yet."

"I know. I was thinking the same thing. Did we make an appointment?"

He reaches into the console between us and takes out a small tablet. He turns it on and slides his finger across the screen, getting to his calendar, I suppose. He stops on a page. "Nine o'clock," he tells me.

I check the dashboard; we're twenty minutes early. We left the office too soon.

"We could drive around," he suggests. "Go to that restaurant at the corner for coffee?"

"No, it's fine just to wait."

There is a lull in the conversation. Traffic moves steadily on the street behind us, and I catch him watching in the rearview mirror as the cars go by.

"How's your girlfriend doing with her dissertation?"

He doesn't answer right away, and this raises my curiosity. Now I'm the one sliding over in my seat to get a better view.

"Well, I guess you wouldn't know since I haven't really talked to anyone." He drops down in his seat, leans back. "We broke up."

"Oh." This is a surprise.

"Well, actually *we* didn't break up; she broke up with me."

I feel embarrassed even though this isn't my relationship we're discussing.

"She claims she needs her space." He reaches up and grabs the steering wheel. "Which I'm pretty sure is code for she's found someone else."

We watch as a car pulls in a few spaces over, right in front of the store. I figure it must be the owner. The driver gets out and walks to the door, unlocking it.

I can't think of a response or a follow-up question to this bit of news from Bus.

He faces me and shrugs. "It's okay," he says, like I did manage some compassionate remark. "I'm pretty sure it's for the best."

I nod and reach for the handle, opening the door on my side. "I'll help you with your bees," I tell him and then step out of the car.

Chapter Twenty-Eight

"I hate to be so suspicious of people or think the worst about society," he tells us, shaking his head. "But there's just been too many places getting hit lately, getting robbed."

The owner, Mr. Starr, appears to be about sixty. Nathan and I have been to this store many times—we both love bookstores, after all—and I saw him working here a while ago, but if we talked, I don't really recall. I haven't been here in a couple years, though, I think Nathan may have visited a few times since the accident.

We knew the previous owners quite well, a couple from Florida who started the shop selling mostly used textbooks. It was a pretty successful business ten or fifteen years ago, but now with electronic books and Amazon selling the required class readings for rock-bottom rates, even the university bookstore struggles to make ends meet. The Florida couple got out just in time; Mr. Starr must do this only for love because I'm sure he doesn't turn much of a profit.

The owner is short, broad-chested, has thinning hair but has still managed a brown-and-gray braided ponytail that hangs down past his shoulders. He's wearing corduroys and a plaid shirt. He looks like a lot of the professors I have known over the years, and it makes me wonder if he's retired from the university, if he's taught classes like Nathan, and if he likes to read as much as we both do.

I don't really have a response to his comment since the previous owners never seemed to have a problem with theft or shoplifting, never worried about such things, so I glance over to Bus, giving him the floor.

"Well, you'll find things often change with just putting these up," he tells the customer with a smile. He motions with his chin to the box of cameras he has on the hand truck he wheeled in. "These let everyone know their actions are being monitored. Sometimes it solves the problem without requiring any other remedy."

Bus sounds confident, experienced. He obviously takes his work seriously.

Mr. Starr puts his hands on the counter in front of him, leans toward Bus and me. "I hope you're right. I'm not wanting to arrest or even confront anybody, and I don't really want to have to bring the police into my business."

And Bus smiles, reaches up and pats our customer on the back of his hand, acting as if he understands; but I don't. I'm suddenly thinking that Mr. Starr might have more than just book sales going on. Nathan always said people who want security systems are either motivated by fear or a strong need for privacy, and he always said it with raised eyebrows, like desiring privacy meant something shady was going on. He has never approved of my field of work.

"This will definitely help," Bus notes.

Both men just nod at each other, and I start to feel left out.

"Bus will be installing the cameras at four separate locations, and then we'll show you how to download the software on your computer. Do you have a laptop?"

"Oh yes, sure," he answers.

"We can also give you the app to put on your smartphone too." I smile, trying to adopt the friendly and knowledgeable style of my colleague.

"Nah, I don't have one of them," Mr. Starr replies. "Still have the flip-style version. I'm old school."

"That's okay, the laptop will work just fine."

There's a lull.

"So I'll just go ahead and get started," Bus notes, breaking the awkward silence.

"Yes, good." Mr. Starr moves around the counter and points Bus in the direction of where he wants the camera mounted. They walk to a far end, but I stay where I am. It's not a very big store, and there isn't much room in the corners. It would be crowded if we all tried to stand around the designated camera spots; besides, there really isn't anything for me to do. In fact, there isn't much for me to do at all, and I start to really hate Kathryn's idea of going out two by two like this. It seems like a total waste of time to me.

I glance at my watch. It's not even nine o'clock yet. I hadn't thought about what I would do while Bus makes the installation, but now that we're here, I am at least glad we're at a bookstore and not the bank, which is where Jon was assigned.

I liked bookstores before I met Nathan, but becoming involved with an English professor means bookstores are a destination at every place one visits and every local spot becomes familiar territory. I can easily say that we have been in all the bookstores, be they used or new, in all of the southeastern United States. We have taken day trips just to visit a little stop he liked or one he just happened to miss and longed to browse again.

Nathan has always loved books—reading them, thumbing through them, buying them. It's just one of the reasons I fell in love with him. The way he talks about books is like hearing a person speak of what is saving his life, the one true thing that keeps him breathing and alive. The talk is intimate and sweet, and he's at his best when he notes the distinct qualities or detailed characteristics of the books he enjoys.

I think of him now in this place. One of the last times we were here together, he was shopping for bee books, and the saleswoman—one of the previous owners, a gentle hippie-type with long, flowing hair who always wore leggings and peasant skirts, strappy sandals, lots of bracelets—grabbed his hand as soon as we walked in. She was so happy when she saw him. Knowing Nathan's interests, she pulled out a stack of books she had saved for him.

I left the two of them at the front of the store and then watched from the mystery section as she showed him each book, holding them out for him, one by one. I fell in love with him all over again, just seeing his tenderness as he held the first and then the second, caressing them, touching them so carefully, asking questions about the author and the information that lay between the covers.

He stood at the counter and read a few pages from each one, and I suppose there were six or eight in the stack. He had, of course, bought them all. Like a smitten lover, he has never demonstrated one bit of self-control when it meant putting one aside or letting one go. He would easily spend every dollar he earned on books. It is a budget item for our household because books matter as much to us both as food and utilities. We can never have enough books.

"You used to come in here." Mr. Starr has returned.

"I'm sorry." I was so lost in thought I didn't hear what he said.

"You used to come in here," he repeats himself.

I reach up and rub my neck, loosen my scarf. "Yes, that's right." I wait for the next observation, the one where he remembers Nathan. I wait for the question of where my husband is, why he's been missing. I draw in a breath.

"You like suspense."

And I'm so surprised that the conversation is taking a different direction, I don't answer.

"Nesbø," he adds, recalling my last purchase that had to have been more than a year ago. "You came in trying to find his series."

"Harry Hole," I reply, still surprised at his memory of my passion and my purchase, still surprised at his memory of me.

"Right." He claps his hands together, obviously pleased at his memory. "We didn't have it, but I was able to persuade you to take a try with another Norwegian."

"Dahl," I answer.

"And?"

I think about the book I bought so long ago and realize it's one of the last books of fiction I have read. For months, I've had my head only stuck in work journals or the bee books. I can't seem to concentrate long enough to handle a novel. I suddenly think of how much I have missed. I start to answer that I liked the recommended book, but the bell on the front door rings, and we both turn.

Chapter Twenty-Nine

"Hello, Mr. Starr." And then she turns to me as if she hadn't expected that I would be where I'm supposed to be. "Emma."

"Hey, Kathryn," I reply, nonplussed that my boss appears to be checking up on me.

She holds out her hand to our customer. "What a pleasure to meet you. I have often wanted to stop here, and now that I have, I can say this is a fabulous store," she says, sounding a wee bit inauthentic if you ask me. She fills up all the space around us, and I back up a few steps to give her more room.

"I'm Kathryn Oakley, the owner of K-Locks. We spoke last week." She stands tall, her shoulders are high, her back straight. She's wearing a navy pantsuit, low heels, a pink blouse. She's had her hair cut in a new style, and there are more blonde highlights than I remember. She's really working every angle she knows to increase business, and thinking about her this way lessens my feelings of agitation about her showing up at my first appointment. She's in trouble; she's making changes.

Mr. Starr takes her outstretched hand. "Thank you," he replies, appearing to be as surprised as me at this visit.

"We are so happy to have you as a customer, and we certainly hope you are pleased with the service you are receiving today." She drops her hand, rests her arms by her sides. She's still smiling from when she first entered. In fact, I've never seen her smile this long, and it makes me wonder how many more minutes she can keep her lips in that stretched position. She's wearing more makeup too—that's also new. I actually feel sorry for her.

"So far so good," the customer responds.

"Is the installation and the delivery of information about your new system going as you had hoped?" She glances around and locates Bus standing on a ladder in the corner near the front window. He must not know she's here, or he doesn't care; I don't think he's turned around since she arrived.

"I can't say I've actually spent much time *hoping* about it," Mr. Starr answers, and I find the response refreshing. He shrugs. "I'm not displeased."

I really don't know why she's here, but I do feel slightly belittled by her presence. I wonder if she has stopped in on the other teams as well or if she was particularly concerned about Bus and me—well, or just me.

"Okay," she responds.

There's an awkward silence that I know *I'm* not going to fill up. I stick my hands in my pockets.

"Okay," she says again. "Well, Emma has been with the company for a long time, and I'm confident that she can answer any of your questions. I'm sure she's gone over all the paperwork and helped you understand the system."

I wait for the customer's reply, knowing I haven't really gotten to the paperwork yet. I was waiting until Bus was finished.

"She has been quite helpful," he answers, without glancing in my direction or adding a wink, which is what most people do when they know they've just scored points for you.

I like Mr. Starr.

"Well, that's just terrific to hear."

Another pause. I guess Kathryn's webcasts didn't give her the opportunity to practice this business call, and seeing how badly it's going, I think maybe she won't try it again. It feels too much like overkill for the customer, and it makes her seem like a hovering boss. Now that I've had this experience, I actually hope she hasn't gone to the bank or the other team's appointment. Jon would hate everything about this.

"I'll just let you get to it then." And without ever changing the smile she has worn since walking in, she sticks her hand out again, and the bookstore owner takes it. She looks over in my direction. "Emma, thanks for your work, and Mr. Starr, thank you again for choosing us for your security needs."

"Uh-huh," he answers, drops her hand, and watches as she turns and leaves.

We don't speak until we see her car pull out of the parking lot.

"She bored or just worried I won't pay for the installation?" He leans against the counter behind him.

"Nah, that was for me. I think she may have been worried I wouldn't show up." I pull my hands out of my pockets to confess. "I haven't been all that reliable lately."

"Well, it doesn't instill much confidence in your boss."

"Don't blame her," I tell him.

He shakes his head like he doesn't want to believe me.

"Really," I say, defending Kathryn and also trying not to lose this business contract. "She's just trying to make sure you get the best customer service. She's a good person," I add, not sure why I need to tell him this.

"Okay, I'll take your word for it." He's studying me now, and I remember our conversation before that storm just blew through. I suspect now's the time for the questions about Nathan. I avert his stare.

"So how long have you owned the shop?" I ask, glancing around and hoping to avoid the inquisition.

"Bought it a couple years ago," he answers, and I wait for him to tell me it wasn't his finest financial decision; but he surprises me. "Best move I've ever made."

"Really?" And then I realize I sound like I don't believe him. "I just thought this would be a hard business in today's market."

He nods. "I didn't say it was the best move professionally." And he laughs. "I just mean personally. I was in need of a change, and this has been great."

"Except for the fear of break-ins," I note.

"Well, yes, that's been a bit disconcerting; but I think that will work out."

"Do you have a good customer base?" I wonder about the university atmosphere and whether or not the locals are supportive of a used bookstore.

"It's not so much the customers who actually come into the store and buy the books; it's the ones selling. I have a pretty good web business—sell a lot of used books to Amazon and eBay."

"Right," I reply, having forgotten those contemporary opportunities for booksellers.

"This is a good area for acquiring used books. College students and faculty collect a lot of them, some quite expensive. I give a respectable price for what they bring me, and I still make a profit on my internet sales." He folds his arms across his chest.

"That's great," I say and mean it. After all, I thought he was just another struggling business owner.

"It is," he agrees. "Hey," he adds, and I snap to attention. "Sometime when you're not working, you'll have to come by and see some of the collections I've acquired. I have a number of first editions and some antique selections that you might find interesting."

"Sure," I reply.

We both turn to the corner of the store where Bus has been working. The ladder slides across the floor as he moves to the other end to install the second camera.

"I better go and see if he needs some help," I say, and I step away from the front counter.

Chapter Thirty

"Thave something for you before you go," Mr. Starr says, and I stop while Bus heads out the door.

We're finished with the installation, the tutorial, and paperwork. It took most of the morning, but it turned out to be enjoyable. I got paid to browse through books, and I had forgotten how much I love book stores, how much I love the ease in shopping in them, the authors in alphabetical order, the genres all shelved together, the big roomy chairs to sit and leaf through pages.

Maybe I like being out in the field more than I thought I would.

"Oh, okay," I say. I step inside the store.

"I found your author while you were browsing." And he walks around the counter and holds out his hands. "I had it in the office, was just waiting for the right person to give it to. And you're here."

I glance down. It's the first book written by Jo Nesbø, *The Bat*, the first in the Harry Hole series, only it's in the original language. It's entitled *Flaggermusmannen*. I recognize it because I remember the cover. I read it years ago, but I bought the paperback. I don't have any hardback books by Nesbø.

"Wow, thank you, Mr. Starr." I take it from him.

"Paul," he tells me. "Please, call me Paul."

I study the book. It's in great condition, and when I open it, I see that it's a first edition, and it's been signed by the author. I look up at him. "Wait, I can't take this." I try to return it to him.

"No." He pulls away from me with his hands raised. "I really want you to have it. It's a gift."

"I can't."

"Sure you can."

I feel his resistance, and I reach for my purse. "At least let me pay you what it costs."

"That kind of takes away the whole notion of a gift, wouldn't you say?"

I shake my head, feel my face flush. "But I can't take this."

"Are you worried about your boss? Because I promise I won't tell. Not that there's even a reason to think she'll come here again anyway."

I'm still shaking my head. "No, it's not her. I know you wouldn't say anything. I just—"

"Then give me a dollar," he tells me before I can finish my sentence, and he goes to the cash register.

"What?"

"The book costs one dollar. It's a business transaction. No ethical dilemma. The book is old, out of season. I'm charging you a dollar."

"But it's signed," I protest. "It's a first edition."

"That's the luck you sometimes have when you're shopping in a used bookstore. Treasures on every shelf," he says with a grin, sounding very much like Nathan.

I look behind me. Bus is waiting in the van. He's hunched over, probably filling out his time sheet.

"I don't know what to say."

"Say, 'thank you, Paul.'"

I open my purse, find my wallet, and hand him a dollar.

He takes it from me, rings up a sale, hands me a receipt.

"Thank you, Paul."

"You're welcome." I return my wallet to my purse, open the book. I don't think it's ever been read. It's in mint condition.

"Of course, maybe you'll need to learn Norwegian to actually read it."

I close the book. "Maybe that's just what I need to do. That way I can read all his other books in their original language. It could be that something gets lost in the translation to English."

"I suspect that could happen."

I study the cover a few more minutes, and then I think of the question that has been bothering me since I got to the store this morning. "Why do you really need a security system?" I hesitate. "You're not really worried about burglars or thieves."

He smiles and glances away, scratches his chin. It's like he's thinking very hard about his answer. He turns to me again. "Your husband used to come in all the time."

I put the book down on the counter.

"I knew about the accident, and I heard later about his passing."

I glance outside at Bus, who has finished his paperwork; he faces me and waves. He must be wondering what's taking me so long.

"It took me a while, but I finally remembered where you worked. Nathan told me about you."

I draw in a breath, turn around to face my customer. "So you put in this upgrade as a gesture of—what? Of your sympathy?" My voice has become sharp, pointed, a weapon I sometimes like to use.

He shakes his head. "No." He pauses, swallows hard. "Not exactly."

"Here, I can't take this," I say, sliding the book over to him. "Thank you for your business." I start to walk away.

"No, that's a purchase. I won't take that back." He doesn't reach for it and stays where he is behind the counter.

"Mr. Starr—Paul," I pick up my purse that I had let drop to the floor and hang it on my shoulder.

He interrupts me. "I lost my wife three years ago."

This was not what I expected to hear.

"That's the personal stuff I was going through, why I needed a change, why it was a good move for me to buy this store."

I'm at a loss for words.

"I was in bad shape," he confesses, his voice softer.

I turn away, keep my eyes down, keep reading the title of his gift over and over.

"And I came across this book and thought about you."

I nod but don't reply.

"Nathan had been trying to find one for you, a while ago, after his accident, but before he ..." He hesitates. "It was about this time actually. I guess he wanted to buy something special for your anniversary or Valentine's or something. Anyway, this came in a couple months ago. Somebody from Raleigh brought in a stack of books, and this was in there, and it made me think of Nathan and of you."

"So you pretended to be a customer of the agency where I work in order to have me come in so you could give this to me?" I hold up the book. "Was all this your idea? To have me come to the installation?"

He shakes his head. "No, that part was just serendipitous. Once I knew you were still there, I was just going to mail the book to you. I did want cameras, though, because I think it's just smart to have them when you work alone; but I had no idea you'd show up here today. I'm sorry all this happened. I see now it was a dumb idea. You'd think I'd know better."

I recognize the look now, the widowed look—the way spouses who have lost their partners seem off-balance somehow, like we're missing a part of ourselves. I have seen it everywhere I've gone since Nathan died. I can't believe I missed it when I came in earlier. I see it all mapped out now in his eyes, across his brow, the thinned straight line that used to be a smile.

"It was my birthday," I tell him, thinking about the gift.

His face becomes a question mark.

"When he came in before, when you saw him last year about this. It was my birthday. It's next week."

He nods.

I pick up the book and hold it against my chest, but before I can say anything, Bus is standing in the doorway.

"Everything all right?" he asks, and I nod, turn, and walk past him.

Chapter Thirty-One

"So I'm thinking of putting them here."

Bus has taken me to the house he has just rented. His girlfriend kept their apartment near campus, and he found this place on Craigslist. It's about fifteen miles from town, a fixer-upper that he got cheap so long as he does the fixing up. It's a clapboard one bedroom, one bath, with a small kitchen and a screened-in porch.

He's showing me the area behind it where he wants to keep his hives. There's a barn about one hundred feet behind the house, one side has fallen in. Weeds have overgrown the whole property, but there is a place where there used to be a garden—a plot bigger than the house, filled with wild clover and *Lamium amplexicaule,* henbit, a ground cover that blooms with purple flowers.

Henbit usually grows about six inches tall and a foot or more across, with purple and pink flowers in small whorls at the ends of the stems. If you research this plant, mostly what you find are ways to get rid of it since it's primarily seen as a weed that takes over gardens and lawns; but beekeepers love it.

"Maybe right along this part of the house."

"You want to keep your bees here?" I'm surprised Bus would want hives right at his door.

"Too close?" At least he's figured that out.

"It could be seen as a bit off-putting for your guests."

"Yeah, well, I don't know about having guests, but I can see having the bees flying in the house all the time might be a problem."

I nod.

"I've never lived in the country like this, never had animals or space to grow things."

"City boy then?" I ask.

"Military brat," he replies. "Apartments or base housing, compounds in Japan and Korea. We didn't have yards and gardens, just playgrounds and maybe a park."

"Well, that's not bad," I say. "Parks are good."

"I guess."

I hear him taking in a deep breath. He's standing behind me so I'm not watching him. I'm studying the henbit in the garden plot and remembering how Nathan transplanted the weeds that our neighbor was throwing in the garbage. He planted them out by the hives at the farm. The neighbor thought he was crazy taking the pesky weeds out of the trash cans at the curb and putting them in a box in his trunk.

"That's crap," he told Nathan when he came out of his house to see what he was doing. "You don't want that growing anywhere."

"Well, crap to you maybe," my husband replied, "but to the bees it's divine."

Henbit is one of the few plants that grow in winter, providing nectar and pollen to hungry bees. He saw it in the trash bin as some heavenly gift since he always wanted to give his bees every chance to survive.

"What about you?"

I turn. "What?" I hadn't made out the question.

"Where did you grow up? You a country girl?"

I shake my head.

"More of a suburbanite, but we always had a yard, not really gardens so much. But my grandparents were farmers."

I think about the farm in eastern North Carolina where my sister and I spent a few of our childhood summers when we were quite young. I rode the tractor with my grandfather, picked vegetables, and watched as my grandmother canned them. Violet built forts near the creek behind the pasture. Even as a kid, she was already intrigued with military life, and when we were finished with our chores she would christen us soldiers, and we would fight pretend battles until the sun went down. We climbed trees and fished from the banks of a river.

We stopped going to our grandparents after Daddy left because Carla couldn't stand to be alone, and since she worked six days a week as a unit secretary in the local hospital, we never got down there with her. Our grandparents took us camping a few of the summers after that, came to visit a couple of times, stayed the weekend for our high school graduations. Once they got older, they rarely traveled. But I still remember the farm where they lived, and even though those memories of my sister and me being there with them are old and rare ones, they are still some of my favorites.

I start to say something about the corn and cotton that my grandfather raised, how he taught me how to pick the small bolls of white fluff from the sharp brown shells and pull the ears of corn with their long, silky hair, but when I turn around, Bus is watching me, and for some reason I decide not to share.

"Where did you go?" he asks.

"What?"

"Just now, you went somewhere in your thoughts."

"Oh, nowhere," I reply, and start walking toward the barn behind the house, wondering how I appear when I am somewhere else, how he knew I was wandering.

I hear him following me.

"You think out here will be good?"

I glance around the dilapidated barn, the weeds growing tall around it, a meandering path heading beyond the barn out to a field. A line of trees stands in the distance.

"Where's that go?" I ask.

"Creek bed," he answers, following my eyes. "I think the owner said it fills up sometimes, but it's mostly dry in the winter."

"Trees?"

"What about them?"

"What kind of trees are they?"

"Big green ones?"

This makes me laugh. "You really don't know anything about nature, do you? What exactly did you learn growing up on those military bases?"

He clears his throat, straightens up, measuring out attention exactly like my sister when she's standing with her unit, getting ready to load up and head out.

"I know about car engines and electrical wiring. I know how to spit shine shoes and how to keep a neat storage locker. I know how to make knots and how to shoot rifles and when to say yes, sir and no, sir. And I know how to be real quiet. But no, to answer your question, I don't know much about nature. I don't know the names of trees."

"Okay," I respond and turn once again to the field. "So a few daddy issues, I see."

He shakes his head and scratches his neck. "Just a few," he answers. "You?"

"He left when I was eight. I didn't even learn the shoe-shining part."

Bus doesn't respond.

"Well, let's go see what they are." And I start walking.

"Wait." And I hear him catching up behind me. "You want to walk way out there? You want to go see trees?"

"I do," I reply. "Bees love maples and American hazels."

"Bees like trees?"

I smile and keep walking. "Bees like trees," I reply.

Chapter Thirty-Two

"You went to his house?"

I haven't even actually made it inside before I feel him right in front of me. His hot breath, his barrage of questions, his jealousy.

"What?"

"The Neanderthal you work with," he says while I am trying to put my key in the lock. "Buster Bus."

He is standing just on the other side of the door. I can't see him but he's there. I'm sure his face is smashed against the window.

"You worked with him all day. You ate lunch together and then you went to his house."

I close my eyes and don't turn the key. I don't know how to respond. I don't understand how he knows what he knows.

"Well, what are you doing out there? Can't you open the door? Do I need to unlock it for you?"

I clench my teeth and don't respond because there's no talking to him when he's like this. Sometimes, since he's come back from the dead, he can be irritable, hard to please, always trying to find out what I'm doing or where I've been. He was never like this before the accident. Even after it happened, when he was sometimes moody and bearish, he was still never jealous or brooded over how I spent my time or whom I was with. This is a new side of my husband, a new monster from the grave that I do not recognize.

"Just step aside so I can get in," I say to him, thinking that if I open the door I will hit him. I unlock it and pull out my key.

"I don't need to step aside," he replies.

"Right" is all I can think to say. I don't make another move.

"Do you have something for me to eat?" he asks.

And I do not.

"Hi, Emma."

It's my neighbor, Louise. She lives across the street from us, and I had seen her coming out her front door, walking toward her mailbox when I first arrived at home. I waved at her, but I figured she had already returned to her house. Now I wonder how much of this conversation she has witnessed.

"Hi," she says again, holding up her hand, the stack of letters held above her head.

"Hey," I reply, holding the doorknob and trying to keep the door closed on Nathan. "Good to see you."

"Tell her to go away."

"It got warmer today," she says, making small talk.

"It did, yes."

"I'm glad. I'm ready for spring."

"Uh-huh."

"Don't encourage her." His voice is angry, sharp as a blade.

"You and Mike doing okay?"

Now that I see her, I realize that I haven't actually talked to our neighbors in weeks.

The four of us were never actually close, but we always liked them. We watched the Super Bowl together one year, grilled out in the summer a few times, sat on the porch some Sundays. We moved in after they had been living here only a year or so.

Mike teaches engineering at the college. Louise is a pianist, plays for the symphony.

"We're fine," she replies.

Since Nathan died, they've invited me over a few times, but I always decline. She's come by with a casserole or cake over the months, stopped by once and had a glass of wine, but I've not really been that interested in socializing with them. It's hard enough trying to be with Carla or Violet or some other single person. I don't have many outings with two; trying to sit down for dinner with a couple is just too hard.

"Don't shut the door on me," I hear him say from inside. "She can't see me."

I keep forgetting that small detail of his invisibility to everyone else, and I take my hand off the knob, turn and face Louise, who is standing in the road, having moved closer.

"Mike's gone to his mother's."

She's walking toward me. She's wearing a friendly smile, but I can see that she's a bit tentative. I've not always been that easy to read, a bit aloof most of my life; and since Nathan died, I can tell people are more careful around me.

"Tell her you can't talk," I hear Nathan say.

I slam my bag against the door like it will shut him up.

"Would you like to come over for dinner?" she asks as she makes her way to the front porch where I'm still standing.

I hesitate.

"I just feel like we haven't been very good neighbors."

"Well, she's right about that because they really haven't been that great." Nathan is talking so loud I just can't believe Louise doesn't hear him. I step closer in her direction.

"No, no," I say in my most reassuring manner. "You've been fine. I always know I can call on you both if I ever need anything, and that means a whole lot."

"Still ..."

"Tell her she can make up for her lack of neighborliness by getting us some more of that chocolate she sent last year when I got home from the hospital. What was that? Salted caramel? Tell her you don't want company, just chocolate."

"Shhh," I say under my breath to Nathan, but Louise notices. I smile. "Shhh," I say again, this time to her, waving her off. "Please, don't apologize. You and Mike have been very good neighbors. We're so lucky that you live here."

She stands at the bottom of the steps, and I realize I've said "we." She stares.

"Well, now you've done it," he says, having caught the slip of my tongue. "She's giving you that pity look now, right?"

And she is.

A kid on a bicycle rides along the sidewalk across the street in front of her house, and we both glance in his direction, both apparently glad for a distraction.

She turns to face me, and now that she's this close, I think she might want to be invited inside.

"So?" Nathan won't shut up.

I'm confused.

"She invited you to dinner. Just say no."

"Oh, um, dinner," I respond. "I actually had something to eat on my way home, so I'm not very hungry."

"You had dinner with him too?"

I try to ignore my husband's question.

"A glass of wine then?" Louise asks.

"Tell her you're tired, that you had a long day. Just get rid of her."

And I start to say these exact words to Louise and then stop myself. "You know, I think that might be nice." And I shut the door behind me and walk down the steps with my neighbor.

Chapter Thirty-Three

When I get home, it's dark, and there are no lights on in the house. I stayed longer than I wanted at Louise's, even had a piece of pie when Mike got home from visiting his mother. They both seemed happy to see me, spend time with me. And I don't know whether it was their hospitality or my spite that motivated me to stay so long. But I realized that I preferred listening to stories of concerts and budget cuts being made to art funding—even Mike's terrible jokes—than coming home and putting up with Nathan's interrogation about my day with Bus because truthfully, it was a good day.

Bus and I made three calls together. The bookstore in the morning, a restaurant located on the road out of town where he lives—which is why we went to his house—and then later in the afternoon we made a visit to a residential customer.

We ate lunch at the restaurant where we had our appointment, where we went before stopping at his place and finding a spot for his bees. It's a small pizza joint, serves westbound travelers and locals who don't want to go into town for a meal. I had never been there before, and the owners, Mr. and Mrs. Edgerton, were a nice couple who had owned several restaurants in other spots across the state.

They called K-Locks because they wanted new locks put on the doors of their establishment after Mr. Edgerton fired an angry employee. They were nervous that he had keys and would return and vandalize the place. Jon took the call and had tried to talk them into a security system, but they explained to Bus and me that the money was just not there for now, and new locks were all they could afford.

I hadn't realized that Bus was a locksmith too, but he installed deadbolts on three doors and even set up a fake camera Mr. Edgerton had bought but not yet taken out of the box. I was surprised to see that it looked like the real deal, and once it was placed on a shelf high in the corner near the cash register, I couldn't tell the difference between the plastic one they bought online and those he had installed in the bookstore this morning. The restaurant owners were so pleased with his service, they gave us a free pizza, and because it was warm enough outside, we ate our lunch at the table on their patio.

Bus played sports in school—football and track—and he was a guitarist in a rock band when he was in his late twenties and early thirties. He met his former girlfriend at a college party when she was an underclassman and his band was the entertainment at a fraternity house. They dated while she finished her four years of study and while he worked odd jobs around campus. He quit the band when the lead singer decided they should move to Oregon.

He loved her, he said, and still thought it was the right thing to do, even though the singer and musicians went on to be somewhat successful, selling CDs, and opening for popular grunge bands. He followed his girlfriend around while she completed two master's degrees and then on to Elon where she teaches classes and works on her doctorate.

He doesn't know much about the other person with whom she is involved, but he's a little suspicious that it's another woman. He claims he always had his doubts about her sexuality, and he began to notice a particular friendship that he thought seemed rather intense. The suspected other woman is an undergrad at the college, a "special student," his girlfriend had explained, and when he talked about that relationship, I couldn't help but think about me and Nathan and how universities seem to become a sort of hot spot for intellectuals to hook up. I think it's all that cognitive stimulation. We can't expect human brains to manage all the activity. There is the rest of the body to consider.

"Are you angry with her?" I asked when he told me that part, when he explained what he thought had happened.

He shook his head, wiped his mouth with his napkin. "What's there to be angry about?" he asked.

"Well, you have followed her around all these years, supported her, waited on her, and then she just ups and leaves you for a student?"

He smiled like he had already thought about my question, already knew the answer. "I didn't have anything else better to do," he told me. "I didn't mind supporting her. I liked following her around. I liked being a student vicariously through her." He shrugged. "She's a nice person; we had a lot of good times together."

I could tell he had more to say so I waited.

"And if she's happier with somebody else, then I'm glad she's found that person. I'd hate thinking she hung around because she felt sorry for me, that she stayed with me because she didn't allow herself to be who she really was or go where she needed to go. I don't want that kind of relationship because I know, in the end, both people are miserable."

I walk into our house and stand in the hallway in the darkness. I don't switch on the light, and I don't hear him anywhere close by, so I think he must have gone to bed. I hang up my coat and then turn and face myself in the mirror that hangs across from the coat rack.

I am old.

I'm not sure when that happened exactly. I've always thought of myself as appearing younger than my age. I was always the one who had to show my ID even when Violet, who is younger, never did. She's always carried a certain authority that I don't have, and it made her appear more mature somehow. I've always had good skin with a few freckles and just never thought of myself as aging like everyone else.

But seeing myself now, all that I've been through, all that I know and think I know, I am finally old.

"And how are the Webbs?"

He startles me. He's standing at the other end of the hall. He waited up.

I pick up my bag that I had put down to take off my coat and walk toward him. "Fine," I answer. I stand in front of him. He's old too. "Mike's mother had a stroke. He's putting her in a nursing home."

He nods.

"He thinks he's going to retire in a year or two."

"He should have retired when I did."

"Funny, he said the same thing; but he likes teaching. Doesn't know what he'll do when he can't be in a classroom anymore."

I study my husband's face, the lines that have deepened across his brow, at the corners of his eyes. His hair is white and there are still curls. There are a few whiskers. I reach up and start to touch him, but I stop. I close my eyes, thinking of how it used to be when I was with him, how it was to feel him close to me, feel his hand in my hand, his leg next to mine, his arm around my shoulder. He kept me young.

"He should work until he dies."

"What?" I open my eyes, watching him again.

His face is stern. He's still mad.

"He should work until he dies. That's what makes him happy. He can't stand Louise, so he should work until he dies."

I step away. "Why would you say that? They've been married, like, forty years or more."

"Longevity in a relationship doesn't determine happiness."

I shake my head and move by him into the kitchen. I see the papers and magazines on the dining room table. He's been reading.

"Do you want me to fix you something to eat?" I ask, putting my bag on the counter. I take a glass out of the cabinet and fill it with water from the faucet.

"No, I'm fine."

"Okay," I say, drink my water, and put the glass in the sink. I think about the book I was going to show him, the one Paul, the owner of the bookstore, gave me this morning. The one he had tried to find to give me for my birthday, the signed first edition; but I change my mind.

"I'm going to bed," I tell him, and I walk toward the other end of the house.

Chapter Thirty-Four

"Emma, there's a Dillard Brady on line one." Kathryn is standing at the door to her office. I am staring out the front window, sipping my coffee. I have drifted off somewhere, thinking of how days have passed since the fight with Nathan and how things are still smoldering between us. I'm thinking of how the landscape is changing, winter slowly giving way to spring. I think about passage of time, how nature moves us along. It's clear and yet so tentative, the way the earth leans into the next season.

"Oh, okay, sure."

She startled me. I put down my cup and pick up the receiver on my phone. I recognize the name. "This is Emma," I say, watching Kathryn as she gives me a look and then retreats to her desk. I guess I should have answered the phone when it rang. Only I swear I didn't hear it. I was thinking about last night, about Nathan and reminding him about my birthday and how I won't be celebrating with him at home—the silence this morning from his side of the bed when I left.

"Hi, this is Reverend Brady, from the Fourth Street Presbyterian Church."

"Yes, hello."

"Hi," he says again.

There's a pause, and I assume I am meant to fill it. "How are you?"

"Well, I'm doing okay." He pauses. "Actually, I'm not doing okay. I'm slightly rattled, and I need some professional advice."

"Oh." I open up the files on my computer to fill out the request form.

Kathryn likes to have a record of any calls, any potential business. I consider the idea that maybe his maintenance committee has finally decided on putting in a system, and I think this is good news for me. I need clients.

"I was thinking about putting up a camera."

"Okay, I can help you with that."

I find the page with his initial contact information, the report from my first visit and start typing in the date of today, the time of his call. "Has there has been another theft?"

"No, it's not that." He hesitates.

I stop typing and wait.

"This is actually personal; I mean it has to do with the church, but this will be a personal expense. Nobody from the church is authorizing this but me."

"Okay." I'm not following exactly.

"Wait a second."

I hear a rattling around, a door shut, and he's returned to the call.

"Sorry, I needed to make sure I'm alone."

I wait.

"Church walls always have ears," he adds.

"Right," I reply, assuming he means that there could be someone there he doesn't want to hear the conversation we are having.

"So, what's happened?"

"It's my office, my computer. Well, actually, it's the church's computer, but I use it. Just me, no one else."

"Was it stolen?"

"No."

"Vandalized?"

"No, not that. I guess that's not what it would be called."

I wait for him to explain.

"It's been"—he pauses before finishing the sentence—"compromised, tampered with."

Oh, now I understand.

"You mean someone is stealing information, passwords and identification?"

"No, I don't think there's been an identity theft, but now that you say that, it does make me wonder. I hadn't really thought about that."

I hear keys clicking on the other end of the line and assume he's on his computer.

"So if nothing's been taken, and you don't see evidence of hacking your personal accounts, what makes you think somebody is tampering with your computer?"

Another pause.

"Someone has been downloading files, checking out websites." He pauses. "Websites that I know I haven't browsed."

I drop my hands in my lap and stop working on his profile. He's going to need to give me a little something more before I write up an invoice.

"Somebody's using my computer to go on the internet and enter websites that, if discovered, would get me in a lot of trouble."

It's becoming a bit more clear.

"You mean like porn?" I'm not sure why I think of this first, but I can only imagine how this would ruffle the feathers of church members.

"Yes, but even worse."

I don't name anything else. I wait for him to say it.

"Horrible things—sites that wouldn't just cause me to lose my job, but sites that I think could get me arrested."

"Shouldn't you just go to the police?" I still don't know what he's talking about exactly, but I think maybe it must be child pornography.

"I-I actually don't know what to do. I just found it, just now."

"Can you talk to anybody at the church? Is there a board or something, a committee?" I wonder if there is somebody he can trust.

"I don't know."

"Reverend Brady, if you're talking about what I think you're talking about, this is a crime. I think you should report this."

"It's horrible; it's unbelievably horrible."

"It's also against the law. It's best to call the police."

He doesn't reply, not just yet. I let him think.

"I'd rather try and find out who's doing this on my own, handle it privately, you know? I'd rather keep the police out of it. Maybe it's someone I need to help."

"I really don't recommend that. I mean, if this gets out, and you didn't report it, well—"

He interrupts. "People will think it's mine, that I look at this stuff, that I would do something like this."

"Yeah, they will. And again, this isn't just something that would get you in trouble with your church; this is against the law. You could be arrested if this is discovered."

"Someone is very sick."

"Yes, it certainly sounds like it."

Dexter comes in the office. I assume he's been out on a call. He glances over in my direction. I raise my chin as a greeting.

"Have you let anybody use your office?"

He doesn't respond.

"Maybe," he finally answers.

"Reverend Brady, why don't I come over and we can talk there?"

"Okay, sure. If you think that's best. I have a group that meets at eleven."

I notice the time. It's just after nine. "I'll be right there."

And he hangs up without saying goodbye.

Chapter Thirty-Five

It's only ten minutes from the office to the church. I park and get out of the car. It's warm today, bright sun, only a light breeze. I stop to observe a plump bumblebee humming above the row of hedges that surround the parking lot. She's furry and stout, active, larger than our honeybees, and I wonder where she's nesting.

I study the ground near the shrubs, trying to find others that might signal the home of the colony, but she's the only one that I see at the moment. I'd like to stay and follow her, watch her dip and buzz, find out where she gets her nectar, but I know I have work to do.

The rear door, the one closest to the pastor's office, is unlocked, so I walk in. His study is open, and I see him before he notices me. He's sitting at his desk reading. Getting ready for his class or group later this morning, I suppose. He appears calm, at ease, not at all the condition I would be in if I just found illegal websites on my laptop.

"Hello," I say as I tap on the door.

He glances up immediately. "Hey, come on in." And he closes the book, stands up. "It's really so nice of you to come down here. And I've probably just made too much out of this."

"No problem," I respond, waiting to be invited to sit. "And I think you're right to have called someone."

"Oh, here," he says and gestures to one of the two chairs situated in front of his desk. "Please, sit down. Can I get you a cup of coffee?"

I take a seat. "No, thank you. I've had three cups already."

And then he follows suit, sitting in his chair across from me.

I scan his desk, see the desktop computer. It's turned on, and there are pictures floating across the screen. I can't make any of them out. He follows my eyes.

"I took them all down," he says.

I nod, understanding he's referring to the websites he's reported. "Okay."

"I deleted them, cleared out the browsing history."

I don't think this was a good idea, but I don't say anything. Now the police will have a difficult time believing him if he's wiped away the evidence, and it just makes things appear worse for him if someone does find the sites.

"I called a friend of mine, and he told me how to erase all the fingerprints."

"Okay." I know for a fact that there's no way to erase *all* the fingerprints, all the browsing history.

There is always information that remains on the hard drive. I learned this when we watched a webcast on computer safety. It was part of our continuing education that Kathryn wanted us to have a few years ago. At one time, she was considering offering computer services—digital safety is what she called it—but all the information was over everyone's head. None of us could follow the instructor; we just weren't that computer savvy. But I remember some of what was explained, and you can never erase everything. I learned that.

"He told me where to find that on my toolbar; it was easier than I thought it would be."

"So you're not going to the police then?"

He shakes his head. "No." And it seems like he has something else to say, like he's learned something new since we spoke.

I wait.

"I think I figured it out." He gets up and moves around the desk to close the office door.

I guess there must be other people in the building.

He takes his seat again. "I remembered that I let someone use my computer a couple weeks ago. I had forgotten about it until after we hung up. They were trying to find information about somebody in the court system, someone in jail."

So this was just another act of kindness from the pastor, like letting the homeless guy come in and get a blanket, sleep on a pew, only this seems slightly more reckless. "You weren't in here with that person when you let them get on your computer?"

"Most of the time, sure. But I left for a little while to check on things in the parish hall. He could have done it then. I guess I can be naïve about people."

"I guess," I reply, thinking my tone sounds somewhat judgmental.

He turns away.

"And you're sure it's that person?"

"I'm pretty sure. I mean, who else would be using it? Who else would come in here and get on my computer?"

"Well, there could be others if he told anyone."

"No, I don't think so."

"What do you know about this person?"

"Not much. I hadn't seen him before, but he knew me, said he had heard about me from some of the guys at the shelter, and then he asked if I could help him. His brother was arrested a month or so ago, and he was trying to find out his court date. We got on the computer together, and we found the court website, found his brother and the charges. And then I left to run downstairs for a few minutes. That part of his story was legitimate, so I trusted him not to mess with anything while I was gone."

"And you think that's when he went on the websites?"

He shrugs. "I guess. It's the only thing that makes sense."

"Did he act strange when you returned, like he was guilty or had been caught?"

The preacher picks up the pencil once again and taps his chin with it. "I didn't notice anything different, but then again, I wasn't expecting anything to be happening. He finished up pretty soon, though, and he knew how to turn everything off; so he was smarter than he let on—I do know that."

"Then it sounds like you're probably right." But something feels off to me, and for some reason I don't believe this is the guy.

"Yeah, I'm pretty sure I've learned my lesson this time." He leans back in his chair, appearing to be very much at ease.

"Did the maintenance committee make changes to the building?"

He appears to think about the question. "After your first visit you mean?"

I nod.

"I gave them your suggestions, and they did put up outdoor lights, and they trimmed the bushes near the doors."

"No security system then?"

He shakes his head. "They decided to wait on that."

"And now you don't want anything in here? No camera?"

He shrugs. "I hate I made you come here for nothing."

"No, it's fine. It's just ..." I hesitate because I'm not really a pushy salesperson, and I know that's how this could sound. "It's just I think you should put one up. Just for a few weeks, make sure the guy or whoever did it doesn't come back. We can put it on a shelf or something, and it'll never be seen. And then, if nothing else happens, we can take it down, give you a full refund."

He nods. "You really think he would return here and do this again? I mean, even if I don't let him in. You think he might break in and try to use it again?"

I shake my head. "I don't know, but what's there to lose? This is illegal activity. You and the church could get in a lot of trouble if anyone found those sites on your computer."

He sits up in his chair, closer to his desk, closer to me. He seems to be thinking about it. "I don't know. I feel like this was just a one-time thing."

"Look, we'll give you a loaner. We'll set it up for free. It'll make me feel better."

"No, it's not the cost. I'll pay for it if you think that's the right thing."

I pull out my phone to text Bus. "I do," I say.

Chapter Thirty-Six

"He didn't really want it." Bus is standing at my desk. He reported that he installed the camera in the pastor's office an hour ago.

I've been working on a few other contracts, and I had forgotten that he was able to do the installation this afternoon. It's been busy today and time has slipped past me. I remember the appointment from the morning. I recall how I suggested the camera to the pastor and how he had agreed reluctantly. I think about how I left, how he asked if I was okay, knowing now how we met the first time, how he met me the night Nathan died.

"I know, but I think he should have it."

"That's what he said, that it was your professional counsel."

"Which one did he get?" I ask, wondering how much he spent, which security apparatus he agreed to.

"The bullet," Bus answers, and I know he means the three-megapixel IP infrared camera. It's our bestseller. It can see one hundred feet in darkness, is easy to set up, connects to any smartphone. He'll be pleased with it, I'm sure.

"Where did you put it?"

"On a shelf, in between some books. I guess he doesn't want anyone to know it's there."

"No, I guess he doesn't," I respond. "Does it face the door or the desk?" I ask, wondering what they decided together.

"Desk," he answers.

Bus appears to be waiting for information about our reluctant customer. I guess he wants to know why he just installed a camera in a church office and not by the outside doors.

"Did he tell you why I suggested the camera? Did he tell you about his call this morning?"

Bus shook his head. "He just said there had been an incident, and you thought there might be another one, and he should have a camera for security reasons."

I nod.

"Was there a break-in?" he asks.

"Yeah." Even though he wouldn't call it that, I do.

"And he didn't report it to the police?"

"No, he decided to downplay it, thinks he knows what happened—who did it—and he doesn't want to get anybody in trouble." I think about the pastor's decision not to turn the guy in, wondering how he thinks it's okay to protect someone viewing child pornography, wondering if it really did happen the way he said or if there's something else going on.

"He seems like a nice guy."

"Yeah, I think he is."

"He paid cash, said he wouldn't ask for a refund." Bus seems like he wants an explanation since that's an odd thing to say after a purchase. He hands me the invoice and receipt. I take them and place them in the file I started.

"Great" is all I say.

He stays where he is.

I see the time and realize now why it's so quiet, why we're the only ones still in the office. It's after four and everyone left early, even Kathryn. I take off my glasses and rub my eyes. I've been staring at the computer all afternoon and I'm tired.

"I bought a couple books," he tells me, apparently changing the subject. "From your list."

"Yeah?" And I remember that when I went to his house, I gave him a few titles on beekeeping, some of the books Nathan really likes.

"I'm reading up."

"Great." I wonder which ones he's ordered, but I don't really want to have a long conversation. The one I'll likely have when I get home in a little while will be all that I'll have energy for today.

"I'm going to order some next week."

"Books or bees?" I ask, turning off my computer, straightening things up, putting loose papers in folders, getting ready to go home—face what I have to face.

"Bees," he answers.

I nod.

"I thought I'd use a supply place from around here. I found them on the internet. They seem reputable. Maybe you've heard of them." And he pulls out his phone to find the name, I suppose.

"You getting a four or five frame?" I ask, referring to the nucleus hives, not waiting for the name of the supply company he's planning to use.

"Five, with an extra laying queen." He scrolls down, doesn't look up to answer. "Brush Mountain Beekeeping," he says, and of course, I've heard of them. We've ordered lots of supplies and bees from them. They're a great company. It sounds like he has done his homework.

"You ready for all that?"

He shrugs, returns his phone to his pocket. "Were you ready?"

I stand up and grab my sweater that I had hung on my chair earlier in the day. It warmed up later in the afternoon, but it was chilly this morning.

I stop and think about his question: was I ready? And even though I know he's referring to beekeeping, I consider all the things that I haven't been ready for, all the stuff that has happened in the last year, none of which I was prepared for.

"Well, I suppose you had some help before you took over." He answers the question for me.

I hesitate, though I'm not sure why. "Yeah, I knew a little before I was in charge."

"You think I should wait? You think I should maybe wait until next year?"

He seems so sincere, so sweet. I smile. "No, I think you'll be fine."

And he seems to relax, rests his hands on hips.

Bus is wearing one of the new, short-sleeve shirts that Kathryn gave out last week. It's bright blue with red stitching, and it fits him well. I realize he's nervous about the bees; he's unsure about starting a colony; and the truth is I think it is too soon, that maybe he should work with someone else, a more seasoned beekeeper before he goes on his own. But then again, how do you learn if you don't just start?

I have all my things in my hands, and I'm ready to leave. I stand there, not sure how to make my exit.

"You want to go get a drink or something?" he asks, and for a second I wonder if he knows it's my birthday but then remember that I told Kathryn with great clarity that I did not want my colleagues to know, that I did not want any attention. I have been pleasantly surprised all day that she did as I asked; but now, I'm not so sure.

I glance up at him. He doesn't know. It's simply an innocent invitation, but I cannot have drinks with Bus. Not tonight. Tonight I have to talk to my husband, work things out with him, figure out what we're going to do, how we're going to make this work.

"Maybe another time," I say.

"Okay, sure," he says. "I understand. We'll see you then tomorrow or something." And he turns and heads to the rear part of the office.

I wait a few seconds and leave as well, making my exit through the front door.

Chapter Thirty-Seven

I notice the daffodils as I walk home. I hadn't seen them this morning, but I was driving then. This evening, though the sun is fading, the days are beginning to lengthen, and I decided to leave my car at the office, put on my sneakers, and walk home. It's warm enough not to wear my sweater, and I guess I'm doing this not just for exercise or enjoyment. I know I'm taking the slow way.

Seeing the flowers bloom reminds me my work with the bees will start to pick up now. I will need to make sure the hives are healthy, and soon I'll likely need to medicate them to try and keep them from developing diseases. According to my husband and all the books I've been reading, American foulbrood is the one issue I should be concerned about. Nathan explained this to me last year, making sure I understood the seriousness of this widespread and most destructive of the bee brood diseases. He showed me what to do.

It was about this time a year ago when I drove him to the hives and watched while he put out the oxytetracycline, the antibiotic that is used as a preventative. He was in good shape then, finished with the rehab, before the pneumonia, excited to return to the things he loved. He was energetic, happy, and I enjoyed going with him to work with the bees. While he medicated the hives, he explained that using the antibiotic as a preventative was the only way to manage American foulbrood. Apparently, once a colony has the fatal bacteria living in it, the only remedy to get rid of it is to burn everything. Nothing can be saved since the spores of the bacteria can live up to forty years.

"Forty years?" I remember asking, so surprised that bacteria could live that long. And I watched carefully as he mixed the antibiotic with powdered sugar and spread just about a tablespoon across the top frame in the hives.

"Yep, forty," he repeated. "Now you put this only along the edges," he advised, sounding like the English professor I fell in love with, so clear, so confident. "Because you don't want the mixture to fall onto the brood." Then he had stopped to make sure I was listening. "That would kill them," he said with a great seriousness in his voice.

I wasn't taking notes at that time since I wasn't expecting to take over the hives a year ago. When we returned last year after the winter season, after the long nights and a fair bit of fretting about their survival, after the surgeries and the rehab and the infections and the victories, we still expected this to be his work, his avocation, his activity, not mine.

I stop with the thought of how quickly things had changed.

Now I realize I will be responsible for medicating the hives to protect against the foulbrood disease and making sure they have enough food. I will check for mites and roaches and mice damage. It will be up to me and me alone to repair and replace old parts of the boxes and make sure there are enough nectar-producing sources still around the old farm to keep the bees healthy. And I glance around at the few but noticeable signs of spring and think that perhaps I have taken on more than I can do. I think that maybe I should have taken Lou Caster's advice, the beekeeper in Virginia Nathan sometimes called and to whom I spoke last summer when

Nathan, dead and hiding in our house, decided to turn over the farming to me.

"Better to sell them and wait a while for your own hives," he had told me, without explaining. "Beekeeping is your husband's hobby; might not be your cup of tea."

But I wouldn't listen. I wanted things to stay the same. I wanted him somehow to get better and take over after I assumed he would regain his strength.

I was not ready to let everything go.

"How hard can it be?" I had asked but not really received an answer. After all I learned last summer, after all I've read throughout the fall and winter, all I now know, it may be harder than I imagined.

A bumblebee is feeding in the small cup of a yellow flower—not a daffodil but something similar, a crocus maybe or buttercup. Nathan would know its name but he's not here to ask, and it doesn't matter anyway. I stop and watch as it dips its long, hairy tongue to lap up the nectar to add to the stores in its nest and to take back and feed their young.

I kneel down, close to it, eye level to the bloom and really unafraid since I know bumblebees are not aggressive and generally sting only in defense of their nest—which is not where this one happens to be—or if harmed, which I don't plan to do. The busy insect pays me no attention, and I just stay there, resting on my haunches watching her work.

She's chubby and furry like the one I saw at the church when I had my meeting with the pastor, and compared to the honeybee she has a broader body and a more rounded tip to the abdomen. I know this one is female because she has corbiculae, or better known as pollen baskets, bulging masses on her hind legs that can contain as many as a million pollen grains. Male bumblebees do not have corbiculae and do not purposively collect pollen, only the queens and workers—females all.

I recall from my reading that at least in some species, once a bumblebee has visited a flower, it leaves a scent mark on it, and I wonder if this one I'm watching so closely today is returning to a place she's been before or if this is her first time to visit, leaving her mark even as I study her.

I know that with a scent mark, other bumblebees will be deterred from visiting that flower until the scent fades and that the mark is a general chemical bouquet bumblebees leave behind in various locations, like their nests and places they have found food. I know that they learn to use this bouquet to identify both rewarding and unrewarding flowers. Because of the smell she leaves behind, she will know this is one she will want to revisit, a place where she likes the ambiance.

Of course, Nathan taught me about bumblebees and the scents they use to mark flowers. He also taught me that bees understand what it means to have a place. He said that whenever they leave their hives, they memorize all the landmarks near them. They remember big things like trees and buildings and tractors; but they also keep in their memories the smaller things, too, like old bottles or rusted cans. Bees have a clear sense of where they live and how they make their return home.

He explained all this to me during an autumn season when we were out at the farm together and I picked up the hives, planning to move them just a few feet from where they had been. I had noticed the morning sun was brighter at another spot, and while he was mowing and cutting weeds, I was going to relocate the boxes. He saw me before I completed the task and immediately stopped me.

"What are you doing?" he asked, running over to the hives.

"Just giving them more sun; I thought you said they liked the sun in the winter, that they needed it."

"They do, but you can't just move their homes like that. You can't just shift things while they're away. They'll be lost forever."

I put the boxes back down in their original location, even though I wasn't planning to move them more than eight or ten feet.

"I know it seems weird," he said, his voice softening. "But their knowledge of where they live, their home, is incredibly accurate, perfect down to the tiniest marker. They can't really find anything beyond what they know, this small but very particular, very familiar place."

I remember how odd I thought that was, how limiting it must be for the insects, and I wondered how many bees were still flying around at that very moment searching for a home that was no longer there, searching for the life that was forever displaced.

I glance up the street at our yellow house, the one we have lived in for more than twenty years together, and see the curtain rise and fall in the front room. And I realize I can only picture it the way I remember it. I only know it with him.

Just like a bee trying to find a relocated hive, without him, I understand, I might be lost forever.

Chapter Thirty-Eight

"Where's the car?"

Nathan meets me in the hallway.

I close my eyes, turn and shut the door, and then open them and glance out the window as a couple walks past the house, looking up, trying to find someone at home, I guess.

"I left it at work," I explain, trying to sound positive, upbeat. "I decided to walk. It's nice this afternoon."

"Aren't you going to Carla's?" The hurt is there, just beneath the surface of his question.

"She's swinging by here to pick me up," I answer, moving past him, dropping off my keys in the bowl by the door.

"So when is she coming?" His breath is hot on my neck. "What time will she be here?" He is close.

"I don't know." I answer without turning around.

"You don't know?"

"Five thirty, I think. Six, maybe."

I walk into the kitchen, take down a glass, open the refrigerator, pull out a bottle of white wine I opened last weekend. "Chardonnay, you want a glass?" I ask, holding out the bottle so he understands my offer.

He shakes his head and watches as I pour. He stands across from me, leaning against the sink. "I wanted to get you something," he tells me.

I take a sip, realizing he's talking about a gift for my birthday, and then I recall that I never told him about the book I had recently received. I still had not mentioned the first edition that Paul Starr gave me, the one Nathan was searching for a year ago.

"It's okay," I answer as I wipe my mouth.

"I can't really make purchases," he explains. "I didn't know how to make you anything. I could have tried, I guess."

"It's okay, Nathan," I tell him again, not sure why I don't bring out the book, why I'm being so secretive about it, why I'm letting him feel so bad about himself. "You don't need to give me anything."

He shakes his head, and I notice the white curls are thinning. There's a bald spot on top of his head I don't recall seeing before. I almost walk to him and put my hand on it, almost walk over to him and throw myself in his arms like I have a thousand times, so easily; but I just take another sip of my wine instead.

"Will you be gone long?" he asks, and he sounds sad, and I see how tormented he is, how hard I have made things for him.

I shake my head and glance at the clock on the stove. Carla will be here in less than half an hour. I wasted time walking home, time that we could have spent together, and I can tell he knows it. "I don't know," I reply because I don't.

"Anybody else going with you?"

And I start to respond, in anger actually, but I don't, and instead I just hold up my hand. "I don't want to fight," I say and finish my wine. "Not today." I set the glass on the counter and start to walk away.

"I don't want to fight either," he says, stopping me.

I nod.

"Do you have a few minutes to talk?"

"Sure," I answer, and I head into the dining room. I sit down and watch as he moves around to his seat.

"I saw a bumblebee," I tell him as he sits down, trying to lighten the mood. "Her pollen baskets were full."

He smiles.

"*Bombus*, the only one extant in the tribe Bombini. It comprises over two hundred fifty species."

"That's the one," I reply.

"Did you know that Emily Dickinson sent a dead bee in her letter that included the poem she wrote, 'The Bumble Bee's Religion'?"

"I did not know that," I answer, happy to hear him talking of bees, of poetry, of anything other than me and my actions—our marriage.

"*His little Hearse like Figure, Unto itself a Dirge...*"

I assume this is a line from the poem. I do not respond. I just watch him as he continues with his recitation.

I used to love hearing him recite poems, the old ones especially—the ones with a language so different from what we speak today, words so unordinary, how he raises his voice, creating a melody of verse.

He stops, makes a face, shakes his head.

"No, don't do that," I tell him, reaching my hand across the table, reaching for his. "Keep going," I urge him.

He just keeps shaking his head, a negative response to my request. "You don't want to hear that stuff anymore."

"Why would you say that? Of course I want to hear you."

"Old poems from an old man. Dead poet. Dead professor." He slides his hand across his head. "It's no good."

I watch him, and I feel so many emotions at once, I can't even pick the one that troubles me the most. I'm sad and angry and I hate this. I hate it as much as I hated it when he died. And even with him here, I realize that this grief has fingers with long, pointy nails, and I am as ripped apart by it as I would be if he had gone, if I had just let him be gone.

"I was thinking we should go to the hives tomorrow." I don't know why I say this. Maybe I think it will help. Maybe I think the bees can save us.

"Tomorrow is Saturday?" he asks.

"Yes, it's the weekend. We can go and check the boxes, check on the bees, make sure they have enough honey. You can help me clean and make the repairs. Maybe you can show me how to divide the hives, help me know if we should do that. There's still so much I haven't learned."

He nods and I see the tears.

"Should I order the antibiotic?"

He doesn't reply, wipes his eyes.

"Nathan."

He shakes his head.

"Nathan ..." I say again, but he gets up from the table and disappears into another part of the house.

I stand up to follow him but the doorbell rings, and I know my mother has arrived. I turn from one direction to the other, confused, torn. I hear the bedroom door close, and there is no dilemma for me. I know which one I have to open.

Chapter Thirty-Nine

She's studying my outfit, the one I wore to work and didn't change. I can tell she's disappointed. She raises her eyes up to my face and reaches out to hug me as we stand in the doorway. She doesn't comment on my clothes.

"Hello, dear," she says. "Happy birthday." She's wearing a dress—a new one, I think—and her hair is perfectly coiffed.

"Thanks, Mom." For whatever reason, I can't help myself, and I take a quick glance in the mirror. Unimpressed, I grab my keys.

She stands aside so I can close the door, but it seems like something is wrong.

I turn the lock and stare at her. "What?" I ask.

She shrugs but I know it's something, so I wait.

"What?" I ask again.

"I just thought we'd go in for a few minutes." She fidgets with the rings on her fingers, her bracelet.

Oh, so that's it. She wants a tour. She wants to see if I've changed anything. And I know if I let her in, she would find her way to the bedroom closet where Nathan's clothes still hang or the bathroom cabinet where we keep his pills and shaving supply or back to the kitchen pantry just to see if my husband's things are still there.

There are always layers with Carla.

"I'm actually really hungry," I lie and head down the front steps without giving her the opportunity to snoop. I am not playing games with my mother on my birthday.

I hear a sigh and footsteps. First round is apparently mine.

I open the door to the passenger's side of her car and slide in. As she walks around, I glance up at the front window. He's not there, and I feel a little disappointed not to see him wave goodbye.

She gets in and immediately announces our venue. We're going to an Italian place in a little town outside of Elon. It's a great choice, I think, since it's dark inside, mostly booths, a jukebox, perfect for intimate rendezvous or mother/daughter dinners that don't allow for heavy conversation or even truth telling. We drive the fifteen minutes mostly in silence.

When we arrive, Carla gives her name, and I discover that she's made a reservation, and we're taken to the banquet room in the rear part of the restaurant where a table is set up with balloons and party hats—three of them—and I wonder if this is another test to see if I expect my dead husband to join us or if there's someone else she's invited. Before I can ask, Violet appears, and I realize I've been set up. I can only hope it's just a birthday dinner and not another intervention.

I hug her and then quickly check to see if anyone else is arriving, if there are therapists in the booths, chaplains or doctors around the corners, but it appears to be clear.

"What a lovely surprise!" I say with as much enthusiasm as I can muster, and I realize I am actually happy to see my baby sister. I know I'm just feeling extra suspicious, and I think with the intervention still lingering in my thoughts, this might count as post-traumatic stress disorder.

"Happy Birthday, old lady," she answers me, pulls away, and then punches me hard on the arm.

"Ouch," and I grab my arm and rub. She has always hit like a boy.

"That didn't hurt," she says, put off by my complaint, and drops into a seat at the decorated table.

"When did you get here?" I ask her and sit across from her, watching as our mother takes the seat between us.

"Flew in at fifteen hundred. Raleigh, civilian style," she answers, sliding her hands down the front of her light brown sweater, calling attention to her "ladies' clothes," as she calls anything that isn't a uniform. "I've got twelve hours to celebrate the day of your birth, and then I'm needed back in DC."

"She's working on a secret mission," Carla whispers and hangs her purse on the back of her chair while my sister raises her eyebrows and puts her finger to her lips, as if she is trying to keep our mother's voice down, as if the secret mission is also very dangerous, even though I can tell it isn't. She's acting way too calm for that, happy even, and it makes me wonder if she had a drink on that civilian flight.

Violet, a bit like me, rarely lets her guard down, but she will sometimes drink a few cocktails when she's away from her unit. I have often thought maybe she's the one needing the intervention, but I wouldn't dare bring this up to our mother.

The waitress arrives, takes our order, and we decide on martinis, and I feel myself relax a little and entertain the thought that maybe the night won't be a total loss.

"So what's up with you?" Violet asks. "You still selling locks and bolts?"

"Something like that," I reply.

"Kathryn says you're doing really well," Carla pipes up.

I turn to her and start to ask why my mother is talking to my boss about my work performance, but Violet must see what is taking shape in my mind.

"Does she do any industrial installations?" She puts a party hat on her head. I'm pretty sure she's had a drink already. My sister does not wear party hats.

I glare at Carla but resist asking the question that Violet knows I want to ask. "Some," I respond, turning to her. "But mostly small businesses, nothing too extravagant."

"She could make a lot of money if she went big," Violet says. "Some of those systems can run up to a hundred thousand dollars."

"I will let her know."

"How about the university—she get that contract?"

I shake my head, and Violet doesn't ask anything else. Clearly, she has done her best work. She's managed to stall the first conflict.

The waitress returns with our drinks. I get ready to take a sip but stop when I see that Carla is holding her glass up like she's planning to make a toast.

I wait.

"I'm so happy to be with my girls," she says, sounding like she might cry. "You are both such blessings to me."

I glance over at Violet, and she rolls her eyes.

"And, Emma, I know how hard this year has been for you, and I'm just so pleased at how well you are doing."

I can't help myself; I put my glass to my lips and take a long drink.

"Oh, okay," Carla tries to hurry up her speech that I'm sure she has taken all day to prepare. There is likely even a script in her purse. She probably has a lot more she was ready to share.

Violet takes a big gulp from her glass, following suit, and we grin at each other.

Carla blows out a long breath of defeat. She is not giving a speech tonight. "Fine, happy birthday."

"Happy B-day, Sister," Violet adds, and we reach across the table and tap our glasses together, both of us taking another long sip.

Chapter Forty

"You sure you're okay?"

Carla has excused herself, and Violet and I have a few minutes alone.

"Is she getting cake?" I ask.

"And organizing the waiters to sing."

"Great," I say, taking the last swallow from my second martini. Violet is staring at me, waiting for the answer to her question.

"I'm fine," I reply.

"That meeting at your house was stupid. I should have told her I wasn't coming." She slides down in her chair, stretches out her sturdy legs. She's had two martinis too. She's clearly at ease.

"It's no big deal," I reply. "I probably needed it." And I remember the letter she read along with the others, the way she wouldn't let me loose.

"Your husband died. I think it's perfectly fine to act weird."

"Is that what you thought?" I hadn't spoken to my sister since that night. She wrote a card, sent a couple of emails, but we haven't actually talked since the intervention. "That I was acting weird?"

She raises her arms, holds up her hands like she doesn't have the answer.

"How would I know, Em? I hadn't seen you since the memorial service. I wasn't exactly the attentive sister I could have been."

"Your plate is pretty full, Vi."

She waves away my comment.

"Carla was so worried, and she talked like you were psychotic or something, so I took an emergency leave to be there, told my superiors that my sister was losing her mind." She grins at that. "And then when I saw you, I thought you seemed all right. I thought everything was okay." She sits up and tries putting her elbow on the table, but it slips off and we both laugh. "Well, as all right as me anyway." She falls back in her seat.

"It's no big deal," I tell her.

"But you weren't, were you? You weren't all right?"

I don't answer right away. I feel the alcohol and also the need to excuse my sister for her forthrightness; I also feel the need to be honest.

"I really wasn't," I reply.

She's staring at me and then glances away, as if it hurts to look in my direction. "And now?" she asks softly.

I shrug. "Still not all right."

She nods like she understands.

"Would you believe me if I told you I still see him?"

There is suddenly a roar of laughter coming from the main dining room, and she doesn't answer right away. It quietens down.

"Like in a crowd, you mean? Like you think you see him at the university or out on the street or something?"

I shake my head.

The waitress returns to clear off the table. She reaches for my martini glass, but I grab it before she can take it. "Still sucking the olives," I say, and she smiles and keeps picking up plates. I'm pretty sure she's making room for the cake she's being asked by Carla to bring in.

She leaves and I confess.

"Like at the house, at the table, in our bed." I reach in my glass and take out the last olive, stuff it in my mouth.

"Like he's not dead?" she asks.

"Like he's not dead," I repeat and chew and then swallow.

She waits a beat. "But you understand he is, right? You understand Nathan is dead."

I face my sister. She knows grief. She knows it better than I.

She was just twenty-four when she was in Iraq with three other soldiers, and the vehicle they were in was hit by a roadside bomb. She had just gotten out of the jeep to pick up something that had flown out—a paper or hat, I don't remember—something she said she had to retrieve, and the driver, her best friend, was trying to be funny, teasing her, and drove forward like they were leaving her out there in the desert. It was a silly game they played with each other. And she was chasing them to where they were heading, about five hundred yards away, when they hit the IED—all of them, all three of them, blown up right in front of her.

My sister knows grief well.

But she's tougher than I am, always has been, even though she's younger. She got bucked off a horse when we were kids, landed hard on her shoulder, broke her collarbone but wouldn't go to the doctor until she jumped back to prove she could still ride.

She got knocked down by a bigger girl at recess, some stupid bully picking a fight with her, and she'd stand up and keep swinging even though the girl would just knock her down again. She did this until the bully finally got bored and quit.

When she was a freshman and didn't make the varsity basketball team, she kept working out, kept running drills until the coach eventually put her on the squad, where she started all four years. My sister took everything as a challenge, even the loss of her closest friends, signing up for another tour right after it happened, staying in, becoming an officer, dealing with these kinds of tragedies every day.

She's just made of different stuff than me.

"Emma, he died. You were there with him. You saw it happen. You know he didn't survive the pneumonia. He died at the hospital, and you were there, and later we cremated him and he's dead."

I nod.

I hear whispers from the other room. I know the waiters are getting ready to come in. I hear Carla giving instructions about lighting the candles.

"I didn't let him go," I say to my sister. "I brought him back because I couldn't live without him."

She glances down at her lap.

"I wanted that so much too," she tells me. "For Trina not to be dead."

I know she's talking about the soldier who was driving, the one she had talked about when she first joined up, the one she called her best friend.

"I made every promise to God you can make." She clears her throat like she's trying to stop the break in her voice. "Just if she wouldn't be dead." She pushes her glass away. "I ran that five hundred yards after the blast, yelling at God that I would do anything, just don't let her be dead. I couldn't live if she was dead."

And just like that, I realize Trina was more than just her best friend.

"But she was. And nothing was or is going to change that." She swallows hard. "You know, before the medics got there, I even tried to find the detonated bomb to see if maybe there was more to it, that maybe I could get blown up too. I ran around trying to find more of them so I would die there too."

My eyes fill with tears, and now I'm the one suddenly feeling like I let my sister down.

"But they were dead. She was dead. And I wasn't."

I hear the happy birthday song starting around the corner.

"And Nathan is dead too," she tells me, and it's like I'm hearing it the first time but I don't stop her.

"But you are not."

Chapter Forty-One

It is quiet when I walk inside. I think maybe that he's asleep or reading in bed, but as I turn the corner into the kitchen, he's there at the table. He's found the book I had hidden—the one the bookstore owner saved for me, and he's acting like he's reading it.

"You're still up?" I ask, walking over to the sink and pouring a glass of water. I watch out the window as Violet drives away.

"Where did you get the book?" he asks.

I drink the water, put the cup in the sink, and walk around the row of cabinets to where he is sitting. I pull out the chair across from him and take a seat. I study him, his gaunt face, the pain in his eyes that I don't know how to name exactly, his long, thin fingers, the pulsing of his heart I can see in his neck. He's so frail.

"You told the bookstore owner about a year ago; he found it, saved it for me. He was a customer."

"Paul," he says, naming the owner of the store that he knew.

"That's the guy."

"Why did you hide it from me?"

It's a fair question.

I just shake my head. "We were fighting."

He glances away, closes the book, slides it over to me. "How was your celebration?"

"It was okay. Carla had the cake and the singing."

He smiles slightly.

"Violet was there," I tell him, thinking he might be interested in that.

I watch him as he takes in the news, and then I remember her story of the loss of her unit, the way she prayed to die.

"Do you remember your thirtieth birthday?"

I nod. "I do indeed."

"You wanted to sleep outside under the stars."

"And you said it was too cold for that."

"It was too cold for that."

I think about that night, the tent he purchased, the sleeping bag, the way he picked me up at work since it was a Friday, and we drove to Asheville and the Great Smokies to a campground. We were the only campers since it was still too early in the season for most campers. We had a picnic with wine and s'mores, built a huge fire.

"Remember the bear?"

I cross my ankles, fold my arms across my chest. "It wasn't a bear," I say, recalling the nighttime visitor that woke us both, the smell of its breath near the tent, the noises of our food and belongings being rampaged.

"I don't care what that ranger said about them still hibernating, it was a bear."

We held each other for over an hour, waiting for whatever it was to leave, wondering if we were going to die, our hearts both racing. And then, as we lay there all wrapped in each other, arms and legs all melded together, we made love, forgetting everything about what might just kill us. It was one of my best memories of sex that I have. We had on so many layers of clothes, it seemed like it was forever before we could actually touch each other's bodies. And it was sweet and desperate and exciting and lovely.

I glance over at him, and I can see he's remembering the same part of the night that I am.

"That was a good birthday," I say.

"It was that," he replies.

"Your fiftieth," I add. "That was a good one."

He looks away, remembering, I suppose. That was the year we traveled to Europe to Marjorca, Spain. It was a place that bore importance to the author, Aurore Dupin, Nathan's literary idol. On that island we were able to visit the remains of the Carthusian Monastery of Valldemossa, where Dupin spent the winter of 1838–1839 with the Polish composer Frédéric Chopin and Dupin's two children.

This trip to the island—during which Chopin composed a number of works—was described by Dupin in *Un Hiver à Majorque*, first published in 1841. While they were there, the composer, already suffering from what was thought to be tuberculosis at the beginning of their relationship, became quite ill. It turned out that spending a winter on the island where it rained and stayed cold and where they were not able to secure proper lodgings was not the best choice for someone with his condition, and being there exacerbated his symptoms. After that winter in Spain, the two lovers eventually separated. It was only two years before the composer's death.

"It was cystic fibrosis," he says to me, interrupting my memories of our summer excursion.

"What?"

"Chopin—it wasn't tuberculosis. It was cystic fibrosis."

It's not that the news surprises me, it's that he knows.

"I asked him," he clarifies and then grins.

I roll up a napkin and throw it at him. "You haven't met Chopin," I reply.

"Could have," he responds.

I wait because there are a lot of questions I have about where he goes, where he's been, what it's like in the world beyond this one. I'm curious about what he knows. I have been for the entire time he's been here, but I never ask.

"Remember that restaurant with the fresh fish?"

Of course I remember that. "Yes," I respond, my mouth watering at the thought of how perfect those meals were, how much I fell in love with the island in the Mediterranean, with travel abroad, with Europe.

He seems to know what I'm thinking. "We should go again."

I study him, consider taking a trip again, trying to hide him. Us. "That would be nice," I say.

There is a long, quiet pause between us, the thoughts of what we are now, the sadness in remembering what we used to be—how even though I can try and make this thing we call our marriage work, it will never satisfy, never really stop the pain of what has been lost.

"I'm glad you had a good time with your family," he says, sounding sincere, pleasant.

"Thank you," I respond.

He watches me.

"I drank two martinis," I tell him. "I'm still feeling a little drunk."

"It's late."

I yawn at just the sound of that, the knowledge of the time that has passed this evening while we were not together.

"I think I will sleep well tonight." And I stand up from the table, push my chair under it. I look at him. "You coming?"

He shakes his head slowly. "I'm going to read a while."

This was what he used to do most nights when he couldn't sleep.

"You got something good?" I ask, wondering what book he has started in the last week.

"Book of poems," he notes but gives no more information about the poet or the collection.

I nod without asking anything more.

"Good night then," I tell him.

He lifts his chin. "Night."

Chapter Forty-Two

I am awakened by my phone buzzing on the nightstand. I roll over, slide my hand across to his side of the bed, but he is not there, so I roll back and pick up my phone.

"Hello," I rub my eyes, trying to see the time, trying to remember the day and whether or not I have overslept. I clear my throat, sit up.

"Emma."

"Kathryn?"

I must be late for work, I think, but the clock on the dresser says it's only seven o'clock, and then I recall that it's Saturday. So I'm not late, and it's not a work day. But now I wonder if I've missed another meeting or get-together.

"I am so sorry to call you on the weekend."

I lean against my pillow, try to see around the corner if Nathan is there. "It's okay, what's up?"

"The pastor."

"I'm sorry?"

"Dillard Brady, from the Presbyterian church."

"Oh, yeah, okay."

"He's called for you."

"At seven o'clock on a Saturday morning?"

"Actually, it was eight o'clock last night. He called our emergency line, and they couldn't get ahold of me until this morning. There's no signal here, and I didn't know I had a message."

"What's going on?" I can't imagine why the pastor is calling me. I can't imagine what has happened.

"He's been arrested."

"What?" I sit up again, throw off the covers, and slide my legs over the side of the bed, making a move to get up.

"Last night, he was arrested, and he's asking for you. He said you would understand."

"Well, I don't."

"He said you could find what he needs to clear this up, that you helped install the system."

And then I remember the camera hidden in his office.

"He said you would be able to get his cell phone from his house and that you will find a key under the biggest stone in his front yard that will get you in." Kathryn pauses. "Emma, why does he want you to get his cell phone? What does this have to do with us?"

I think about the phone and the app he had installed so that he could see what images the camera was collecting.

"He's got live video feed," I tell her, standing up. I try to find my pants that I wore last night.

"From one of our systems?"

"A camera—a small one we mounted in his office. Bus did it because the pastor thought someone used his computer without authorization, and apparently they were browsing some pretty heinous sites. That's all I know."

"Could he be arrested for what was on the computer?"

I remember what he told me, what he found in his files. "I think it was pretty bad, sounded like it was illegal."

"On a minister's computer?"

"I guess."

"But how did anyone find it?"

I think about the question. It's a good one. After all, it's one thing for someone to browse the sites, it's another for someone to use the pastor's computer and then report him for what they found. It's a mystery, but I'm still not sure why he's called me, why he doesn't just tell the police, call a lawyer or a friend.

I hear a tapping noise, a pen or pencil on a desk or table, and wonder if Kathryn is at the office or at home, and then I recall her mention that she had plans to go out of town for the weekend.

"Well, I don't think you should go to his house and break in," she advises me. "Why don't you call the police to go with you?"

"I don't know if that's the best thing," I say, still trying to see or hear any noise from Nathan coming from the other rooms. "If I can find his phone, I know how to locate the video. I helped show him how the apps work. And technically I'm not breaking in if he tells me where he hides the key and gives me permission to use it."

"Then let me meet you there," she offers.

"Aren't you at the beach?"

"I can be there in about two hours. He can wait that long for us to get the phone."

"Kathryn, I don't really want to make the poor man stay in jail any longer than he has to. He's asked for me because he must trust me not to tell anybody or not to involve the police any further. I can go alone."

"Then let me call Bus."

"I don't really need anyone to go with me."

"It'll make me feel better," she says. "Let me just call him and have him meet you there. At least there will be two of you. I don't like you going to this residence without backup." She sounds like a police officer now.

"Okay," I say in resignation. "But you don't need to worry about it. I'll call Bus and ask him to meet me at the pastor's house."

She hesitates. "All right, you call him, but if he can't go with you, call someone else. Don't go in that house by yourself."

"Sure," I say, not really meaning it.

"Thanks. And, Emma, I realize that this is over and beyond the call of duty," she says. "In fact, I think this is the first time we've ever had a customer be arrested and then use our surveillance as evidence in the case."

"Well, I guess if that's the way this thing turns out, you might have a lot of new business coming in."

I hear the wheels turning in her head from across the phone lines. "I think I'm going to come back a day early anyway, just to see if I need to answer any questions at the station or help in whatever way."

"Sure, Kathryn."

"Keep me posted, okay?"

"Right." And I click on the end button and walk over to the closet to find something to wear and then head into the bathroom, but not before peeking around the corner to see if Nathan's at the table.

When I'm out of the bathroom, I head into the kitchen to see if there is coffee, but the pot is empty and cold. I decide to take a bottle of juice with me instead.

"Nathan?" I call out his name as I find what I want in the refrigerator, thinking he must be asleep somewhere.

I check the sofa in the den, the study, the area around his desk. I open the blinds and look outside, trying to see if he's on the porch or in the backyard. And then I notice the guest room door is closed, and I just stand at it and listen. I put my hand against it, close my eyes, and I'm pretty sure I hear him breathing. I wait a few seconds and then tiptoe away and head into the kitchen. I find paper and a pen and write him a note, telling him where I'm going and when I plan to be home, and I place the note near the edge of the counter where I think he will see it.

I grab my bottle of juice, my purse, walk out the door with my keys in hand, and get to my car, turn it on, and back out. I stop briefly to glance up at the window to see if he's there, but the curtains remain closed.

Chapter Forty-Three

Kathryn texted me the address, and I turn on my GPS and head in the direction in which I am instructed. I take a few turns, drive past the church, where I notice no cars in the parking lot, and go a few miles and eventually arrive at the place. There is one car in the driveway. The blinds are open, but I don't see anyone moving around inside.

"Be careful," she texted, and I read it and then power down my phone. I don't want to talk to her again or have her pester me for updates.

I turn off the engine and decide to wait just for a few seconds. I'm still trying to sort through what has been asked of me so early in the morning.

I didn't call Bus. Whatever I'm getting into by coming here, I don't want him with me. I know I lied to my boss, telling her I'd phone him, but I don't really think what I have been asked to do is such a big deal. And I know I don't have time to wait for Bus to drive all the way into town from his house.

I don't need a babysitter. If the pastor has asked that I go into his home and retrieve his phone, I don't really see why I need help. Even if there is someone in the house, I can just explain why I'm there and handle it alone, without backup. I'm not breaking in; he's told me where the key is. And I'm pretty sure there is nothing dangerous about this request or action. I just go in and get the phone. Kathryn is overreacting.

As I'm just about to get out of the car, I realize that I have a slight headache, a hangover I suppose, from last night's festivities. I find aspirin in my glove box and take two with my juice, hoping that will help. And then I stop and lean my head against my seat and close my eyes, thinking I'll just take a few seconds to let the aspirin start to work and to finish my juice.

I slept all night—and hard. I never heard Nathan come into the room or get into bed, and now I wonder if he did sleep in the guest room or if he wasn't there at all and I just thought I heard him breathing. I realize that I can't tell any more. I don't know when he's really there and when I'm just pretending that he is, when he's actually been in our house, reading or drinking coffee or listening to music or if I have simply become accustomed to what I think I see and hear.

I know now that I can't tell at all anymore what is real and what is imagined because it's clear that what I think has been real—that Nathan is still with me—is not actually that at all, and if I accept that, then this leads me to think maybe nothing is real; nothing that I think can be trusted. But even then, I just don't know. I take in a couple deep breaths, trying to clear away the cobwebs and the night's dreams, the leftover drag from my birthday.

"He's dead," Violet said before I was serenaded by cocktail waitresses and college students working as bartenders and sous chefs. And I know that.

I mean, I guess I know that. I know my husband is dead, but that doesn't mean he isn't still with me. It doesn't mean I don't still talk to him, sleep with him, live with him. Does it? Isn't there something else other than just life and then death? Isn't there something more? Couldn't he be dead but still be with me, in some form that only I see, some spirit being that only I recognize?

Isn't it possible that love creates a bond that transcends this reality?

I open my eyes, my head swimming.

Later, after we said our goodbyes to Carla at the restaurant, my sister and I drove around just talking. Violet swore she was sober enough to handle the car and frankly, I didn't really care if she wasn't. We talked about lots of things—about her service, about the way things are in the Middle East, what she thinks is happening, and she told me more about the bombing in Iraq, more about what happened to her afterward. Where she went, what she did. She even owned up to her love of her comrade Trina, that the tragedy was more than just losing soldiers with whom she served.

She drove along while I sat beside her, the windows opened to keep us awake, our car alone on the road, and she confessed that after the incident, she would hear her lover sometimes late at night or think she saw her walking ahead of her in the desert, glancing back with a smile. In the first few months, she thought she saw her everywhere. But, she also told me, she understood that what she saw was just a mirage, just the deep longing of her heart to have again the love she lost, see once more this woman she loved. She had to accept that her beloved was gone and was not coming back.

And I leaned over and asked her the question, the cold wind whipping through the car—what if it was her? What if Trina was there late at night, talking to her, telling her things about where she was, what she knew? What if she was the one walking ahead of her on desert sands, that she wasn't some mirage or deep desire, what if it was really her? And Violet had pulled off to the side of the road, put the car in park, and taken me by the hands firmly but also with great tenderness and said, "It wasn't her, Emma. It wasn't."

As I sit in my car, I think about the year this happened to my sister, that span of time that my mother and I didn't really know where she was or how she was doing. We had been informed of the bombing and of the deaths. Her survival. But she had not come home as they said she would. She had been hospitalized briefly in Germany, minor injuries, they said, and then written us that she was fully recovered and ready to return to her unit. Neither of us had any idea of what she had suffered, what she had been through, and she never asked for our help. She had simply grieved alone.

I remember discussing it with Nathan after it happened, when she was hospitalized and planning to come home, and he had suggested that I go to Germany to be with her, that maybe she was not as well as she professed; but I had to work to do and my life to live, and I had chosen not to go. I think I just believed that she would be home soon, that she would leave the hospital and immediately return to the states. I believed there was no reason to go to Europe when she'd be sent home in a few days. And besides, I told him and myself to justify my reasons not to travel, she was fine, she had told me so.

And then, when she didn't come home, when she chose instead to return to Iraq, I assumed she was completely over it—all better. I thought she had healed up and was ready for battle, stitched up and out on the field again. I thought then that grief was just a wound that needed to close, and with enough time, a few months at the most, a person could just go right back to their life as if nothing had changed, a soldier returning to war.

Of course, I know now that I was wrong, terribly wrong, but I also know that even if I had gone to be with her, flown to Germany and talked to her doctors and sat by her bedside; even if I had found out how she really was, how broken her heart was, I still wouldn't have been able to fix it for her—change it, make it different from what it was. Grief is a beast hunting you down, terrorizing you; and you might have support and care, but if grief is coming for you, it is always your beast to wrestle. No one steps in to take your place.

We have to fight it all by ourselves.

Violet chose to deal with it like a soldier at war and to battle it, over and over until she was bloody but victorious while I, on the other hand, just surrendered. As soon as I saw the size of it, the weight, the girth, the unrelenting strength and power it had, I just lay down and let it have me. I didn't even try to fight. I would not wrestle this demon.

"You're stronger than you think," she told me last night before she drove off. "You can do this. You can live without him. You're already doing it, Em."

She said those words, and I simply smiled at her, smiled at the thought of her, at the thought of what she believed about me, hoped to be true about her big sister; and then I turned to face the house and saw his shadow behind the curtain—my husband, the ghost waiting for me to come home.

"Thanks for the birthday celebration," I told her and closed the door. "Thanks for coming home and drinking with me." And I had patted the car door like it was her arm and walked away.

I shake my head, trying to clear away the memories and don't see the police car until it has parked right behind me.

Chapter Forty-Four

I watch in my rearview mirror as the officer on the passenger's side gets out and opens the rear door behind him. Reverend Brady exits the vehicle. He even waves at the men as they pull out of his driveway and head up the street. And then he turns to glance in my direction. I get out of the car.

"Are you okay?" is all I know to ask.

He shakes his head, runs his fingers through his hair, takes in a deep breath like something horrible is over. "Come in," he tells me, and I follow him to the front door. He reaches in his pocket and takes out a key.

"Have you been in already?" he asks as the door opens, and he stands aside so I can walk in.

"No," I answer. "I just got here."

He nods and holds the door, glancing up and down the street before closing it. "Please," he says, motioning over to the kitchen. "Would you like some coffee?"

I follow him into the kitchen where there is a plate of food sitting on the counter, a glass of water and a table setting on the bar. There are pots on the stove. It looks like an unfinished meal.

"They picked me up about six last night," he informs me, dumping his dinner into the sink and then turning on the disposal. He waits a bit and then takes the pots off the stove and adds some dish soap and water and puts them on the counter to soak, then he starts to make coffee. I take a seat on a barstool across from where he is working.

"And they let you go just now?"

He nods while he pours water in the coffeepot. He stops, places the pot on the counter. His head is down, hands clenching the sides of the sink. "You know, do you mind doing this?"

I stand up. "No, not at all," I reply.

"I just feel like I want to take a shower."

"Sure." And I walk around the counter and pick up the pot.

He just stands there for a few seconds, and I don't know what he needs or what is going on with him. "They put me in a cell with two other men."

I nod because I don't know what to say.

"One of them I knew from the soup kitchen," he tells me. "The other one ..." and his voice drifts away. He reaches up, wipes his face with both hands, and then turns around. "I won't be long." And he quickly heads down the hall.

I fill the pot with water, find the coffee, and fill it so that it will make eight cups, hoping that's enough. I find mugs, take two down from the cabinet, and search inside his refrigerator for milk or cream, the other cabinets for sugar. I don't know how the pastor likes his coffee.

I wash the dinner plate and the pots from the stove and then place them on the towel I find hanging on the handle of the stove. I wash the counter, straighten things up a bit, and then return to a seat at the bar.

I hear the shower running and pull out my phone and turn it on. Kathryn has texted twice and called. I text her, tell her that the pastor is home, and that I'm okay. I turn it off before receiving her reply.

While I wait, I glance around the house. It appears as if Reverend Brady lives alone. I think about the photographs of the two children, but I don't see any evidence that there are children living here. There are no toys lying about, no swing sets or bicycles in the yard, no art work on the refrigerator. I don't know who the children are in those photos at the church, but it certainly appears as if they don't live here. Everything is neat and tidy and has the feel of the home of a single person, a single person who wants order in his home and keeps the clutter to a minimum.

"I'm sorry," he is saying as he returns to the kitchen, drying his hair with his towel. He checks the coffeepot. "Seems like you found everything."

I get up from my seat and make two cups. He leaves the towel around his shoulders and adds milk to the one I handed him, holds out the carton to me, and I add some to my cup as well; then I return the pot. I follow him to the sofa in the den, waiting to see where he sits, and then I take a seat across from him in a large recliner.

"They came and got my phone," he tells me. "Last night, just after I called your boss."

I nod.

"It took them a while, but they finally believed me, found the camera at church, saw the footage on my phone, and let me go."

I take a sip of my coffee, shake my head. "Why were you arrested? What are the charges?"

"Possession of child pornography," he reports and then closes his eyes.

"But who found the files? Who reported you? Was it the guy you let use the computer a while ago?"

He takes a sip of his coffee and shakes his head.

"No, turns out he doesn't have anything to do with this."

I place my cup on the table beside the chair. "What do you mean?"

"Somebody was trying to set me up," he says. "Somebody downloaded the sites and then called it in."

I can't believe it.

"I thought there was someone following me when I left the church and went to the grocery store; I just had that feeling, you know?"

I nod.

"And then I came home and was fixing my dinner when the police showed up, claimed I was under arrest. They handcuffed me and took me to jail. They confiscated my home computer, my files, my laptop, all of it." He motions over to a desk in the corner where a monitor sits with a keyboard, all the wires hanging. It was clear the computer had been disassembled. There was no tower, no hard drive apparatus.

"And they let you go this morning?"

"It took a little time to clear things up but yes, just a couple hours ago I was released."

"Because they saw video feed."

He nods, takes another sip of coffee.

"And you knew the video feed was there?"

He nods again. "Found it yesterday, but I didn't really think anything about it. I just thought he was trying to find a file or search for something on the internet, maybe use my printer. I didn't know, but thank God I hadn't deleted it. I kept the evidence."

"And this person confessed?"

"This morning, just before they released me. He told the police he did it because he thought I was evil, that I was bringing evil into the church, and he didn't know how to prove it, so he just made this up so the church would fire me. So I'd be taken out of the ministry, accused and branded."

The pastor holds his coffee cup with both hands, he's shaking. "I'm so glad I had the camera," he tells me. "I'm so grateful you talked me into it."

"Me too," I reply, thinking this really did save this man's life. A little camera—a video recording has saved this man's life. I pick up my cup, take long sips.

We are both silent for a few minutes.

"What about the guy?" I ask him. "Did they arrest him?"

He nods.

"But I'm not pressing charges. I'm not letting them use the video against him. The police officer said it was my possession and that they couldn't use it against someone else because they hadn't added my phone or a camera to the search warrant. They can't use it against him unless I give them permission."

"What?" I really can't believe what I'm hearing.

"He's sick. He's not mean; he's sick. I can't hold him accountable for his actions because he's sick, and I know because I've been sick too."

Chapter Forty-Five

*T*hope he will explain since apparently I don't understand mercy.

I put down my cup again, fold my hands in my lap, and wait. I am eager to hear how a falsely accused person can let go of harm so easily.

"You think I'm wrong?" is what he says when he notices my silence.

I shrug. "I think you're being magnanimous."

"Magnanimous," he repeats the word I just used. "Magnanimous," he says it again. "That's a big word."

"It is that," I reply, knowing we are not just talking about how many syllables there are.

He smiles.

It's the first time I've seen that expression since arriving at his house. The shower and the coffee must be helping.

"Leroy Taylor lost his family in an automobile accident about six years ago—drunk driver, about the time I started at Fourth Street Pres."

I know he's referring to the church, even though I've never heard the abbreviation of Presbyterian.

"It was devastating to many in the community. I had just arrived here, never met the family, couldn't even find the hospital the night it happened. It was a terrible time."

The pastor glances down at his hands. He stretches out his fingers, spreads them apart, and then balls his hands into fists as if that might help stop the shaking.

"Leroy was driving in another vehicle behind his wife and kids. They had driven separately to some event, and he was following them home. He saw the accident—happened right in front of him." Dillard shakes his head, closes his eyes, as if the memory still troubles him.

"He blamed himself, said he should have been in front, said he should have been the one who died that night—not his wife, not his two children."

Now I close my eyes, unable to imagine that brand of grief.

"It turns out I haven't been much assistance to him. In fact, it seems I just make things worse."

"How's that?" I ask.

He faces me, ponders the question. "Over the years, I suggested professional help. I've been running a grief support group for years since my daughter died, and I personally invited him. I send him books, offer to meet with him individually, anything and everything, but he just can't get through the dark valley."

"But how do you make it worse?" I'll ask this first and then circle back to the information about his daughter's death.

"The forgiveness factor," he tells me.

I wait for more.

"The driver of the other vehicle."

"The drunk driver?" I ask.

He nods.

"You've tried to talk him into forgiving the person who killed his family."

"And himself, yes."

"Well, I can see why he's mad at you."

Dillard turns away as if what I said hurt him.

"I mean, I understand your position and all, but forgive the guy? Can he even do that?"

"I think to move through grief, it's required."

And that's when I think he sounds like an expert. And then, I remember the mention of his daughter, and I realize that he is an expert, of a kind.

"Who did you have to forgive?"

He looks at me. His hands aren't shaking any longer. He understands the question. "The doctors," he answers and pauses, glances toward the window where the morning sun is pouring through. "God."

I think about Nathan, about how he had finally reached a point after the accident where he was doing well, where we stopped worrying about paralysis or brain damage or death caused by his internal injuries. I think about how we had celebrated the end of the long, horrible year—the plans we were making. We were so sure we had made it through. We were so sure that the doctors had healed him, that we had overcome.

"Lindsay died eight years ago." He waits. "My daughter," he clarifies.

I shake away the memories while still holding onto the grief.

"She was nine. She'd be graduating this year from high school." He says the last sentence like he's just thought of it, like he hadn't calculated the numbers until just this very minute; but of course, that can't be true. You know all the dates, all the milestones that will be missed.

He picks up his coffee cup and takes another sip.

I start to drink from mine, but then I realize I finished off my cup. I could get up and fetch the pot, but I don't. I just stay right where I am.

"She had been to a number of doctors, had all kinds of tests. My wife thought she was just trying to get out of homework." He takes in a breath. "It was cancer—a weird tumor in her stomach, hard to see, hard to find. And she died during surgery, and I blamed the first doctor for missing it, the second doctor for not being aggressive enough, the third doctor—the surgeon—for being too aggressive." He exhales. "And my wife blamed herself and me too. She couldn't help it; she blamed me because I couldn't fix it. We could never resolve things for the marriage. We divorced about a year later. We have a son; he lives with her because, well, because apparently he blames me too."

He shakes his head. I guess it must be weird to hear the story told that way.

"And after two years of being angry and bitter and trying to find some relief through lawsuits and letter campaigns, I finally had to stop."

"For her sake?" I ask.

He turns in my direction, stares at me like I just grew another head. "Her sake?" he repeats.

I don't respond.

"No, this was totally for my sake. I was drowning, losing everything. No—forgiveness, as they say, was the salvation I bought for myself." His voice trails off a bit. "It was the only way I was going to survive." He waits, speaks up this time. "You don't understand?"

I shrug and then ask, "Aren't you still mad?"

He puts down his coffee cup, leans forward in his seat. "No," he replies. "No, I am not still mad."

"Because you forgave everybody?"

"Because I wanted to live."

I suddenly remember Reverend Brady months ago, sitting with me in that waiting room while I heard the news that Nathan was dead, how he didn't say anything while the doctor explained what had happened to his heart, how he sat, kind of like he's sitting now, elbows on his knees, head down. I didn't think much about it at the time since I wasn't paying much attention to anything but this news I was being given, this devastating, unexpected, unbelievable news; but I suppose he was praying. I suppose that's what chaplains do in these situations.

"You tell Mr. Taylor this?" I ask, thinking I can understand why the guy hated him now. Nobody likes to be told they aren't living. Nobody wants to hear that forgiveness equals life when everybody you love is dead.

The pastor smiles slightly, as if he realizes what I'm implying. He raises his eyebrows, nods, sits back.

"And now you realized that you can't really ask a man to forgive his family's murderer if you can't forgive him for setting you up to be arrested?"

"Wouldn't make much sense, would it?" And he finishes up his cup of coffee, stands up, walks over, picks up mine, and heads into the kitchen.

Chapter Forty-Six

My sleep is fretful. I toss and turn with pieces of dreams stringing together. Car wrecks, hospital waiting rooms, grainy images on videos that I can't quite make out. Voices repeating lines I heard from the pastor.

"They're all dead ... She blamed herself ... He's sick ... Because I want to live ... There has to be forgiveness."

Over and over I am besieged.

I glance up at the clock, and it's three in the morning. There are still four hours to go before sunrise, before light breaks through this night's darkness.

Nathan is beside me, or at least I think that's him. He's curled up, and the covers are bunched around him. I cannot even see his head on the pillow, but I'm pretty sure he's there. I reach out to touch him but don't stretch out my hand quite as far as I can. I stop just short of where I think he will be, and I place my fingers in the space between us and think about what it might be like if he's not there anymore, if I reach across the bed every morning, day after day, and he's never there again.

I pull my hand back, ball it into a fist and hold it against my chest, and I start to cry. If he hears me, he doesn't respond. He doesn't try to comfort me.

We fought most of the weekend. Saturday, once I got home from Dillard's house and Sunday while it rained.

We argued about what to eat and where I keep things in the cabinets. He yelled at me for working overtime and how easily I make myself available to my boss and coworkers—that I never ask for his consent or consider what it means to him when I'm gone. We fought about the bills I don't pay on time and the food in the refrigerator that I forget to throw out. He pointed out the dead mouse on the porch that he mentioned to me last week that I should remove and is still there, and he hates it when I leave the radio on and then exit a room.

He accused me of actually trying to stay away on Saturday, of making up reasons not to be at home on the weekends, that I hadn't allowed him to have any part of my birthday celebrations. He brought up the book that I was given and how I kept it from him, never told him about it. He even questioned whether I had actually gotten a call to go to the pastor's house and suggested I had made up the whole story just to be gone all day.

It was brutal and nonstop, worse than any fight we ever had before he died. I ended up drinking a lot of wine Saturday night and fell in the bed without resolution. We woke up Sunday morning and started it all over again. First it would start with a pet peeve, an annoyance that I cause him, and then it would be about how I don't give him enough attention, how I keep putting everything and everyone ahead of him, ahead of us. He said he was the drone bee, and I was the queen, and I saw him as just draining the resources and tried to keep him out. He said I was done with him. I was only interested in the worker bees, Bus and Kathryn, the productive ones, the ones still alive.

"Choose," he screamed. "Me or them, choose."

And I covered my ears and yelled at him to leave me alone. I wept for hours while he ranted.

I realize now that I cannot keep pretending this is going to work.

I get up from bed and walk into the dining room. I stand at the window, watch the rain as it keeps pouring down. I think how Nathan and I used to love rainy days on the weekends. We called them "designated reading days," and there was only one rule: there were to be no work manuals or books he taught in his literature classes, no security systems magazines, no sales journals. When he retired, the bee books and the gardening journals were even off-limits. It was fiction only—commercial. Mysteries or romance or sci-fi, and literary only if they didn't have anything to do with the British writers.

It was not easy at first—more difficult for Nathan than for me—but after a few years and enough seasons of rainy Saturday mornings and stormy Sunday afternoons spent together, after enough Norwegian thrillers and flawed but brilliant detectives, we both felt great pleasure at hearing weather reports that promised tempestuous days ahead.

"You're up," he says as he stands at the door. His hair is sticking up all over. He looks like Einstein, and I laugh a little.

He understands the reason for my laughter and tries to smooth down the sides. His robe opens, and I can see his ribs. He's so skinny, and I wonder what I have done to him.

"You can't sleep?" he asks, covering himself. It's as if he's ashamed of his body. I've never seen this side of him. He has never cared about how he appears to me, his belly fat or his gray hair. He used to be so comfortable in his skin.

I shake my head, turn again to gaze out the window. In a few minutes I feel him behind me, his breath on my neck, his arms, thin as wire wrapping around me. He rests his chin on my shoulder.

"I was thinking about designated reading days," I say.

"We should have one," he responds.

"What will you read?" I ask him.

"Le Carré," he answers. "I do love a good French spy."

"Well, who doesn't?"

There is a long pause as we stand together this way, and I catch the reflection in the window, seeing only myself as he is hidden behind me.

"I'm sorry," he tells me.

"Yeah? For what?" It could be for anything, after all.

He breathes. In and out—I feel it. I feel him.

"Screaming mostly, I guess."

I wait.

"Being so needy, so angry that you have a life when ..."

He stops and I know the rest.

"Maybe I should get you a dog," I say as a suggestion for his loneliness.

"I don't want a dog," he answers.

I feel his grip on me loosen a little.

"Not one of those nervous ones like your mother always kept?" I am trying to be light.

"No, I do not want a Chihuahua or a Poodle."

"A big one, then? A Great Dane or a Lab? A rescue like Pistol. They're good company. You could teach him how to fetch things."

"Emma."

I turn around and face him. We are so close, and I raise my hand to his chest so that I can feel his heart beat. "See," I say, like I'm proving something to us both. "See, there's that."

He pulls my hands into his, holds them right at the place of what I know to be life—the pounding of his heart, the blood coursing through his veins. I close my eyes, making myself pay attention to what I want so desperately to be true.

"I'm sorry," he tells me again.

And I remember the pastor and his deed of mercy. I remember what he said about forgiveness and life and the way grief can make a person sick; but it is not what I want to think about at three o'clock in the morning, standing in the dining room window, holding onto my dead husband. I open my eyes and see his face, see the pain of death and sorrow and the ache to be somewhere other than he is, someone other than himself.

"It's okay," I reply.

And I try as hard as I can to make myself believe that too.

Chapter Forty-Seven

"So he has the evidence?"

It's Monday morning. I'm at work. Everybody at the office is standing around my desk. They've all heard parts of the story, and they're interested in the news about the minister, about how our camera saved him from jail and how he has proof of being set up, and the latest, how he isn't using the video to have the perpetrator charged.

"On his phone," I answer.

It was Jon who asked. He's standing up at his desk, peering over the divider. Kathryn is beside my chair. All the others are behind my desk waiting for more information. "And he's not handing it over?" My coworker asks. "He doesn't want to press charges?"

I guess Jon doesn't have much experience with mercy either. I shrug. Even knowing what I know, it's still mostly a mystery to me too.

"Well, I'm just so glad they believed him, went out of their way to secure the phone and make a record of the video for themselves." Kathryn has her arms folded across her waist. She's shaking her head like she's hearing this for the first time when we both know she got a full report Saturday afternoon. She's trying to play up the good work of the police force. She always likes us to know how much she appreciates the boys and girls in blue.

"Yeah, that would have been rough for the padre to be in jail." Dexter doesn't know the whole story.

"Oh, he spent the night in jail," I tell him, and he pulls away like he can't believe it.

"They kept him overnight?"

I nod, and we all turn to Kathryn. It's not the public relations news of the police force that she wants to discuss.

"Okay, everybody, that's enough recap of the weekend. I just wanted to say what a great job Emma did in working with this client, informing him of the benefits of a camera and the video feed to his smartphone, and we want to recognize and thank Bus for getting the system installed and placed in a secure location." She stops and actually holds up a hand in my direction, like she expects me to lean over and give her a high five, like we're at a football game celebrating a touchdown; it's practically embarrassing, and I feel my face get warm.

She puts down her hand. "Great work, you two."

Bus glances away.

There's a polite round of applause.

"So just remember this story when you're on your sales calls. The security cameras and other parts of our systems aren't just useful in catching bad guys, they also provide information in protecting the good ones!" And to this, she adds her own bit of applause, two sharp claps of her hands. "Now let's get on those calls that came in over the weekend and let's make Elon secure."

I am facing Jon, my back to my boss, and I roll my eyes. He smiles and takes his seat, and I face the front of my work station. Everybody returns to their desk or to the break room except Bus. He remains where he is, looming over my desk.

"That's some crazy stuff," he says.

"Uh-huh," I respond and then start up my computer.

"Why didn't you call me?"

"What?"

Kathryn texted me after she talked to you, told me you would be calling, asked if I could meet you at the pastor's house.

"Oh."

He's waiting for more—an excuse for why I didn't ask for his help, why I didn't answer his message, return his call.

"It turned out to be totally fine," I say. The smile is plastered across my face.

He nods suspiciously, stays where he is.

I glance down at my screen, waiting for the computer to boot up, waiting for him to join the others or head out for his installations; but he's not moving. I try to focus on my computer screen. Our time sheets are due in an hour, and I'm behind by about three days.

"I was waiting for you to call; I was planning to join you."

"I'm sorry about that," I say, not turning to face him.

He watches me. I feel him.

"But like you heard, it turned out to be no big deal, and well, truth be told I didn't see any reason to ruin both our weekends. I figured I would just show up and find the phone at his house like he said and then take it to the district attorney. There wasn't any reason that you needed to be there."

I hear the sound of my voice, and I think I sound strident or irritated. I soften. "And then, the pastor was released and showed up anyway. So there wasn't cause for either one of us to have to go." I end my explanation by turning around and giving the same dumb smile with which I started.

He just nods; he's not buying the fake expressions. "Well, I'm glad everything worked out," he notes and starts to walk away.

"Bus," I call him, and he turns around. "It's no big deal."

"Right," he responds and heads to the break room. I watch as he joins the other two guys standing near the counter and talking.

"What's eating him?" I ask Jon because I know he has heard all of this go down.

He holds up his hands, steps away from the divider. "Hey, I don't even want to know what you two lovers are quarreling about."

"Not funny," I say and enter in the times for last week, and then I add the overtime from Saturday. I can use the extra cash, and since my boss sent me, I think it's only fair to list it. I glance up again. Bus is no longer standing where I can see him.

I know that I probably should have called, just to tell Bus what was going on. I should have returned his message from later in the day. Instead, I had deleted it, and I see now that it wasn't fair to him. I blow out a breath and shake my head at the thoughts of this past weekend. Everything feels like a blur today anyway. And it seems like all I did in those two days was just make everybody mad.

It wasn't just Nathan. Carla called and wasn't happy because she claimed Violet was driving while intoxicated Friday night, and we were very lucky that nothing happened. She claimed I was to blame for the entire course of events because I was the older of the two and should have been more conscientious. I could've gotten us killed or gotten Violet in trouble with her commanding officer or court martialed. She wasn't making any sense, and I know that she was just mad because we left her out of our little after-party.

And now, apparently being added to the list of those distressed by my actions is Bus. I should have touched base with him to let him know what was going on at the pastor's house. He was waiting by his phone all day. He left messages.

I see him now sitting at the table, hunched over his laptop. I think of him standing in front of me sulking, hurt. I think that maybe I should go over to him, try to smooth things over, apologize.

Maybe I should tell him the truth. Maybe I should say that my life is way too complicated to bring him into my weekends. Maybe I should tell him that my husband is jealous of him, and I don't have the energy to hide the dead from the living and the living from the dead. I didn't call him this weekend because really I just didn't want to have to lie to them both.

I notice as he takes a call on his phone, gets up from the table, and heads out the front door. I return to the time sheet on my screen, check my work, and hit send.

I am relieved to watch him go.

Chapter Forty-Eight

It's almost five and I'm the last one in the office.

Kathryn left at three because she had an appointment with an important potential client. After years of attempts to get her foot in the door, the powers that be at the university finally answered her calls and were willing to make an appointment with her. She was bidding on security systems for the recently built athletic dorms. If she gets this contract, we all know that it could lead to a very large and lucrative arrangement for K-Locks. It was the "mother lock and lode," as she liked to call it.

Once the appointment was made, she was so excited, she made an announcement giving everyone the last two hours of the day as comp time.

"Go and pray or light candles or send positive energy up to the universe, whatever it is that you do, and let's make this thing happen," she had said enthusiastically as she stood at her office door while we all watched.

I'm pretty sure that nobody is praying or lighting candles, but they did all take the two hours and left work. Everyone is gone but me. I still have some paperwork that I would like to see done before going home.

Things have been busy for me today. I made two sales since lunch—domestic customers but still good commissions. I just want to get them both ready for installation and for that to be finished as soon as possible.

Kathryn wants us to start going out in the community with the new marketing idea. She thinks sales will go up for everyone once word gets out about the camera in the pastor's office, the one that saved him from jail, the one installed by us. Word already got out at the police station, which she hopes will soon spread around town, garnering Kathryn and K-Locks a lot more business.

The phone rings. I pick up after a few rings, not sure I want to answer the phone.

"I hate to bother you."

"No bother, what's up?" I ask, recognizing Dexter's voice. I keep typing in the information as I complete the second contract. I'm almost finished.

"There's a swarm," he says.

"What?" I'm not paying very close attention. I want this completed and sent out to the customer.

I glance up at the clock. I already know I can't use this for overtime. Kathryn made it clear after the last pay period that overtime has to be approved before we report it. Talking to the installation staff after five o'clock after already getting two free hours will not count, I'm sure.

"A swarm. Of bees. At this client's house." He speaks in phrases, trying to slow it all down for me, I suppose.

"It's a little early, I think."

"Well, apparently, they didn't get the memo because there's a lot of them."

"You see the queen?"

"Haven't really gotten that close," he answers. "I don't do bees."

"Right." I fill in the last blanks and then scroll up to proof my work.

"I tried beating a metal spoon against pots," he adds. "I heard that would do it."

"It doesn't work," I tell him.

I understand what he tried is called tanging, a means sometimes used to get swarms from flying overhead to move closer to the ground. Nathan explained that most experts don't really think this is effective since it is widely accepted bees do not hear airborne sound.

"Bees," he had explained, "are only moderately sensitive to the sound waves that can move through solid objects like the ground."

"The sounds," he told me one summer, "are actually detected through the only ears anybody knows about." And here he had smiled, like the news was something deliciously private. "They're on their tiny feet."

And I had entertained the image of teeny-tiny human ears growing out of little black, pointed feet.

When I asked him once about swarms and getting them down or taken away, he said that in everything he had read, there wasn't really any perfect solution and that the swarms were likely going to fly down anyway. He also explained that swarms are not dangerous, and if a person would just wait, they would eventually fly away. I tell this to my coworker.

"Oh." Dexter doesn't sound too interested.

"Where are you?"

"The Lewis house."

"Lewis?"

"The elderly woman whose husband died last year. Bus usually deals with her. In fact, she called him, but he's at the doctor's, I think."

"Hospital," I correct him. Bus is finishing an installation at the emergency department. I know about it because I handled the first call that came in, and then Kathryn took it and gave it to Bus.

I am trying to recall Mrs. Lewis. There have been a lot of calls in the last couple weeks. A few more minutes have passed, and I realize I was just being optimistic to think I would get out of here by five.

"Bus said to tell you she was the old woman who thought you were nice, the first client that the two of you actually worked with together."

"Wait, are you talking to Bus?"

"Text. He texted me to call you." He blows out a long breath like he's tired of trying to explain. "Can you tell me what to do about this situation or not?"

I just stop trying to work on the contract and think about Dexter's request and this customer, and then I remember. It wasn't that long ago that we spoke. Mrs. Lewis, the one whose husband was sick, and before he died, made her buy a security system. Bus stops by there a lot, helping her out with all kinds of things. He's quickly become like a family member or a handyman; I'm not sure exactly how she thinks of him, but I heard him tell Kathryn about it one time. She lets him count some of it as work-related and put it on his time sheet.

"Oh, right," I respond. "Mrs. Lewis on Church Street."

"That's the one. So should I try to spray them with a wasp spray or something?"

"No, don't spray pesticides." I sit up in my chair; I hope he hasn't already done something stupid. "They're actually harmless," I tell him.

"Mrs. Lewis says she's allergic, and she's very nervous."

"Okay, just let me finish this paperwork I'm doing, and then I'll swing by there on my way home." I think about home, what's waiting for me there, who's waiting for me there. "Can you go and get me a hive box from Bus?"

"That might take a while."

I wait for him to decide.

"Okay, I'll do it. What does it look like?"

"It's a box—a single one that's stapled to a bottom board. He keeps them behind the old barn."

"You've been to Bus's house?"

"He knows I have bees," I answer, feeling slightly defensive, even though there's really no reason.

"Right," he says, sounding somewhat smug.

"Can you get it or not?" I ask. I don't have time for stupid boy games.

"Yes, I can get it," he answers. "I'll meet you in about half an hour. That's how long it takes you to get to his place and back, right?"

Now he's just being an ass.

"I'll be at the customer's house about the same time," I say, not taking the bait.

"Thanks, Emma. You know I'm just yanking your chain, right?"

"Yes, Dexter, I know. I'll see you in a bit." And I hang up and wonder if I have time to stop by the house and ask for Nathan's advice.

Chapter Forty-Nine

I didn't stop at home. I decided not to ask Nathan. I decide to handle this on my own, see if I can wrangle the swarm of bees without supervision or assistance. In fact, I have an idea that if I go home later and tell him this, get the opportunity to brag about this accomplishment, how far "his student" has come, it might improve his mood, lighten his load.

He's still sullen and withdrawn even though we haven't had a fight in a few days.

I leave the office and head in the direction of Church Street. In only a few minutes I find the house and pull into the driveway. I don't see a company van so I assume Dexter hasn't returned from fetching a hive box. I park and immediately see Mrs. Lewis peeking out her front window, so I smile and wave, turn off the engine, and open my door.

The curtain falls, and in a few seconds, the front door opens, the screen door remaining closed.

"Are they there?" she whispers like she doesn't want anyone to hear.

I walk toward her but stay at the bottom of the steps.

"The bees?"

"Yes, the bees, are they still there?"

I glance around, but I don't yet spot the swarm. "Were they out front?"

"No, no, they're out there by the shed." She points to the side of the house with her chin.

I try to get a view around the carport where she's motioning, but I can't really see anything from where I'm standing.

"Shall I go and see?"

She hesitates. "Will you be okay? Maybe you should come in and wait until Dexter gets here. He said he wouldn't be too long. You can just wait with me, and we'll be safe inside until he returns."

I understand the implication Mrs. Lewis is making. Since I'm female, she thinks I need the help. She seems to have forgotten that I'm the one Dexter called. I'm actually the bee person, the expert asked to come and help with her swarm.

I think about correcting her, setting her straight, but I see that wouldn't really change things for Mrs. Lewis, and besides, I'm feeling somewhat charitable. Let her think what she does. I would probably have the same prejudices if Nathan hadn't taught me about beekeeping and if I hadn't learned how many women do this work.

"No, I'll be fine," I say reassuringly.

"Oh, I don't know," she replies.

"I'll just take a peek around the corner, see if they're there, see if I can tell what kind of bees they are."

"Well, be careful," she tells me.

"Yes, ma'am."

I leave the front sidewalk and walk through the carport and into the backyard.

It takes me a few minutes, but it isn't very long until I see them, thousands of them, flying low to the ground now. I stop and take in the sight and the sounds all around them. There's so much movement, so much activity that the air almost feels electric, and I suddenly recall the first time I ever saw Nathan wrangle a swarm of bees.

It was early summer a few years ago, before the accident, and he was called to the grocery store near the farm. He had been there several times since starting his new hobby, had even sold some of his honey there, and the manager of the place knew him and knew about his bees. When an employee saw a large swarm near the dumpster, the manager found Nathan's number and called. We were there in less than an hour. And I, along with about thirty store employees and customers, watched as he slowly and carefully captured the bees.

It was such a sight of beauty, as simple as it was, and I was so happy to be with him, to be his assistant as he placed the hive on the ground, a feeder inside with frames of worked honey, and covered the area with a white sheet so that when they landed on it to go into the hive, he could find the queen. He needed to make sure she was safe in the box, he had told everyone, before putting the entrance screen into place and stapling it.

We all watched silently as he did his work, and then there was a great cheer with enthusiastic applause when the swarm was gone. All those watching had gathered around him like he had just made magic, asking questions, patting him on the back. I had not seen him that proud in years. It was as lovely as the wrangling itself.

He explained everything to me as we drove to the farm where he ended up putting the new beehive he had just collected. "There are some hives that swarm more than just once, sometimes several times during a season. It all has to do with the queen because sometimes there may be more than one. So instead of killing one another, a new queen will leave the colony, taking some of the bees with her."

He drove along, checking the rearview mirror of his truck, making sure the hive box remained steady on the bed. "The bees ingest a lot of honey in preparation for leaving. It's like they understand they won't have access to food for some time, and once they've left, once they've swarmed, they no longer remember the former hive. They somehow forget where it is, like that information is wiped from their brains." He shook his head like he still couldn't understand such behavior.

"And then they find temporary places, with the large group always protecting the queen. Scouts are sent out to search for a new home, and it may take a few hours or it might be a day or two, but they always return successfully, letting the bees, including the queen, follow them to their new residence."

"How do they let the queen know?" I asked, wondering how he had learned all this, wondering how many swarms he had collected that I had not witnessed.

"It's the dance," he answered, glancing over at me with a smile and a wink. "The bee dance."

"There's no such thing," I responded, thinking he was only teasing me. "Bees communicate chemically—they leave something on their food so the other bees recognize the markings. I read that on one of those websites you sent me."

"Well, yeah, they do tag the honey when it's being processed; but they also talk to each other by dancing. They relay information about new places by dance steps and body movements."

"Okay, tell me more," I said, sliding closer to him, taking his arm and putting it around my shoulder. "Tell me about the bee dance." And I felt like I was seventeen, falling in love for the first time, falling in love with him all over again.

"It's highly choreographed with important details, and nobody really knows what each step means, how it all gets interpreted; but it is a series of movements that the other bees understand because once they watch it, they immediately follow the scouts to their new location."

"Have you ever seen it?" I wanted to hear how it felt to watch such a thing, how it was for him to see it.

He shook his head. "Never have," he answers sadly. "Only seen videos, pictures in books."

"A bee dance," I repeated softly. "They dance their way home."

He squeezed me and then we both checked the rearview mirror, and I felt suddenly a little sad, wondering if we had interrupted the performance of a scout troop at the grocery store dumpster or if we had separated them from their colony forever. I wondered if we had messed up the bee steps by taking the swarm away.

I hear a tapping on the window and turn to see Mrs. Lewis standing in the kitchen. She is pointing to the swarm I have just found. I nod at her and return my attention to the bees, and I feel the sting of grief once more, knowing the dance steps I'm doing will never get me home.

Chapter Fifty

"You found them."

It is not Dexter's voice I hear. I turn around and see that Bus has joined me. He has a bee box in his hands.

"Where's Dexter?" I ask.

"I was home when he came to get the hive. I told him I'd bring it. He wasn't too happy about this call and having to stay, so he was glad to have me take over." He glances behind him and acknowledges Mrs. Lewis who is waving at him from the window. "She's allergic to bees," he tells me.

"So I've heard," I reply and wonder when he found this out, wonder how much he knows about our customer, how much she knows about him.

"She's called me for help with things like this before. I've taken down lots of wasp nests from her garage, gotten bees out of her mailbox."

"You didn't kill them, did you?"

He shakes his head and then gives me a look like my question troubles him. "I killed the wasps, got rid of the nests—don't see much good in them—but the spiders and the bees I never kill. She knows that."

His answer makes me sorry that I asked, but I do think about the bees he took from the mailbox and imagine that they could have been scouts for this colony. I guess he captured and released them somewhere else, but I hope it wasn't so far from here they didn't make it back to their queen.

"Dexter tried tanging them," I say, deciding to bring him up to speed about Mrs. Lewis' visiting hive.

"Well, that doesn't work," he replies and then shakes his head like he can't believe his coworker tried it, and his knowledge about this surprises me. "He didn't tell me that."

"Yeah, he did that before he called me. I explained that it's just an old wives' tale that the noise would bother them."

He makes a kind of clicking noise, his tongue against the roof of his mouth. "I should've taken the call," he says. "I was trying to finish over at the hospital. I had about twelve cameras to install and then put in a keypad to fit all the doors. The nurses were all antsy that the installation wasn't completed and that they might not have a security system in place for the night."

"Uh-huh." I'm not really sure why he thinks this is important information for me to have; but I just keep listening.

"Apparently, it's a pink moon tonight."

I wait because I don't quite know where he's taking this.

"It's what they call the full moon in late spring. Native Americans call it pink moon because of the pink flowers that were blooming at the time."

"Phlox," I add. I know the names of full moons and their origins. I've always liked moon lore. I could tell him that coastal tribes called it Full Fish Moon in April because the shad start swimming upstream to spawn, but I withhold my trivia for now.

"Right."

"But I don't understand what a full moon has to do with cameras in the emergency department at the hospital." I need him to get on with his story. I take a quick look at the bees. They're still swarming near the shed.

"Oh, right. Well, they claim they're busier on nights when the moon is full, especially in the spring."

"Is that true?" I had not heard this before.

He shrugs. "Full moon madness, they call it." He pauses as if he's just thought of something. "Hey, do you think the moon has anything to do with bees? Do you think the fact that it's full caused this swarm of bees?"

"Well, they were likely swarming before today," I say. And then I consider his questions and remember hearing that some beekeepers actually follow a lunar calendar with their farming—implement what is known as biodynamic beekeeping techniques, which includes information about phases of the moon and weather patterns.

It's been documented that bees are known to be more aggressive during hot humid days with thunderstorms and that they do in fact swarm more when there's a full moon. I glance again over at the bees and wonder if there's something to any of this and if this swarm vacated its hive because of the phase of tonight's moon.

And then for some reason I had not anticipated, I find myself thinking about the night Nathan died—how bright the moon was when we left for the hospital and when I returned before morning. How he mentioned earlier in the day that it was going to be a full moon that night, and maybe we could go on a honeymoon, then kissed me even as his fever was rising. I began to realize that he was starting to talk nonsense because he got the wrong name of the moon. May is Milk Moon. June is the Honey Moon. He knew that stuff but it seemed as if he had lost track of the dates, the time.

"We deserve another honeymoon," he had said, smiling, his face flushed, his breathing hard and labored. "We deserve a real sweet June Honey Moon."

"And that's exactly what we'll have," I told him, trying to hold my fears at bay, trying to keep from touching his forehead or focusing on his ragged breath. I was trying to pretend he was getting better, not worse, that he was just tired and not weak. I was trying to make myself believe that my husband was just confused and was not becoming more ill.

"You okay?"

I'm shaken from my memories. I turn and face Bus. "Yeah, sure," I say and then glance away.

"So, I brought some honey. Should I put it in the hive box? That's what you use to get the bees to go in, right?"

I do not respond right away; I'm trying to let go of the thoughts of that night in May. I hear a tapping behind me, and Bus and I turn to see Mrs. Lewis waving her arms and then pointing toward the shed.

We follow her direction and notice the bees as they are starting to move away. They swarm up and around, up and around, an elongated shadow dancing across the sky until they are as high as the shed; and it is the most beautiful thing I have ever seen. I am full and empty at the same moment. Life at the height of such intense beauty and me without my husband to witness it. And then in an instant, the small dark cloud just drifts away. It's almost as if they were never there. All of them are suddenly and completely gone.

Bus takes out running after them, and before I know it, I'm chasing them too.

"Wait!" I shout out, and I don't know who I'm calling, whether it is Bus I want to stop or whether I feel a need for the bees to let me catch up; but I run after them, through the field behind Mrs. Lewis' house and down an alley until I see where Bus has stopped.

"They're up there," he says, sounding a bit out of breath. And he points to a tree, a large one, its limbs full of buds, green ones, an elm I think; and I can see the hollow place in one of its wide arms, the bees moving inside.

I stop and hold my sides. I'm a bit winded from the run myself.

"Should we try and get them down?" he asks.

"No," I reply. "They'll be fine." I straighten up. "The scouts found it for the queen. They picked her a good spot. It's their new home. It was the dance. They're fine."

And I blow out a breath, turning again to Mrs. Lewis' house, turning back toward the rising of the full pink moon.

Chapter Fifty-One

He is not there when I get home, or at least I don't see him. Sometimes it's like this. I come home and I don't miss or need him; I have something pressing on my mind; and he only turns up later when it gets dark or when I'm suddenly sad. Of course, now I understand that it's all up to me whether he stays or leaves, whether he appears or remains hidden. He comes when my heart calls.

I am tired from the day, tired from selling security systems, pushing hidden cameras and motion sensors to people who live and work in fear. I'm tired of quoting prices to business owners trying to decide whether to put in new locks or grant a pay raise to employees.

I'm tired from chasing bees.

I'm tired from the weeks of rain and the slow start of spring—of winter's hold on my soul, of grief's long war. I'm tired of dull secrets and fretful dreams, of dancing with no partner, of living through the worst year of my life. Like a lie that can take you anywhere but home, I feel as if it has all caught up with me now, and I realize that I cannot keep going the way I have been trying to go.

I put down my lunch bag, my purse, close the blinds in the windows, pull the curtains shut, and decide to take a bath, thinking the soak will do me good.

I start the water in the tub and pour myself a glass of wine, and I think about the ending to my workday, about the bees at Mrs. Lewis' house and how late I had stayed with our last customer.

After finding the bees making their new home, Bus and I returned to Mrs. Lewis to tell her the news, and she had immediately invited us in for glasses of iced tea and pieces of apple walnut cake she had made and wanted to share. I tried to refuse the invitation, explaining that I needed to get home, but the refreshments were already made and put out, and she would not take no for an answer. Finally, I just relented and joined both of them inside.

As we sat together in the living room, I noticed how she and Bus carried on like old friends. She teased him about needing a haircut, about taking out his earring; he laughed at her story of being chased by a bee all around her house, how she ran and screamed, waving her arms, she explained, "like a Pentecostal at revival."

I discovered that Beverly Lewis is more than just an old scrambled widow, as I had first thought—she is witty and warm, and I'm glad she and Bus have such a friendly connection. It's easy to see they care a great deal about each other. He would jump up from time to time to fetch napkins or get more ice, and she kept calling him her sweet boy and telling me how lucky she was to have him in her life.

She told me about her husband, Bennie, pulled down photographs from the wall, opened up her wedding album. They never had children, she said, appearing a little sad about that; but she cheered as she reported that they had great fun together traveling in a motor home across the United States, meeting people all over the country. It was a good marriage, she said, as she handed Bus the pictures to return to their places.

She wanted to know about my marriage, and she asked about my husband, wanted to know his name and what he did for a living. I didn't know how to reply since I wasn't sure what she did or did not know about me; and I sat silently as Bus quickly and easily changed the subject, protecting me, I suppose, or maybe protecting her—understanding that for one widow to hear the story of another sometimes just ends up making them both sad as they add their sorrows, calculate the losses.

He told her I kept bees and that I was going to help Bus get started, that I had been to his house to see his hives and was helping him find the right place to keep his colony. She had lifted her eyebrows at this bit of news as if she was concerned about her friend meeting with a married woman or, thinking about it now, maybe it was nothing, and I just read more into it than was there. I'm not sure; but I had used that moment in the conversation to leave the room, standing from my seat and picking up the empty dessert plates and taking them to the kitchen.

I stood at the sink and listened to the two of them as Bus told the older woman once again where the bees from her shed had gone, describing the large tree at the end of the alley behind the field that stretched far away from her house—the hollow place in the limb and how they would likely not return.

"The swarming," I heard him explain, sounding as if he had done some reading on the subject, "is just to get to the new place to live. They don't do it to be aggressive or to cause trouble; it's actually a dance. They're moving their queen to a new residence. It's just how they relocate."

"Well, it sounds just like Bennie's family on vacation every summer. His sisters and nieces would buzz around the beach house, trying to assign bedrooms for everyone, bringing in their suitcases and ice coolers. It was just like a swarm of bees; and Bennie's mother was most definitely the queen."

I heard her high-pitched laugh. "But you don't want me to get started about Felicity Lewis. Now there was a woman who knew how to sting."

Bus's laughter rang from the next room, and I washed the dishes, put them in the drain, and returned to the room to say my goodbyes.

Just as Bus had predicted, Mrs. Lewis tried to pay me for coming over, but I had refused. And she said that the only way she would not insist on me taking the money was if I promised I would come to her house again with Bus to dinner one evening. She made no further comment about my husband, and as I agreed to the invitation, I wondered if she forgot that I was married or if there had been something else shared between the two of them while I was in the kitchen, some secret code that I had not broken. I wondered if Bus somehow let her know in their brief time alone together that I was no longer married.

I light a candle, turn off the lights, and test the temperature of the water. I grab a towel from the closet, take off my clothes, and slide in the tub.

I close my eyes. Immediately, I feel myself relax. I haven't soaked in a while.

It isn't long before I hear the music coming from the front of the house, and I feel him standing at the door. I look up and see him. I can tell even with a candle's light that he is sad. I sit up.

"Come be with me," I say, and he starts to undress, and I move forward so that he can have the back part while I lean against him. We have taken baths together for years. We know how to fit in the old tub we share.

I feel him stepping behind me, and he makes no comment about how hot I have gotten the water, something he almost always said before. I feel the water rise as he takes his place, and I close my eyes as he maneuvers his legs around me, and we settle in to each other.

I drop my head behind me on his chest, and I place my hands on his as they rest on the bottom of the tub.

"How was your day?" he asks, his lips right at my ear.

I nod but do not speak.

"It was nice today," he adds. "No rain."

"It was. Did you know it's a full moon?"

"I did."

"Pink moon," I say.

"The flowers."

I nod again, and for a few moments, I am not the wife of a dead man.

I am at peace.

Chapter Fifty-Two

"I was called to a swarm today," I tell him as he washes my back. I am leaning forward and rubbing his legs, the tops of his feet. Nathan has long toes and bony ankles. I slide my fingers across them.

"Did you box them?"

I shake my head. "They flew off on their own."

"That's for the best," he says.

"I watched them dance."

He cups his hands and pours water, starting at my shoulders. I feel the streams of suds running down.

"You saw the dance," he acknowledges, sounding far away.

I try to turn around so that I can see him. "It was ..." And I stop. I do not want to hurt him.

"Like nothing you've ever seen," he finishes my sentence. And I nod.

I lean against him again, turn on the hot water with my toes. There's room for a little more in the tub.

"Where was it?" he wants to know.

"A residence. They were swarming near her shed, and then they flew to a tree about a quarter mile away. I followed them."

He wraps his arms around me and places his hands on the tops of my legs, and we wait until I turn off the water to continue.

"The customer, Mrs. Lewis"—I drop my foot and there's a splash—"is allergic. She called our installer and he called me."

"Bus?"

I feel myself tighten, worried this will lead to a fight.

"Dexter," I answer.

He doesn't react or respond.

"But Bus showed up." I don't know why I have chosen to tell him this.

I feel his chest rise and fall. "They're close," I say.

"Who is close?"

"Bus and the customer, Mrs. Lewis. She counts on him, kind of like a handyman." I pause. "A son."

No reply.

"Her husband died a few months ago," I add, not sure why I'm giving so much information, why I want to tell him everything tonight.

"She needs him."

"Yes."

There is a long pause, and I close my eyes and listen to the soft sounds of the music from the other part of the house. He has it on the station from the university, the one we always listen to for our NPR news, the classics, and jazz in the evenings.

"Do you?"

I open my eyes. I was thinking of the song playing, thinking it was from the album John Coltrane made with Thelonious Monk, the recording made in 1957 but not released until 2005.

I know about jazz from a music appreciation class I took my senior year of college. I like jazz, and I especially like Coltrane. I feel the hint of loss remembering how young he was when he died. He was forty, younger than I am now, died of liver cancer.

"Do I what?" My thoughts about jazz drift away, and I suddenly remember the question.

"Do you need Bus?"

I lean forward and turn around again to look at him, and even though I was planning to say something, to rebuke his suggestion, tell him that he was just being crazy or jealous, I quickly turn back and face away. He seems so desperate, so lost. I remain sitting up, but I'm no longer eye to eye with him.

"It's okay if you do," he says, giving me permission for something for which I have not asked.

I shake my head and find my voice. "I don't need him."

He pulls me to him.

"I'm fine," I say. "Everything is working out just fine. Nobody is paying attention to me or what I do. I come home and we're together. It's all fine." I hesitate, and I sense the coming of sadness. The marching of old boots.

"I'm fine," I say again, trying to convince us both.

I cling to him as we sit in silence.

"That's 'Bye-Ya,'" he finally says, referring to the song playing on the radio. I recognize it because we have the album. It's in with all the others Nathan and I collected over the years, all the albums I have not touched since he's been gone, all the albums he hasn't touched since he's been back, at least as far as I know.

"Yes."

I heard it not long ago on a new album performed by a latecomer to jazz. I can't think of the musician's name, and I don't bring this up. Nathan only prefers the originals. He would have hated the remake.

"I'm glad the swarm found a home," he says. "It's supposed to be cold again the rest of this week and rainy. They might not have survived that."

"How long can they make it swarming away from a nesting site?" I'm sure he's told me this, but I don't remember the answer.

"About three days. That's about as much honey as they can carry. After that, they starve. The queen will be killed, and they will all eventually die."

I think about the swarm in the elm tree, and I feel happy they found a place to live. I think about this phenomenon, about queens and scouts and the decisions animals make to leave home. I think about the in-between places all creatures find themselves from time to time.

I think about Nathan, how I have kept him from where he should be, how I'm responsible for this temporary place I've forced him to stay, and that I've made him stay too long and that he's starving and that is why he's losing so much weight, why I can feel his bones.

I feel him shift beneath me, and I realize that I must be hurting him.

"You want more hot water?" he asks.

And I start to cry.

I feel the familiar and jagged way the grief tears at me, at us both.

He wraps his bony arms around me as I try to hold it all in but I cannot. I know what I have to do. I have seen enough. I know enough. It is only fair to him.

"I will be okay," I say, not really believing it but wanting to, and I know that at times like this it has to be enough.

"I don't want it," I stammer. "But I will be okay."

And there is a tight squeeze on my chest as I feel his hands over mine, all four of them pulled tight across my heart.

"I will be okay," I whisper again, a third time. And alone, I lean back against the cold porcelain and weep so loud I do not hear the falling rain.

Chapter Fifty-Three

I wake up, and I do not reach across the bed for him. I know he is not there. I know this time things are really different. I know he is gone.

I lay there a few minutes longer, thinking about last night, about how it felt to come to bed alone—how it was to wake and feel this intense loneliness, to realize that I no longer have a spouse and partner, that I am utterly and completely alone. And that for the rest of my days on this earth, my life is forever altered, forever changed. I am now an orange.

I feel the weight of my decision and choose not to go to work, deciding I will go somewhere else, that I will ask for help. Even though I realize I have turned a corner, I also realize grief can flip a person right back to the exact same place on the path she has been before, the exact same place she thought she had passed and conquered.

Grief offers no kindness.

I sit up, listen to the cars passing on the road in front of the house, hear a group of children walking to school, their voices coming through the windows and walls. I have seen them before. There are three girls and one boy, the one I see riding past on his bike from time to time; and I hear the boy teasing a girl, the pretend fights they have most mornings, the way she acts so incensed but also unable to hide a certain appreciation for the attention.

I smile without seeing them because I know that girl. I know her youthful and innocent appreciation. I know the game we all have played.

I breathe in a deep breath and go into the kitchen, start a pot of coffee, find my phone, dial the number.

Kathryn answers on the second ring.

"K-Locks," she says, and for some reason I wait before announcing myself.

"Hello?"

And I think she may hang up.

"Hi, Kathryn."

"Oh," she sounds slightly surprised. "Hey, Emma."

I glance out the window and see the kids I had heard earlier crossing the street. One girl is smiling, swinging her hair from side to side, and I know she's the one being teased. The boy is running circles around the group.

"You okay?"

"Yeah."

There is a pause.

"I really am this time."

She doesn't respond, and I suppose she doesn't quite know what to make of my reply. I know I have been hard to read this past year. I have given all kinds of clues and answers. I have been moody. I've been elusive and irritable. I have been all over the map. And in this moment of thinking of my erratic behavior, I am suddenly deeply grateful for my boss, deeply grateful for her patience, her generosity, her friendship. I haven't been fair to her, really to anyone.

I am suddenly aware of her graciousness.

"I want to thank you, Kathryn," I tell her, letting the curtain fall.

"For what?"

I hadn't thought this through.

"For not pushing me where you thought I should go." There is a catch in my voice, and I realize this had not been the intention of my call. I am as surprised by what I am saying as she must be.

"I don't know what you mean," she replies. And of course she doesn't. She has given her acceptance of me so unconditionally, so fully, so unquestionably, she wouldn't know what I mean, and this touches me even more.

"I'm better now," I respond. "I've not been for a while, and I think you knew that, but I'm better."

There is a moment of silence.

"I'm glad, Emma. I know it's been hard."

"Yes."

She clears her throat.

"Hey, I got the contract," she announces, changing the subject, changing the intimate direction of this conversation. "From the university," she clarifies. "We've got the athletic dorms, and if this installation goes well, they'll consider us for all their future security needs."

"Kathryn, that's great. I'm so happy for you."

"Well, be happy for us all because I'm spreading the wealth. Everybody gets a raise."

I think I hear applause, but I can't be sure.

I glance over at the clock and see that I'm late by fifteen minutes. The others could be there and listening. I hadn't realized I had overslept.

"So what's up with you?" she asks. "You running late?"

"Well, I am running late," I confess. "But I'm actually calling to see if I can have the day off." I wait for a beat. "I need to take care of some things here at the house, and I need to go to a meeting I've heard about."

I had gotten the information about the grief support group from Pastor Brady when I was at his house. He gave me a flier, and even though I tossed it in the trash can as soon as I got home, I remember the dates and times. Mornings and evenings, a time and space for everyone. "Sure," Kathryn responds. "Do what you need to do. We'll hold down the fort."

I hear some rustling of papers. "In fact, there was a message for you from the night crew, which led me to want to give you some time off anyway."

She pauses, still searching for the note, I suppose.

"Here it is." And she starts to read. "Mrs. Ben Lewis called last evening. She said that you came to her house on your own time and single-handedly rescued her from a swarm of killer bees."

This makes me smile.

"She noted that you were brave and courteous and that you deserve a promotion for your good work." She's quiet, and I guess she's still reading. "There's more; Margaret took the message and wrote down every word, but basically she just wanted me to know what a great thing you had done. So you get the day off, Emma Troxler, with pay, so go enjoy yourself, and we will see you when you get back."

"Thank you, Kathryn."

"No, thank you.

There's a moment before we hang up, and I think she may say something more, but I realize that Kathryn and I have said more to each other than has been said in a very long time.

"Okay, bye, Kathryn."

"Bye, Emma."

And I end the call.

Chapter Fifty-Four

It's about what I expected, this small band of bereaved. Since it's during the hours of a weekday, it's an older crowd, retired, I presume, and mostly women; although there is one man sitting alongside the pastor. Dillard stands up when I walk in.

He's wearing a look of surprise, which quickly turns to delight. He's so easy to read. Like a book with pictures.

"Emma," he says and moves over to me, taking me by the hand. He's so tall he looms over me, but I don't mind. There is a sense of safety standing near him. "I didn't think you'd come." He smiles. "I'm so glad you did." And he motions to an empty chair, and I walk over and take the seat.

"Would you like some coffee, dear?" It's one of the women sitting on the other side of the circle who asks.

I glance around at where there might be coffee and notice the small table in the back of the room. "Yes, ma'am, I think that would be nice." And I watch as she gets up, heads over to the pot, and pours me a cup.

She holds up the pitcher of cream and a container of sugar, and I point to the cream. She smiles, pours me cream, stirs, and brings it to me.

"Thank you," I tell her, taking the cup from her.

"So, this is Helen," Pastor Brady tells me, introducing the woman who is taking her seat. "She makes the refreshments for us."

"And I'm Barbara," the woman beside her says, holding up her hand.

"Rachel," the other one adds.

I nod at them all, feeling self-conscious that I am late, that I am no different from them, that loss has evidently tripped us all up.

I turn to the man beside Dillard, but his head is down, so he doesn't seem to know what is happening. He's missing the introductions; but recognizing raw pain when I see it, I just look away.

"This is Bill," Reverend Brady says and the man snaps up. There are tears in his eyes, and I make a guess that this may be his first time too.

"Hi," I say, sitting at attention. "As you heard, I'm Emma."

There are a couple of nods, a couple of quiet greetings made in my direction. It's awkward for a bit, so I take a sip from the cup of coffee handed to me by Helen, try not to fidget in my seat.

"So," Dillard says softly, turning to Bill. "Carolyn died last week, so we want to welcome Bill this morning but also let him know that this might be very hard for him today since he is just starting this grief process."

He speaks directly to him. "If you need to go at any time, it's okay. Just do as much as you can today. There's no expectation for you to participate or even stay the whole time."

The man wipes away a tear and nods.

Dillard waits for a few seconds and then begins. "Last week we talked about feeling angry after the death of our loved one. I remember that I told you about the argument I had in the carpool line at school after Lindsay died, how I almost got arrested for punching a guy."

The women smile politely.

"That, of course, was only one time I'll tell you about. There were certainly others."

No one is facing him.

"I don't know. Do you think men may feel anger more than women? Do you think men might have an easier time with that emotion than with sadness?"

The women shrug. No one answers. And I wonder if all the meetings are like this, the pastor making his own confession while everyone else just listens, refusing to name their own demons.

I glance over at Bill, but he's still staring at the floor.

"I've felt angry," Barbara confesses, capturing everyone's attention. "I didn't say anything last week because I didn't really know that I was feeling that way." She nods. "But I've been angry."

"Can you tell us what that was about?" Dillard asks.

Barbara doesn't reply at first, but no one hurries her along. No one tries to answer for her. Dillard doesn't ask another leading question.

There is a long pause as we wait, and I think maybe Barbara has said all she intends to say, but in a few moments, she continues.

"Jim refused to go to the doctor when he knew he was having symptoms of a heart attack. He had heart problems twenty years ago, and he knew what was going on. And after last week, when you talked about anger as a part of grief, I realized that I was really mad at him for not having his checkup, for not telling us. I'm so mad that he didn't take care of himself." She stops. "That he wasn't concerned about taking care of me."

Helen reaches in her purse and hands Barbara a tissue.

"I was never really allowed to be angry, so I don't think I even knew that's what I was feeling. But I am." She wipes her eyes. "Angry at him, I mean."

Helen nods.

"Have you felt anger, Helen?" The pastor asks.

"Oh, sure," she says, and with no prompt, she begins. "I've been angry at my husband for not getting me to my daughter in time, angry at my son-in-law for taking her off life support. I've been angry at the stupid girl playing on her phone who drove into her, angry at the nurse for acting like she knew how I felt, angry at my grandson for making his mother pick him up from school. Oh yeah, I've been plenty angry." She wraps her arms around her waist.

Barbara appears slightly uncomfortable, like somehow her sharing has taken down a wall or fence she had so carefully put into place, like Helen is walking through a door she opened.

"I just don't see what good it does," she continues. "That's why I didn't say anything last week. I don't know how it helps. I just get angrier when I talk about it. My husband says I should just let it go." She shakes her head. "And I'm trying. But I just can't do that. Not yet."

We all sit in the wake of Helen's emotion.

"Rachel?" Dillard certainly isn't afraid to call names.

The woman sitting on the other side of Barbara doesn't answer. She gives a slight shake of her head.

I feel all the eyes on me, and I slide down a bit in my seat. I had not planned to share. I don't know why I came to this support group, but I certainly had not planned to share anything about what I feel, what I carry around with me everywhere I go.

"Well, anger is a part of the grief process, and it's certainly acceptable to feel that way."

Pastor Brady doesn't push the question on me, and I'm grateful.

"I'm not angry." It is Bill speaking, and we turn to him. We all seem surprised that he's saying anything.

I think about how I felt one week after Nathan died, and I'm shocked that he can even string together words. I don't think I left the bed the first week; I only answered questions I had to.

Can I get you something to eat? No.

Do you want me to call the office? Yes.

Should I stay the night? I don't care.

"Maybe I'll feel that later, but I'm not angry. It was nobody's fault." He faces Barbara. "And unlike your husband, my Carolyn had been to every doctor we could find. She took good care of herself." He drops his head again. "I'm not mad. I just can't figure out how to live without her. That's what I don't know. That's why

I'm here. I just don't know what to do now that she's gone." He places his hands over his face and weeps.

And nobody moves. Nobody gets up and takes his wide, heaving shoulders into their arms and holds him. Nobody pats him on the head and tells him it will be all right.

The three women, two of them angry, one of them not sure, the minister who told him he could leave—nobody makes a move toward him. And in this newfound knowledge one gains from loss, I understand why we don't.

This pain cannot be hugged away. It cannot be held by anyone else. To run in and put your arms around someone too quickly is to say, "I cannot bear your sorrow. I cannot watch you break."

It is not a lack of care that keeps us from jumping up and running over to this man lost in his despair; it is the exact opposite. We honor his pain by letting him name it and keep it in front of us. We respect his brokenness by refusing to pretend that we could make it go away with touch.

I glance away, wishing this was knowledge I didn't have.

Chapter Fifty-Five

"That was intense," I tell Dillard as we're walking to our cars. The others in the group decided to go out to lunch together; they asked me to go, but I'd rather go for a walk, maybe to the hardware store to pick up a few supplies I will need for the bees. I'm not sure why Dillard didn't join them.

"Yeah," he replies, without much more.

"I guess they're all like that."

"No." He shakes his head. "Not all of them."

We stop on the sidewalk, watch a butterfly wafting near the row of bushes in the parking lot.

"Some of them are filled with great silences."

"Makes sense," I reply.

"What made you come today?" he asks.

I shrug. "Things changed."

He waits for something more.

"It's been almost a year," I tell him, unsure if he is aware of the impending anniversary date of Nathan's death.

He doesn't respond.

"And I really haven't done the work I needed to do," I add. "The grief work, the acceptance piece."

He nods. Maybe he's surprised I know the language.

"I finally realized that last night and thought I could probably use some help."

"We all need help," he replies.

The butterfly moves away from the bush, heads out into traffic, and I feel a little anxious that it might not survive the passing cars, the speed and pace it will fly into.

"What happened to Carolyn?" I ask.

"It was cancer. She had been sick a long time. Hospice was in the home for almost a year."

"I guess that doesn't really matter, does it?"

He turns to me, acting as if he doesn't follow.

"How long a person is sick, how long someone might think they have left."

I pick a leaf off the shrub where I am standing. I think about Nathan, about how I thought he might die after his accident, how I ran to the hospital after getting the news, thinking he was already dead, thinking I was going to find him in the morgue and not the emergency department. And then how we went through all those weeks together, me never sure he would survive an operation, day after day, checking on him, thinking it might be that day that he dies, only to find myself completely unprepared when the day did actually come, when he really did die—how ill-prepared I felt almost a year ago as Pastor Brady sat beside me in a waiting room, and I heard the devastating news.

"No, I guess it doesn't matter."

"He got to say goodbye. That's something," I say.

"Maybe," he answers.

A car pulls into the parking lot and then makes a U-turn. Neither of us makes a comment.

"Did you?"

"What?" I hold the leaf I pulled to my nose. I try to see if I can tell what it is by the scent, try to see if I can tell whether or not a bee has been there.

"Say goodbye?"

I realize he's talking about Nathan, about the night at the hospital when we first met.

I shake my head. "Not the night he died," I say, wondering what Dillard remembers about standing with me when I was taken to the curtained-off room where my husband lay on a gurney, where Nathan had taken his last breath without me, his skin already turning ashen, his lips blue.

"I heard your conversation," he tells me.

I glance over at him, not sure how I feel about that.

"I heard you tell him not to go. I'll always remember that—your voice, your pleading, how hard you begged."

"So you know now why I'm here."

He nods. "I know."

"I thought I had talked him out of leaving me. I thought he came home with me that night, that he never died."

"I guess in some ways he didn't."

"I guess."

"After Lindsay died, my wife wouldn't clean out her room for months. I'd ask her about changing things in there or letting some other little girl have her clothes and toys." He stops, faces me. "I thought it would be better to do that, to get her belongings out of our sight, so we wouldn't be reminded of her every single time we walked past that room, every single time we walked down the hall where her coat hung on the hook by the door; her rain boots placed beneath them or out in the backyard where her bike leaned against the shed; her sandbox, swing set. I thought it would just be better for everyone if we gave it all away."

He shakes his head. "Please know I'm not proud of that. I see now that I was wrong, and I know why she can't forgive me. I was terribly wrong about everything after she died."

I nod and think of Carla, of the gentle ways she has tried over the months to help me get rid of Nathan's stuff, how violently I have reacted every time, how I have hated her for thinking she could make things better by taking away the last of him.

"She told me later when we broke up, when we decided to sell the house and both of us leave there, that she couldn't change anything in Lindsay's room because she kept having this terrible thought that what happened might just have been a dream—a bad one, sure—but just a dream and that Lindsay might come home. She worried that if something was suddenly different and if all of this wasn't true, that our little girl hadn't actually died, that she might come home, and then she'd be so mad that we gave away her dolls, that we bagged up and took away her clothes, gave all of her toys to Goodwill. She said that she wanted everything to stay the same because she wanted to make sure Lindsay would know we hadn't stopped loving her and that we never stopped wanting and expecting her to come home."

"Magical thinking," I say, recalling Joan Didion's famous book about the death of her husband and the critical illness of her daughter, the book the social worker left me after my intervention. I read it a few weeks ago.

"Magical thinking," he repeats.

We stop and listen to an airplane flying overhead, to the birds chirping nearby, the traffic, life moving and teeming all around us, all of it seeming so untouched by death, so unknowing of how a world can come to a screeching halt for someone left behind.

"That sounds like such a lovely thing until you understand what it means," he notes.

"That's for sure," I reply, knowing the heartbreak that the pretty words describe.

"So you're going to come again?" he asks, referring to the support group, I suppose.

I nod. "Somebody's got to stand with Bill," I add. "It doesn't get any easier for a long time."

"Right, that's exactly right." He steps down and waits for me to join him. "See you next week then," he says.

"Next week," I reply, and head to my car.

Chapter Fifty-Six

"Are you sure you want all of this to go?"

Carla is lugging a black plastic bag out of the house and onto the porch. She stops and puts her hands on her hips. She's tired because we've been working for hours. Her hair has flattened because of the humidity, and there is a part of me that would really like to take a picture of her. I don't though, because I know she will get mad and claim she has to leave so she can fix her appearance, and I really do need her help.

"All of it, yes," I answer and then turn and walk inside, knowing she can drag the bag to the truck. It will take both of us to lift it onto the bed, but we'll do that later.

I called my mother a few days ago when I knew it was time to clean out Nathan's things. She was quiet at first, asked if I was sure, and then she said she was delighted to help. Today, however, she may be rethinking her enthusiastic acceptance of the invitation. It's about ninety degrees outside.

I did a lot of the discarding already, by myself before she arrived, with some assistance from Bus. I called him because I thought there might be a few things he would like—some furniture from Nathan's office, lamps and wooden boxes, a file cabinet, odds and ends. I knew he didn't have much in his rental house, and I was right—he was interested in everything.

We used Nathan's truck to haul the things over to Bus' place, and he bought me dinner at the Mexican restaurant near the edge of town, a spot he often frequented and where he was known by name and where he spoke Spanish, ordering us all kinds of dishes that I had never tasted. He tried to pay me for a few of the pieces of furniture and accessories, the desk and chair, the bee books I didn't want; but I wouldn't take his money.

He is actually part of the reason I can do this.

"You're getting rid of these?" he asked as I yanked out the crates of books and records and loaded them on the truck. He pulled out a Rolling Stones album and held it up. It was a classic and just seeing it in his hands, just recognizing it and remembering how much I loved it, how much Nathan loved it, I was tempted to hold onto it, but I shook my head. If I started with Mick Jagger I would have to find and secure Meatloaf and The Eagles.

"Take it," I instructed him. "I'm not keeping vinyl."

Immediately, I am brought to the present moment.

My mother's voice: "Emma, I know I tried talking you into this lots of times, but this seems so, so ..." she searches for her word. "Drastic," Carla says as she walks into the house, the door slamming behind her. "Don't you want to at least keep his plaques, his memorabilia?" She's holding up an award he won for his last writing project, some small trophy from a contest. "Don't you want to hold onto his books, keep a nice library for yourself?"

"No," I answer. "We can recycle the metal and the wood from the plaques. I don't have any place for them. We're taking the books to Mr. Starr." I had already called him, and he said to bring everything I had. He said he could find them good homes.

"Well, what are you going to do in that room?" she asks, walking into the small room we made into his office when we first moved in, the room where I am now standing.

I realize that I almost never went in there for the twenty years we have lived here. It was always Nathan's private space, and because he was so messy and had so much junk, I just decided from the very beginning to stay out of it. Now that I'm cleaning it, now that I see just how much he kept in here, I know that was a sound decision.

"I don't know yet. Maybe it'll be a reading room, or maybe I'll make it into a studio of some kind, a place to paint or write. Maybe I'll take up sewing. I don't know."

And I don't. I only know I can't keep it as it was, and to me, that means having to discard everything in there. I have to start from scratch. If I plan to make it mine, the only way I know how is to get rid of everything that is his, empty it out and begin again, like moving the bee hives fifteen miles away from the previous place until the bees erase all their memories of how things were, where things were. Only after some time can you return the hives close to where they had been. It's clearly not just bees that have to create new memories in order to make a fresh start.

"You know all the stuff I read says that you shouldn't do anything too big or overwhelming the first year. Maybe we should just rent a storage building for a while, give you some time to think about it."

She walks over to where I am standing, and we both take in the emptiness, the space. I think I might decide this will be my new bedroom. I like it that much.

"Don't you want to keep some of his stuff from his office?"

"I don't need his stuff to remember him, I told you that. I've kept the things that matter. The rest of it is just junk to me. I don't want it here."

I glance out the window into the backyard and see the shed, which I plan to take over this summer. I intend to start a new garden soon, but I will clean things up first, pull up the weeds that have taken over by the fence. I may plant a few butterfly bushes or honeysuckle vines, milkweed, something bees will like.

I reach to my neck and take hold of Nathan's wedding ring. It's on a silver chain I found a few days ago, and I like the way it feels close to my heart. I think of the other things I have put aside, the collectibles and belongings I have kept. I have a few of his college

T-shirts that I will wear as pajamas, his favorite bee books, the ones all marked up and filled with notes. I will keep an old sweater he'd had since he was a graduate student, a literary journal that printed his article on Aurore Dupin's many affairs, a pipe his father owned, a shot glass from a trip we took to the Keys, his shaving mug and straight razor, a watercolor he kept from his grandmother's estate, a bowl of fruit his uncle had painted as a boy—the uncle who died in the war; some trinkets, good luck tokens, poker chips, books of matches, just a few silly things that remind me of special times; a coffee cup, a playbill, nothing too worthwhile, just a few sentimental items.

I don't need much to speak to me of our marriage or our love. I never have. Without him to share the memories, they mean so little. If I can't have him, these things have no value.

My mother, who has been standing beside me, surprises me when she suddenly throws her arm around me. She'd like to say that she is proud of me, I can tell; I know Carla. I know what she tried to say for years and just can't ever say. I accepted my mother's limitations a long time ago.

"You sure you want to stay here?" she asks.

Carla tried to make me an appointment with a realtor last week. It was some woman she knew from the library board, a reputable real estate broker whose name I had heard, but I had refused the meeting, told her I didn't intend to sell.

"As I have explained to you already, I very much want to stay here," I answer, hardly understanding how she would think I would want to be anywhere else. "This is my home."

"This was your home," she reminds me. "Your home together. Yours and Nathan's. Isn't it too sad to be here alone?"

I pull away from her, and then I take in a breath and try to explain it once again to her.

"This was our home, and now it is my home. I'm happy here. I was happy with Nathan, and I will be happy here living alone." I close my eyes.

I feel her right beside me. She has edged closer.

"You are very brave, Emma," she says, the most complimentary thing she has said of me in years. "Very brave."

"Thank you, Mama," I say, and this time, I wrap my arm around her.

Chapter Fifty-Seven

I am walking out of Kathryn's office when I run right into Jon. He was standing at the door waiting, I suppose.

"You going in there?" I ask, thinking he needs to see the boss, thinking he has been waiting for me to leave so he could go in. I start to open the door again.

He shakes his head. "No, I was waiting for you."

"Oh?" I walk to my desk and he follows.

"What do you need?" I ask, wondering if he took a call while I was in the meeting or if he has a question about the sale he just made.

"Is it true?"

"Is what true?" I open the top drawer, take out some folders, have a seat in front of my computer.

"Are you leaving?"

"What?" I stop what I'm doing, give Jon my full attention. I am surprised that the news is out. I only just spoke to Kathryn. I only just explained it all to her.

"Did you turn in your resignation?" He stands next to me, shifting his weight from side to side. "Are you leaving K-Locks?"

"What did you hear and from whom?"

"I didn't hear anything," he says.

"Then why are you asking that question?"

I had planned to tell Bus after I told Kathryn; I hadn't expected the others to know already. Kathryn said she would wait until tomorrow to make the announcement for everyone to hear.

"I can just tell something's different. You've been acting strange for some time—since it's gotten warm, since you quit wearing your wedding ring. It's like something's changed for you."

I turn my chair to face the computer and think about the last few weeks—the cleaning out of Nathan's things, the painting of his office, turning it into my reading room, building new shelves. I think about the garden I've started, the small rows of lettuce and onions, the buttercup-yellow color that I chose to paint the shed. I think about taking off my wedding band and wearing Nathan's around my neck.

I think about the morning grief support group—Bill's quiet suffering, the way Rachel wrings her hands and can't yet share anything about her sister's murder, how Barbara never brings tissues and Helen always has more than she needs. I think about the casual way we all decide to go out for lunch together after the meeting, the way I have come to think of all of them as friends.

I think about Dillard and how broken he still is over Lindsay and the divorce, how he misses his son terribly and wonders if he will ever get another chance with him. I think about that room where we meet—the four beige walls and tile floor and how it holds our pain. I think about how it is that on some days I walk out of there feeling like the meeting didn't do anything but pry open the wound of loss, and on other mornings I actually feel a bit better, as if I may not, in fact, die from sorrow.

I think about Carla and our friendly chats, Violet and how she wanted my advice about asking someone out, Bus and the bees and how I can sit at my dining room table without losing my breath. How I can laugh again.

"Well, I guess now that you bring it up, I am different." I face him and think about the files I need to close, the customers I need to call, the accounts I will need to turn over to someone else. I put those thoughts aside, however, and give all my attention to my coworker who is still standing beside me. "And yes, I have resigned."

"I hate that," he says, shaking his head. "I really like working with you, Emma." He shoves his hands in his pockets.

I'm touched. I really didn't expect my leaving would matter to Jon. I thought he'd not feel a thing at my departure.

"Well, you know I'm just going to be a couple miles down the road. It's not like I'm moving out of town or going to be living somewhere far away. We can still see each other from time to time."

"You don't like working here anymore?" he asks, and I realize that he never really heard anything from me about Nathan, about grief, about how it's been for me all this time.

"I've just decided it's time for a change. You know? Try something different for a while."

He nods and turns away, and I'm guessing he's thinking about his original plans to start his brewery, how he put aside those dreams and ideas, how he started here as a means to just save some money but has now put down roots in this business, how he has discovered that he is very good at selling security systems.

In fact, I'm pretty sure that when I leave, Kathryn will give him a promotion and a raise. I believe she was actually holding back on that development because she didn't want there to be any ill feelings between the two of us.

I know my departure will be a good thing for Jon. I even gave him a recommendation for a promotion when I turned in my resignation. He's good at this work—may even be the one who eventually buys the business from Kathryn, takes over when she's decided it's time to retire. I have noticed the camaraderie building over the months between Jon and our boss. My leaving will bring about some good things for K-Locks, I am sure.

I smile at Jon, see how young he is, how open his heart is. "It's been strange but good for me to do this work all these years. I've learned a lot about security systems, setting alarms, and ..." I pause, realizing that as I'm saying these things, parts of my life seem to be coming together, seem to be making perfect sense even as I thought it was all falling apart, even as I thought nothing I did made any sense at all.

"I've also learned that I used to think that if a person put in enough locks or installed the right camera that they could keep all their fears at bay." I nod at what I now know.

"But you can't really keep the bad stuff out—not all of it, not forever. You can't outsmart trouble or sorrow. You can't lock it out."

I glance up at Jon, and it's easy to see I lost him. This isn't a familiar language to a business major.

"I like books," I say.

And he nods. This he understands.

"You're going to work at that secondhand place?"

"Paul Starr Books," I clarify.

"You going to be the manager?"

"I believe that will be my new title."

Mr. Starr and I are still working out the logistics, but he claims that he's become much busier with internet sales and called a couple weeks ago to say he needed someone to run the store while he does the acquiring and shipping. He thought of me. And for reasons I don't quite understand, I said yes. Simply put, I like the idea of working in the store, organizing titles, keeping a website fresh, helping readers find what they're looking for. I like the idea of being close to all those books.

Jon chews on his bottom lip. "Does he have an alarm system?"

This makes me smile.

I remember my call there with Bus, how I officially met the store owner that day. "In fact, he has several cameras installed; but you never know what future needs he might encounter."

"You'll call me first, right? Give me the first shot at a bid to install and provide service? There's a new small business package Kathryn's working on that might just be what he needs."

"I promise I will pass along your name and number to my new employer and I will not let another company even make a bid." I stand up and hold out my hand for a true business deal closing.

He takes my hand. "Okay then."

"Okay then," I say.

Chapter Fifty-Eight

"This is really what you want?" Bus is driving the truck, and we are heading out to the farm.

It's Sunday, the last one in May, and the sun is high and hot. It feels like summer already, even though there are a few weeks to go before it officially begins. The traffic is light, and I've rolled down my window, have my arm resting on the door. We're drinking coffee and listening to the country music station that Bus likes.

It's the anniversary date of Nathan's death, and Bus knows it. He knew it before I told him; I don't know how, but I suppose it couldn't have been that hard to figure out. I've had a difficult week—lots of tears, big mood swings. I took yesterday off from the bookstore. Paul pushed me to do it. He knows about these anniversaries. He knows about the first one, how it can rip apart all the work you think you've done. He was clear with me to do something important to commemorate the date and not to expect more from myself than I can do. He's become very important to me in just a few short weeks. He's like a guide for me on this journey of grief.

"It is," I answer him.

I turn and watch Bus as he drives out of town and down the country road that will lead me to the bees. He is kind, tender in his dealings with me, never asking me to take another step when I'm not ready, never applying pressure to make this more than it is.

I lean against the seat, close my eyes. I feel his hand on mine.

I've asked him to do this with me. We'll move the hives later, but I have to do this first, and I didn't want to be alone. Not this time. Not today. I just needed someone to come along, to drive me, to stand close by.

We've cleared away a nice patch of land near the barn at his place to keep the bees. We decided the trees were too far away, and it would be nice to keep the hives closer to the house, where the sweet clover is thick, there are a good variety of wildflowers very near, and it won't require such long walks to get to them.

Bus ordered bees a while ago, and they arrived right away; but it wasn't long before they all flew away or died. There was some evidence of Chalkbrood, a disease caused by a fungus. I guess they were already infected before he got them because in the package of live bees, there were blue flakes, clear signs of the illness.

We read up on it together since I didn't know anything more about Chalkbrood than he did, and we learned that it is not usually a serious disease and doesn't require treatment; but for these young bees being shipped, it was just too much, and they didn't survive. That's when we decided to move Nathan's bees to his place. That's when we made the decision to keep the bees together. We are both beginners, really, and still learning, and it just seemed like the right thing to do.

He takes the turn and heads up the road where the hives are located, and I can only hope that I haven't waited too long.

I did check on the bees a few days ago, and everything seemed okay. Nothing appeared to be out of the ordinary. They were healthy, and I saw lots of them coming and going from their boxes.

It is just an old wives' tale, after all. And yet, I feel this is important for them. It is important for me.

"You can drive all the way up there," I tell him as he slows, waiting for instructions. "I walk sometimes, but you can take the truck all the way to the hives."

He glances over at me. "Just keep going?"

I nod, and he pulls ahead.

The farmer's son was disappointed that I was moving the bees later next month but then decided that maybe it's for the best after all, and it might be the impetus he needs to make some decisions about the place. He's thinking of selling it anyway. He's decided he's not really cut out for the farmer's life.

"It's nice out here," Bus says, taking it all in. This is his first time.

"Yes, it is," I agree.

"Nathan found it on his own?"

I nod, recalling how excited he was when he realized it was the perfect place to raise his bees, farm the honey. We had brought champagne out here, toasted to our good luck, offered thanksgiving to the sun and moon, the wind and earth. He was so happy then, and I can't help myself, but I think of him watching from some cloud somewhere, and I hope he is happy now.

"You can just park right there," I tell him, pointing to the spot where Nathan always stopped the car, an empty space not far from the hives.

Bus stops the truck, puts it in park, turns off the engine, and we just sit there for a few minutes, drinking our coffee, listening to the sounds of all that is coming to life around us. I hear crows and cardinals, a blue jay, I think, and I close my eyes to breathe this place in again, to remember what it has meant for all these years, and then I let it all wash over me. I do not hold back the tears, and Bus just places his hand near me.

It takes a few minutes, and then I am finished. I take in a deep breath and turn to him and nod. He gets out, and before I realize what he's doing, he hurries over to my side of the truck and opens the door, offers me his hand, and I slide out.

"Thank you," I say, not just for the politeness, not just for helping me out of the truck, but for coming with me, for understanding. I mean all that, but I don't say it. Not yet. Not today.

He nods.

I drop his hand and walk alone to where I know the bees will be coming in and out of their entrances, the old ones standing guard with their full venom sacs, the young ones working so diligently on such a warm spring morning. I'm not exactly sure how many of them I will actually encounter. It's still early, but I imagine most of the bees are out already collecting nectar.

It has been a long, cold winter, and I'm certain they are out of honey and hungry.

As I come to the boxes, I think about the poem, about Whittier and his thoughts about the young girl Mary, how he must have been in love with her and how cruel the news of her death must have felt. I think about the sight of her bees, about realizing that she is no longer there. I think about the poet and the sting of death, how hearts will heal but never quite beat the same way again.

I kneel down beside the first box, knowing that to stand in front blocking the entrance could mark me as an enemy, a predator, breaking the path of the bees coming and going, interrupting the important tasks at hand. I don't wish to cause harm; and since I'm not suited, I don't want to get stung.

I place my hand on top, press my lips on the cool, dry wood. I tap lightly.

"Nathan's dead," I tell them. I wait a few seconds, tap two more times and say it three times before moving on. Hive by hive, box by box, I break the news. "He's dead. He's not coming back. He's never coming back."

After my final whisper to the last box, I rise from my knees and feel the morning breeze as it cools my face and the places where the tears have fallen. I hear the rustle in the leaves, the birds singing, and I am at peace.

I stand here, still and freed, the weight of this report lifted from me, and a bee flies right in front of my eyes, close enough that I get a good look at her.

She's beautiful and strong and healthy, longer than most, a thicker belly, making her clearly distinguishable from all the others, and instantly I recognize her as one of the young queens.

She buzzes close to me for just a second, alone and unguarded, and then before I can take a breath or reach out my arm for a landing place, she flies off. She is gone. And with that final blessing bestowed, I gather myself, turn, and walk away.

Acknowledgments

I am greatly indebted to Homer Walsh, who shared his beekeeping work and a few jars of honey with me. Also, the lessons of Sue Hubbell in her book, *A Book of Bees,* were immensely helpful. She writes so clearly and beautifully about the bees, and she was why I first became drawn to the work of beekeeping.

Thank you to the good folks at Warren Publishing: Mindy Kuhn, Amy Ashby, and my astute, kind, and professional editor, Karli Jackson.

I am thankful to all the people in my life who encourage my writing, who ask about stories I might tell, who care that I don't quit. I am grateful to my husband Bob, who has always been at my side with unwavering support for all my endeavors. I am forever grateful to my friends and loved ones. I cannot imagine life without the sweetness of so much goodness. Thank you once again to Sally McMillan, my agent for over twenty years. What a glorious ride we've had!

And finally, thank you to the many family members of hospice patients who openly and bravely shared with me their stories of grief. I am so very honored to walk some of the journey with you.

Questions for Reflection

1. What has been the most helpful story of grief you have ever read?
2. What is the importance of Emma telling the bees that Nathan was dead?
3. What do you know about the grief process? What has been your most difficult loss?
4. Emma works for a security business; how does grief affect a person's sense of security?
5. As a society, how do you think we do in dealing with death and dying?
6. What role does forgiveness play in healthy grief?
7. Have you ever experienced "magical thinking" regarding someone you have lost?
8. What makes grief complicated?
9. Emma finds support in a group at a local church. Where do grieving people find support?
10. Is there a right way to grieve?

CPSIA information can be obtained
at www.ICGtesting.com
Printed in the USA
LVHW021214131220
674071LV00003B/310

9 781735 860053